# FRIEND

WEATHERHEAD BOOKS ON ASIA

WEATHERHEAD BOOKS ON ASIA

WEATHERHEAD EAST ASIAN INSTITUTE,
COLUMBIA UNIVERSITY

For a complete list of titles, see page 225

# FRIEND

## A NOVEL FROM NORTH KOREA

**PAEK NAM-NYONG**

*Translated by Immanuel Kim*

COLUMBIA UNIVERSITY PRESS
New York

Columbia University Press wishes to express its appreciation for assistance
given by the Pushkin Fund in the publication of this book.

This publication has been supported by the Richard W. Weatherhead Publication
Fund of the Weatherhead East Asian Institute, Columbia University.

Columbia University Press
*Publishers Since 1893*
New York    Chichester, West Sussex
cup.columbia.edu
Copyright © 2020 Columbia University Press
All rights reserved
Library of Congress Cataloging-in-Publication Data
Names: Paek Nam-nyong, author. | Kim, Immanuel, translator.
Title: Friend: a novel from North Korea / Nam-nyong Paek, translated
by Immanuel Kim.
Other titles: Pŏt. English
Description: New York: Columbia University Press, [2020] | Series:
Weatherhead books on Asia
Identifiers: LCCN 2019037295 (print) | LCCN 2019037296 (ebook) |
ISBN 9780231195607 (cloth) | ISBN 9780231195614 (paperback) |
ISBN 9780231551403 (ebook)
Classification: LCC PL992.613.N37 P6813 2020 (print) | LCC PL992.613.N37
(ebook) | DDC 895.73/4—dc23
LC record available at https://lccn.loc.gov/2019037295
LC ebook record available at https://lccn.loc.gov/2019037296

Cover image: Pyongyang, North Korea. Panos Pictures © Noriko Hayashi
Cover design: Chang Jae Lee

*For my wife, my comrade, my friend, Angela Kim*

# CONTENTS

# FRIEND

# THEIR LOVE

# 1

The Superior Court was nestled between mountains on the outskirts of the city. A line of tall fir trees guided the road up to the gates of the courthouse. Through the gates, a vast, serene courtyard welcomed visitors. Surrounded by coniferous trees, the courtyard provided ample fresh air to visitors contemplating the long flight of broad steps to the courthouse. The large windows, regal columns, and tall doors gave the building a majestic entrance. Although the Superior Court handled unsavory civil and criminal cases, the monumental facade of the building gave an impression of both grandeur and quiet dignity.

Many people in the city neither knew the location of the Superior Court nor knew of its existence. Those who abided by the law or lived in a harmonious family had no reason to come here.

Distress weighed on Judge Jeong Jin Wu as he stared at the divorce petition on his desk. Much like a fisherman trying to untangle knots in a fishing line, Jeong Jin Wu was upset by the burden of having to deal with another family's misery.

A woman in her thirties kept her head lowered to avoid looking at Judge Jeong Jin Wu. The fragrance of her light, elegant perfume complemented a fashionable sheath dress that revealed her slender white neck. Judge Jeong Jin Wu's secretary had tried to put the woman off with the excuse that the judge was away on a business trip and would discuss her divorce petition when he returned in a few days, but the woman had remained in the corridor of the court for many hours as if her feet were nailed to the floor. Thus Judge Jeong Jin Wu had little choice but to summon her into his office.

The woman trembled as she wept. Jeong Jin Wu waited for her to compose herself before handing her the divorce petition.

Name: Chae Sun Hee
Age: 33
Address: Gang An District, #19
Occupation:

Upon seeing "Occupation," Sun Hee felt her heart plunge into despair, and, not having the strength to carry on, she laid her pen down. Perceiving Sun Hee's distress, Judge Jeong Jin Wu decided to complete the form for her. He well knew her occupation. She was a professional singer, the lead mezzo-soprano for the Provincial Performing Arts Company. Once every few months, he would go to the theater and listen to her sing.

Sun Hee possessed the power of drawing the audience into her world of music with her angelic voice. Receiving bundles of flowers and standing ovations on a nightly basis—that was the life of a celebrity like Sun Hee. However, today she had brought her marital problems to the courthouse, something the audience would never have suspected.

*Why does she want a divorce? Do she and her husband not have a good sex life?* Judge Jeong Jin Wu thought. *Or perhaps her husband is impotent. No, it can't be that. She has a son.*

On his way home from work one evening, Jeong Jin Wu had seen Sun Hee and her son walking to Gang An District, a single-story housing complex located not far from his apartment.

*Her husband must've had an affair with another woman.*

Jeong Jin Wu hoped that it was not a serious love affair. It could have been irreconcilable differences or problems with her in-laws. He hoped it was a petty argument that brought her to the steps of the courthouse. Many young newlyweds, who had entertained fanciful dreams of marriage and family in their youth, entered through the doors of the court with the most trivial of problems, claiming these were the most intolerable tragedies.

But Judge Jeong Jin Wu was slowly beginning to realize that Sun Hee would not have come to him with a petty issue. Sun Hee's entire person—her vacant eyes, her forlorn countenance, her downcast spirit, and her anxious disposition—revealed deep-seated concerns that had been accumulating for many years.

Sun Hee pulled out her handkerchief to wipe away the traces of her distress. With her soft hands, she cleared the hair from her face and tried to compose herself. She let out a quiet sigh and looked up apologetically.

"My occupation is . . ."

"That I already know. Please tell me your husband's name."

"It's Lee Seok Chun."

"His age?"

"He's thirty-five."

"His occupation?"

"He works at the Gang An Machine Factory. He's a lathe operator." Sun Hee's voice quavered from her sobbing, but, nevertheless, it was the beautiful clear tone of a singer.

After writing the information on the form, Jeong Jin Wu asked, "You have a son, right?"

"A son? Yes, my son. Oh dear . . ." Sun Hee wept again. The thought of her son's miserable fate pained her heart. Jeong Jin Wu knew all too well from his years of experience that women who filed for divorce generally had great difficulty talking about their children.

Divorcing couples often overlook, neglect, and abandon a child when they aim their distress, rage, and despair at their spouse. But when a mother stands before the judge, her maternal instinct rises. The mother fights for custody and fears for her blameless child's fate. At the same time, there are women who do not even consider a child an innocent victim, and they prioritize their divorce with no regard for the pitiful fate of the child. Jeong Jin Wu hoped Sun Hee was not that kind of mother.

"How old is your son?" asked Jeong Jin Wu in a softer tone.

"He's seven."

"So, he must be in first grade."

"Actually, he has an early birthday, so he will finish kindergarten this fall."

Sun Hee stopped sobbing and began combing her disheveled hair with her hand. Her voice stopped shaking, and it appeared that she had calmed down.

"When did you get married?"

"Is that important?" asked Sun Hee, with a slight frown.

"Marriage is a legal contract. Therefore, I need to know the date."

"I believe . . . it was," Sun Hee stuttered, "May . . . 10 . . . 1974."

Sun Hee turned her head away and stared at the corner of the table. That date undoubtedly called up many good memories, so different from the way she felt today. But she was trying hard not to think about those bygone days.

As Jeong Jin Wu was about to write down the date, he looked up at the calendar hanging on the wall behind Sun Hee. He thought to himself, *Today is April 24, and in a few weeks, this woman would have been married for ten years.*

"Very well, Comrade Sun Hee. Can you explain your reason for wanting a divorce?"

Sun Hee was dumbfounded by the judge's question, for it was rather obvious to her why someone would come to the court and file for a divorce.

"Why do you want to divorce your husband?" the judge rephrased his question. "In other words, what is the basis of your divorce?" Jeong Jin Wu pointed to the document with his pen and explained calmly. "Here on this legal document, there is a section called 'Divorce Petition Summary.'"

Sun Hee proceeded to speak in a resolute tone. "You see, Seok Chun and I have not been on good terms. It's been like this for several years." Her voice quavered. "I've tried hard to be patient with him, but I can't live like this anymore." It seemed that she was going to cry again.

Jeong Jin Wu asked, "How are you not on good terms with your husband?"

Sun Hee did not respond.

"I cannot convince the court to schedule a divorce hearing without a legitimate reason," the judge said, in an attempt to reason with her.

Suddenly, an uncontrollable anger erupted in Sun Hee. She raised her voice.

"I can't live with him anymore! There is simply no way! We were not meant to be. Our personalities are completely different."

Jeong Jin Wu had become accustomed to such irrational outbursts over the years of interviewing divorce claimants. He took a moment before proceeding.

"What kind of personality does your husband have?"

"He is insensitive and speechless like a big dumb rock."

"Being insensitive may not be good," Jeong Jin Wu assured her. "But being a man of few words can be seen as a positive quality."

"If he were a *true* man of few words, then I could live with that," Sun Hee argued. "But we can't have a decent conversation without him cursing at me. He either gives me the silent treatment or nags about little things."

Sun Hee quickly changed her expression to gain sympathy from Jeong Jin Wu.

"Comrade Judge, please help me. I've been living a loveless life with Seok Chun for many years. It's embarrassing to be seen in public with him. I would've come to the courthouse sooner, but, my son, you see—"

Jeong Jin Wu poured a glass of water for Sun Hee.

"Comrade Sun Hee, please explain in a calm and orderly way."

"You see, our lifestyle is not on the same rhythm."

"What do you mean by 'not on the same rhythm'?"

"Like music. Marriage is like music."

Jeong Jin Wu listened attentively. Sun Hee stared directly into his eyes and said, "Comrade Judge, think about it. Would a tambourine and a flute sound harmonious? Wouldn't it sound strange to combine a male and female vocal quartet?"

"That may be the case with music from an artistic point of view—"

"There is no life devoid of art," interjected Sun Hee. "Marriage is like art, and when things aren't right, it's awful. Seok Chun despises me and doesn't even treat me like a human being. Of all things, he criticizes the way I dress! When coworkers from my theater come over to our house, they either close the door and go to the other room or just leave because they don't want to be around my husband. Comrade Judge, how can I live with a man like that?"

Jeong Jin Wu could not understand her explanation, so he said, "Your husband wouldn't just do that to a nice woman like yourself without any reason. Why do you think he did that?"

Sun Hee lowered her eyes and fidgeted with a corner of her dress.

"I don't really know. It's not like I didn't love my husband. I've always tried to respect him and understand him."

Judge Jeong Jin Wu was not convinced. Close to losing his temper, he retorted, "How is it possible to love your husband and live a loveless married life at the same time?"

Sun Hee opened her eyes wide and stared at the judge. She was taken aback by the judge's cold glare and incisive question. Her eyes lost their luster and looked flustered.

"I have been faithful to my husband! I have stood by him and his work. I've been patient with him while he has been working on a single project for the past five years. I didn't care if he didn't bring home his salary or if he didn't help me around the house. I've endured it all—the insults, the physical violence—and lived with him for all these years. I guess I could've tried harder to make our marriage work."

Sun Hee paused for a moment to catch her breath. "No, no. I can't do that. I can't stand it anymore! I am a singer. I love singing, and I love my audience. I will not sacrifice my dreams, my future, for the sake of my husband."

"Why didn't your husband bring home his salary?"

From his long experience, Jeong Jin Wu had learned that financial difficulties could lead married couples to file for divorce. But he restrained himself from jumping to conclusions and asked the question only in order to understand the truth of the divorce case objectively.

Sun Hee snickered, revealing her contempt for her husband. "He made some technical errors and ruined many parts, which cost the factory a fortune over time. He felt guilty, so he tried to compensate for the damages with his salary. He's still paying for those parts."

Sun Hee kept rubbing the corner of the table with her finger. Tears gathered in the corners of her eyes, but her gaze remained resolutely fixed.

"Very well, Comrade Sun Hee. Now, why didn't your husband come with you today?"

"Seok Chun said that it's humiliating to come to court. He said he doesn't have time to explain our family problems. But I know for sure that he agrees with the idea of a divorce."

Jeong Jin Wu wrote down a summary of Sun Hee's side of the story on the divorce petition, but he knew that this was only one side of the story.

Sun Hee glanced over at the legal document and held her breath in anticipation. After letting out a soft sigh, she carefully asked, "When do you think the divorce hearing will take place?"

Jeong Jin Wu looked up from the form and said, "Divorce is not a performance, where you go on and off stage. I have to meet with your husband and listen to his side of the story, and then I have to consult the People's Committee and his factory administrators, and then after that—"

"You don't believe what I've said?" Sun Hee interrupted.

"The law does not approve a divorce claim based on one person's appeal. It bases the argument on objectivity and justice." Jeong Jin Wu had to put his foot down in this matter.

Sun Hee held the corner of her dress as if she had done something wrong, and after a moment, she got up from her seat.

"Comrade Judge, allow me to divorce my husband. I beg of you. I believe I've explained my situation clearly, but you don't seem to understand."

This was a common plea from divorce claimants. Jeong Jin Wu closed the legal file and, with a gentle voice, said, "Comrade Sun Hee, please calm down. The divorce process takes a long time. Go back home and continue doing what you've been doing. Divorce is one thing, but you have a child at home who needs you."

Sun Hee wiped the tears along her long, thick eyelashes one last time, bowed in deference to Jeong Jin Wu, and left the office. The door closed quietly behind her, and the clicking of her high heels faded down the corridor.

The office's serenity was restored. The warmth of the sunlight came in through the tall window, but Jeong Jin Wu was not at ease.

Sun Hee's gloomy countenance and her family problems had cast a dark shadow over his heart. He walked over to the window to catch a glimpse of Sun Hee leaving the court.

Jeong Jin Wu crossed his arms and paced back and forth across his office. The hardwood floors creaked at every step. Each creak felt like stakes being driven into his heart. He sat down in his chair, and then the telephone rang.

"Judge Jeong Jin Wu speaking."

He heard a deep, composed voice on the other line.

"This is Chae Rim from the Provincial Industrial Technology Commission Board. Where has the senior judge gone? I've been trying to reach him, but he's not answering."

"He went to Pyongyang on a business trip," responded Jeong Jin Wu.

For some reason, the name Chae Rim sounded all too familiar to him.

"Will he return soon?"

"It doesn't seem like he'll be back before Wednesday."

"I see . . ." Chae Rim dragged out his response in disappointment and then heaved a sigh.

Jeong Jin Wu sensed something was troubling the man.

"May I ask what this is about?" asked Jeong Jin Wu.

"Well, you see . . . I'm the chairman of the commission board."

"Yes, and so?"

"It's nothing really. But, by any chance, has anyone stopped by the court to file for divorce?"

"Yes, many people have."

"Was Chae Sun Hee one of them?"

"Yes," responded Jeong Jin Wu, paying closer attention.

"Comrade Judge, I don't know how to say this, but . . ."

"It's all right. I'm listening."

"Right, so have you decided what to do about her case? You will divorce them, no?"

Jeong Jin Wu was taken aback by these questions because they sounded like orders.

"Comrade Chairman, I don't know what kind of relationship you have with Chae Sun Hee, but it sounds like you are showing too much interest in legal matters. My advice to you is not to interfere in another family's case and certainly not in the judicial system."

There was no response from the other end of the line.

Jeong Jin Wu continued, "I cannot make a decision based on listening only to Chae Sun Hee's story. I need to hear Lee Seok Chun's story as well and provide an impartial solution. This will, of course, take some time."

"I see. Comrade Judge, would it be all right to stop by your office sometime tomorrow or the next day?" Chae Rim requested.

"Come by anytime." And with that, Jeong Jin Wu hung up the phone.

An unsettling anxiety came over him, provoked by the intrusive attitude of the chairman on the other end of the receiver. Jeong Jin Wu's first impression of Chae Rim was certainly not positive. He was much too concerned with the divorce case procedure, and it also sounded as if he was accustomed to using his official position to get things done his way. In this case, Chae Rim seemed to have some personal interest in Sun Hee's divorce litigation, demonstrated particularly when he demanded that the senior judge expedite it. Jeong Jin Wu had experienced many foolish people thinking they could use their political power or personal networks to manipulate legal proceedings to their advantage. He only hoped that the person who had just called was not that kind of a person, though he had his doubts. Jeong Jin Wu considered those types of people who took principles lightly to be far more troublesome and exhausting than those undergoing a divorce.

Jeong Jin Wu dragged his feet toward the sofa and fell onto it. He closed his eyes and tried to rest, but that familiar name flashed in his mind again.

Chae Rim. That disquieting name reminded him of a horrible experience.

*When and where have I heard that name before? It's such an unusual name . . . Oh, that's right!*

Jeong Jin Wu remembered. *Chae Rim!* He had been a tall, handsome manager of sales at the Electrical Hardware Factory. He filed for a fault divorce on the grounds of his wife's adulterous affair, but when that charge was proved to be false, he changed his grounds to irreconcilable differences. Jeong Jin Wu was the one who divorced them. That was six years ago . . .

There were only a few people inside the courtroom that day. The seats for the audience were nearly empty, with the exception of those occupied by family members. There were not many people interested in another couple's divorce hearing. On the bench, Jeong Jin Wu was seated between two other judges. There was also a prosecutor, sitting next to a clerk. In the very front row sat Chae Rim with his head held high, looking confidently at the magistrates and the nation's flag that hung right above them. A look of imperiousness beamed from his eyes. There was not a trace of despair or agony on his face. Next to him sat his wife with her head lowered, waiting nervously for the judgment. This day was going to be the last time that they would sit next to each other.

Chae Rim had filed for a fault divorce on the grounds of his wife's alleged affair with her manager.

Glancing at the couple, Jeong Jin Wu thought to himself, *What's the crime in walking home from work with her production manager a couple of times? It's on the way, and as comrades, can't they share problems or talk about factory matters?*

Jeong Jin Wu saw through people like Chae Rim. He figured that Chae Rim was filing for a fault divorce not because she had walked home with her manager but for some other reason. The truth was that Chae Rim, a promising technician, dared not be seen in public with a country bumpkin like his wife.

Chae Rim had despised her for it. He had criticized every aspect of her character and amplified every one of her flaws. He had hurled insults such as "You're an idiot for heating up the beer for guests," "You're short and ugly," "You have no social skills," "You're stupid." He had even physically abused her, leaving imprints of his rage on her body.

Jeong Jin Wu had issued an order for an investigation of Chae Rim for domestic violence, but Chae Rim's factory officials intervened and forced Jeong Jin Wu to drop the case.

Jeong Jin Wu was still bitter about that incident and felt that the divorce litigation should be dismissed. He wanted to punish Chae Rim for his violent and insolent personality, but he knew that the court would not approve of sentencing someone based on personality. He glared at Chae Rim and then looked at Chae Rim's wife.

Chae Rim's wife did not even have the courage to look up at the family members on the bench. While her husband attended the university in the city, she planted young trees in the mountains for a reforestation company. In the summer, her skin would get sunburned from the scorching heat. In the winter, her skin would crack from the cold and merciless wind. Her body would become soaked by the rain, and she would shiver all over in the snow, but this had become routine for her. She lived a lamentable life. When she received her meager wages, she would set aside a small portion for herself and her children and mail the rest to her husband in the city. Unlike the other working women, she did not purchase cosmetics or clothes suitable for the different seasons and varying weather conditions. She convinced herself that, aside from one formal outfit, she did not need more clothes, especially with the kind of work she did. Her only motivation was for her husband to graduate from the university and become an outstanding technician. She lulled herself to sleep with hopes of finding a home around his workplace and living a comfortable family life in the city. With those dreams, she continued planting trees and raising her daughter and son on her own.

However, her naive dreams were shattered when she encountered the abysmal reality of her husband's indifference toward her. Chae Rim was not the person whom she had loved and cherished. She never heard anything remotely romantic or affectionate from him. When she would come up to the city from her village, he would not buy her a single article of clothing that would make her fashionable like the city dwellers. He never expressed affection to her; he never opened the door to his heart. When it seemed as if he opened his heart, it was like an empty storage room with a cold breeze passing through. She felt that her husband did not consider her his wife but rather a housekeeper and a nanny for the children. Yet she reassured herself by thinking that his was a dignified occupation and that it required him to always be busy. She had accepted this fact and continued living her life for her husband. But this came to an end when she received the divorce papers from Chae Rim. He accused her of committing adultery and expected her to comply with these grounds for divorce. When she denied the allegation, Chae Rim altered the grounds to irreconcilable differences in order to facilitate the divorce litigation.

During the hearing, she made her demands clear. She stated quietly that she could no longer live with her husband, and with that, she began to cry. She did not expect love from her husband— she had given up on that long ago. She simply wanted him to respect her as a human being, but even that seemed futile. It was only abuse and degradation, an onslaught she could no longer endure.

Judge Jeong Jin Wu took pity on the wife after realizing what she had done for Chae Rim and their children. For the sake of her inalienable rights as a human being, he divorced the couple. It was clear to him that she was the victim of this marriage.

Her eyes in their shadowed sockets seemed nearly hollow from the countless times she had cried. She had wept burning tears of regret for having lived a life of misery, tears of misfortune. However, today was different. These were not tears of frailty or defeat; these were tears of firm determination for a new day ahead of her. She was the kind of person who stood resolute in the face of adversity, and like a wild chrysanthemum, she would emerge from the shrubbery of the dead forest.

Jeong Jin Wu decided to respect and support her civil rights with all his legal might. He felt it the duty of the law to protect the woman's rights from her husband's contemptible behavior, which had disrespected her dignity.

Jeong Jin Wu divorced the couple. Yet it pained his heart, knowing that he was destroying a family, a unit of society. And the couple's children? Indeed, Jeong Jin Wu was not able to free himself of the heavy guilt of breaking the terrible news to the children.

A couple of days before the trial, their children had been called into his office. Jeong Jin Wu offered them two chairs, but the children were so inseparable that they both sat in one. The daughter was ten years old, and the son was seven. They both attended the same elementary school. Jeong Jin Wu did not want to waste too much of their time, so he did his best to keep the conversation brief.

"Your mother and father," Jeong Jin Wu began, "will no longer live in the same house, so with whom would you prefer to live?"

For the sake of nurturing the children and looking out for their interests, Jeong Jin Wu knew it was always best to have them be with their mother. But he gave them the opportunity to decide for themselves.

The children could not respond to the judge's shocking question, which would decide, once and for all, their fate. These children had never imagined that their parents' relationship was in such a dire condition.

After a while, the daughter spoke up, her tears falling like rain-drops. "I . . . I will live with my mother."

"Me, too! With my mom. I don't want to be separated from my sister," replied the brother in utter fear.

It had already been six years since that incident. Judge Jeong Jin Wu got up from the sofa. He tried not to recall that heart-wrenching moment, but the image of the frightened children had not diminished in his memory. The decision that had been made in the court was for the daughter to live with her mother and for the son to live with his father. It would have been better for both of them to be with their mother, but Jeong Jin Wu did not want to overburden her, now that she was a single parent. Jeong Jin Wu had to consider the son's future and thought that a boy would need a male role model. For that reason, the siblings were separated.

Jeong Jin Wu did not know what had happened to that family since the court hearing. He knew only that Chae Rim found a younger wife, and that his ex-wife had continued living with her daughter without remarrying.

*The daughter must be sixteen years old already and the son thir-teen,* Jeong Jin Wu thought.

Jeong Jin Wu hardly ever ran into that family even though they all lived in the same city. Not too long ago, he had inadvertently run into the ex-wife, but she had avoided him. There was no opportunity for him to talk to her. He thought that unless the couple filed for an appeal to revise the custody arrangement, there was no reason for either a judge or the law to interfere in their personal lives. Even if they were to appeal, he would not be able to handle the case because of all the accumulated work he had to do.

Judge Jeong Jin Wu never forgot all the individual divorce cases he had presided over in the past. They left painful impressions on him because he was not dealing just with legal cases but with people's lives. Each case required the judge's discernment and power of reason to administer sentences, but the human heart, so frail and delicate after a divorce hearing, also required compassion and encouragement from the justice system.

Jeong Jin Wu thought, *Chae Rim, the chairman of the Provincial Industrial Technology Commission Board. Could it really be him? Would he come see me after the unpleasant memories of the place from six years ago? Is it the same Chae Rim whom I divorced that day? No, the Chae Rim I divorced six years ago was a manager at the Electrical Hardware Factory.*

Jeong Jin Wu shook his head in disbelief.

*It must be someone else. Who could go through that kind of divorce and then return to the court as if nothing had happened? But knowing him, I wouldn't be surprised. Then, is he related to Chae Sun Hee? They do have the same family name. No, it must be another man.*

Jeong Jin Wu attempted to banish unpleasant thoughts about Chae Rim from his mind as he paced back and forth. The hardwood floor creaked louder than it ever had before.

# 2

It began to rain in the evening. It was unusual weather even for this region.

Judge Jeong Jin Wu wanted to wait for the rain to pass because he did not have an umbrella in his office, but he grew impatient. Although Gang An District, house number 19, was a bit out of the way, he decided to stop by on his way home from work.

He ran to find refuge under the newly budding trees, but he could not escape the rain. Cold drops rolled down his face and onto his shoulders. It was not long before his clothes were drenched.

He crossed a narrow bridge over a small creek and saw many single-story residential houses.

There was a young woman in a raincoat and rain boots coming toward him. She held an umbrella over his head and kindly helped Jeong Jin Wu find Lee Seok Chun and Chae Sun Hee's house. It was a quaint, two-bedroom house with a traditional Korean roof.

A young boy stood outside, shivering and staring vacantly at the way the rain fell from the eaves. Next to him was a shaggy dog, lying on the ground, also soaked by the rain. The lethargic guardian of the house did not bark as Jeong Jin Wu entered the front yard.

Judge Jeong Jin Wu asked, "Young man, where are your parents?"

"They're not here yet," the boy replied. He coughed. "Who are you, mister?"

The boy's hair was wet from the rain, and his arms were covered with goose bumps from being cold. He had dimples in his plump cheeks, and his large lustrous eyes resembled Sun Hee's. His eyes sparkled with innocence and curiosity, but, unlike other children his age, he also showed signs of anxiety and melancholy. He was the epitome of a child raised in a dysfunctional family.

"Well, you see. I am . . ." Jeong Jin Wu was about to introduce himself as the legal administrator presiding over the divorce case of claimant Chae Sun Hee and Lee Seok Chun, as he was accustomed to do in most introductory situations. But he thought it would be ridiculous to say such a thing to a child, so he did not complete his sentence. Instead, he said he was from Seok Chun's factory.

The boy squinted at Jeong Jin Wu with suspicion, and after coughing a couple of times, he said, "I've never seen you before. Besides, my father's shift isn't over yet."

"Well, you see. Uh, I arrived first. And, uh, your father, he will be home . . . uh, as soon as he . . . uh, as soon as he finishes cleaning the lathe machines."

Jeong Jin Wu had just remembered that Seok Chun was a lathe operator from his meeting with Sun Hee. The boy now looked at Jeong Jin Wu with trusting eyes.

"Then do you also work the lathe?"

"Uh, something like that. Aren't you going to finish kindergarten and go up to elementary school this fall?"

"Yes, it's because I have an early birthday." Then the boy let out a deep sigh, like an adult. Perhaps he felt he was old enough to be with the bigger kids.

"Remind me of your name, young man."

"It's Lee Ho Nam."

"That's right! Ho Nam. Is anybody home, Ho Nam?"

The boy shook his head and stepped to the side to show Jeong Jin Wu a padlock on the front door. Ho Nam sneezed and coughed more frequently. His cheeks were red, glowing like embers. Worried about the child's health, Jeong Jin Wu placed his hand on Ho Nam's forehead. It was as hot as a heated floor.

"You seem to have caught a cold, young man. Your clothes are all wet. Do you feel achy?"

Ho Nam insisted that he was not sick.

Jeong Jin Wu looked around at the neighboring houses, but it appeared that the neighbors had not yet returned from work. As Jeong Jin Wu was contemplating what to do, the young woman who had directed him to Ho Nam's house earlier approached.

Jeong Jin Wu called out to her, "Comrade, thank goodness you're here. Where do you live?"

"It's a bit of a walk from here. It's the collective unit next to the river."

"Is the neighborhood community center far from here as well?"

"Yes, it is."

"Comrade, do me a favor. When the boy's parents come home, tell them that I have taken him to my apartment."

Without letting Ho Nam hear him, Jeong Jin Wu quietly told the young woman that he was a judge from the Superior Court and gave her his address. He had originally planned to have a talk with Lee Seok Chun and the neighborhood leader, but he had to postpone that for the sake of making sure Ho Nam was looked after.

Ho Nam coughed continuously. Jeong Jin Wu took out his handkerchief and wiped the boy's wet face and hair.

"Hey, Ho Nam. Would you like to go to my house and wait for your parents there? It's not too far from here."

Ho Nam considered Jeong Jin Wu a trustworthy man, so he accepted Jeong Jin Wu's hand and left with him. Each time Ho

Nam took a step, water in his boots made a squishy sound. Jeong Jin Wu removed the boy's boots and poured the water out. Ho Nam coughed again.

"Do you want to get on my back?" asked Jeong Jin Wu.

"Sure!" Ho Nam exclaimed.

Ho Nam was fatigued from standing and waiting in the cold rain. He jumped onto Jeong Jin Wu's back without hesitation. The dog started wagging its tail and followed them outside.

"Bear, you stay," ordered Ho Nam. "Hey, mister, would it be all right to take Bear with us?"

"I'm sorry, but it's not a good idea. I live on the third floor of an apartment building."

"Bear, you stay. I'll be back soon."

The dog whimpered as it retired to a spot next to the door.

The journey to Jeong Jin Wu's apartment became tolerable when the rain momentarily stopped. For a seven-year-old boy, Ho Nam was quite heavy. Jeong Jin Wu's back was cold and wet, but it warmed up with Ho Nam on it, particularly with his high fever. At times Ho Nam slipped down Jeong Jin Wu's back, but then Jeong Jin Wu would lift him back up. Jeong Jin Wu saw dark clouds rolling toward them. He picked up his pace to avoid the second wave of the downpour. Drops of water fell from the leaves and tree branches. Ho Nam pressed his face against Jeong Jin Wu's back each time drops of water fell onto his neck.

"Hey, Ho Nam."

"Huh?"

"Don't you go to Provincial Performing Arts kindergarten?"

"Uh huh."

"Why do you walk home by yourself?"

"Because I'm a big boy," Ho Nam replied.

"Isn't the kindergarten far from your house? That's why the other kids come home with their parents, right?"

"Yes . . . but . . . I'm fine."

It was a brusque yet forlorn answer. Jeong Jin Wu was able to infer from Ho Nam's answer that he longed to walk home from school with either one of his parents. No, if Ho Nam had a choice, he would have liked to walk home with both of his parents.

"Hey, do you like your mother more or your father?"

Jeong Jin Wu could feel the warm, soft breath of the child brushing his ear. Ho Nam had been pressing his face against Jeong Jin Wu's back, but then he lifted his head and quietly confessed.

"I like them both."

It was admirable that, although Ho Nam had witnessed the hostility between his quarrelsome parents, he did not have a strong preference for either one of them.

Jeong Jin Wu lifted the child a bit higher on his back and walked faster as the rain began to fall again.

Ho Nam soon fell sound asleep on Jeong Jin Wu's back. Jeong Jin Wu realized that the boy's fever was getting worse as he felt his back getting hotter.

Jeong Jin Wu was certain that his wife had returned from her research trip and was waiting for him at home.

*She must have prepared dinner by now—she always prepares a delicious dinner. Tonight, the boy will feast on a wonderful meal. Let me see . . . After dinner, we will bathe Ho Nam in hot water and place him on the heated floor. Then he will feel much better. Let me see . . . After that I will call Seok Chun at his factory to tell him about Ho Nam. And if Sun Hee receives the note from the young woman at the collective unit first, then she will probably be the first one to arrive.*

Gratified with his plans, Jeong Jin Wu approached the front entrance to his apartment building and set down Ho Nam, who was not quite awake. He caressed the child and called out his name until he regained consciousness.

As they climbed the stairs to the third floor, Jeong Jin Wu explained his simple plan to Ho Nam. Jeong Jin Wu could hardly contain his excitement. When they got to the door, Jeong Jin Wu noticed it was locked. His heart sank. He took the key from inside his mailbox and opened the door to an empty apartment. He did not smell delicious food from the kitchen nor did he see his wife.

Plans to feed Ho Nam a hearty dinner and wash the boy with his wife's help were fanciful thoughts that existed only in his imagination. The reality was utterly abysmal. Jeong Jin Wu found a note left by his wife.

> I just received news to come back to Yeonsudeok right away. I took the late bus. They said that the weather is going to get colder tonight and there are already signs of frost. It might even snow. I'm worried about all the seedlings in the laboratory. I hope you understand. I should've made dinner before I left. I'm really sorry.
>
> Love,
>
> Eun Ok

Fury stirred in Jeong Jin Wu's heart. Already annoyed with being wet from the rain, he was even more infuriated by Eun Ok's request that he understand her situation.

*Why do I have to do everything around the house? Am I the housewife?* he thought.

Eun Ok had been working at the agricultural laboratory for more than twenty years and was gone for more than twenty days out of a month. Jeong Jin Wu could not recall a single day when she was just a modest housewife, cooking, cleaning, and raising their son like other ordinary housewives. She was also in her fifties, and he began to wonder how much longer he would have to wait and be patient with her.

"It's not like her research is groundbreaking. She's just cultivating vegetables," Jeong Jin Wu mumbled bitterly.

"Hey, mister, your mom comes home late, too?" interrupted Ho Nam, having grown bored standing next to the shoe rack.

Jeong Jin Wu forced a genial smile for the child's sake.

"The mom of this house went on a research trip again. So, my little guest, once you've taken off your boots, come inside."

Ho Nam hesitated at first but then took a few steps inside. When he saw his wet footprints on the floor, his face flushed with embarrassment. Jeong Jin Wu smiled.

"Don't worry about it. Take off your clothes so I can give you a bath."

Jeong Jin Wu changed from his wet clothes to dry ones and helped Ho Nam get out of his clothes. Ho Nam's undergarments were also soaked. Jeong Jin Wu filled the bathtub with hot water from the kiln and meticulously cleaned the boy's body.

Jeong Jin Wu also had a son, but he had grown up and was currently serving in the military so there were no children's clothes to offer the child. He had Ho Nam sit by the warmest area of the heated floor and covered him with a thick blanket.

After taking some cold medicine, Ho Nam sat cozily under the blanket and sipped on hot water. Jeong Jin Wu went into the kitchen to prepare dinner and checked on the boy frequently. He saw large beads of sweat rolling down the boy's face. Ho Nam's temperature had subsided. It appeared that the child was recovering, which relieved Jeong Jin Wu.

He went down to the bookstore that occupied the building's ground level and made a phone call. The supervisor of the Gang An Machine Factory told Jeong Jin Wu that Seok Chun had not yet left work. Jeong Jin Wu gave the supervisor his address and told him to have Seok Chun stop by his house after work.

It rained violently.

Jeong Jin Wu climbed the stairs slowly, his heart heavy. He would have to prepare his own meals again and manage the makeshift greenhouse in the master bedroom again. He would have to control the humidity and the temperature of the greenhouse, water the vegetables, and prune them whenever necessary. He would also have to record the growth and development of the vegetables. Eun

Ok had not written, "Take care of the greenhouse" on the little note that she had left, but he knew what she meant. "There are already signs of frost" also meant for him to keep the windows closed and take extra care of the vegetables at home.

Whenever Eun Ok would go on these research trips, she would leave Jeong Jin Wu with all the household chores along with the task of caring for the plants in the makeshift greenhouse in their master bedroom. Her frequent absences had become the norm in Jeong Jin Wu's life and the chores routine.

Jeong Jin Wu was exasperated and angry. The whirlwind of fury had turned reason deaf and blind, converting wrath into malice—but he knew there was nothing he could do.

# 3

Lee Seok Chun had finally arrived at Judge Jeong Jin Wu's apartment. They sat across from each other on the living room floor. Seok Chun was a man of medium stature, robust and broad-shouldered, a thirty-five-year-old in the prime of his life. His face was sharp, with a chiseled jawline, his lips thick, and his eyes deep-set but soft. His fingers were calloused from handling steel at his factory, and his hands were large, with the visible contours of his veins extending up his arm, but they trembled as he caressed his sleeping son. Seok Chun heaved a sigh of distress that was strong enough to bring down the walls.

"Comrade Judge, if we get divorced, then what's going to happen to my son? The court will most likely hand him over to his mother, right?"

"That's not necessarily the case. The child will go where it's most advantageous for his well-being and future."

"Then allow me to take my son. I beg of you. I will take care of him."

"You expect me to hand this child over to a father who can't even manage his own life?"

"But with my son, it's going to be different. I can look after him," said Seok Chun with an expression of determination.

"Comrade, don't work yourself up like this," replied the judge in a conciliatory tone. "This is not a courtroom. Calm down and let's talk about this. I called you here because I wanted to know a couple of things. First, if you would, begin with the time you met your wife. And second, tell me how the two of you grew to lack the same rhythm."

Seok Chun figured that Sun Hee had mentioned "rhythm" to the judge, and he smirked disdainfully. He took the cigarette Jeong Jin Wu offered him and let it hang from his thick lips. He stared at his sleeping son.

"The very first time I met my wife was when I was in military service and was sent to the Superior Steel Production Factory to help out. That was about ten years ago. There were three of us, me and two other steel mechanics. We were supposed to install some fraise and a band around the polishing cylinder made by the Gang An Machine Factory."

A dark shadow veiled his soft eyes as he began reminiscing.

At the end of the month, the Superior Steel Production Factory celebrated the hard work of the three mechanics and two technicians from the Gang An Machine Factory. The technicians, along with Seok Chun and his friends, were called up onstage. The board members of the Superior Steel Production Factory first acknowledged the efforts of Seok Chun and his friends before they honored the technicians.

Seok Chun blushed when he looked at the cheering audience. He suddenly began to feel both anxiety and satisfaction about the acknowledgment that he was about to receive from the people for doing something so ordinary. He felt like a young fledgling that was attempting to spread its wings and fly for the first time. He did not feel as if his legs were planted on the stage.

Three young women carrying bundles of flowers came up onstage. One of the young women was a friction press worker. She had a wide forehead and a slender physique. It was Chae Sun Hee. She wore a muslin dress that wrapped around her body like a morning fog. Sun Hee appeared graceful with her elegant dress, shapely figure, and beautiful face. She was holding flowers, which looked like they had blossomed from her chest.

When Seok Chun saw Sun Hee approaching him, his elation suddenly subsided. He felt apprehensive, and his heart began to race like the heart of someone who had stolen something.

*Shit. Why of all women does she have to bring me flowers?* thought Seok Chun.

He tried his best not to look in Sun Hee's direction. He could not forget the day he first met her, a month ago.

When Seok Chun and his friends finally arrived at the village in the mountains after a long bus ride, they met Sun Hee on the side of the road, and she directed them to the factory. The road to the factory was neither complicated nor heavily congested, and if she had just given them directions, they would have been able to find the factory without a problem. But she extended her generosity to the men, got on the bus, and guided them to the front door of the factory. Her hospitable personality was the reason the manager of the factory had chosen Sun Hee, and not the accountant, to help the men settle into the factory and the village. That night in the dormitory room, Seok Chun lay in bed without feeling the least bit foreign in this new environment but slept soundly as if he were at home.

In the morning, the sunlight peeked through the window blinds and woke Seok Chun from his deep slumber. Seok Chun, still half asleep, opened his heavy eyes and imagined Sun Hee's face, her vibrant smile, her tender voice. He did not know what had possessed him to think about her. Perhaps it was because she was the first person he had met in the village. Perhaps it was her white face, large beautiful eyes, long eyelashes, and attractive figure that had captivated his youthful heart and left a deep impression on his mind. Like a wild chrysanthemum, she was divine, and the more he thought about her, the more he became infatuated with her.

He got up from his bed and flung open the windows. The warm sunlight and cool breeze filled the room with life. A melodious river flowed from the mountains in the distance beyond the hills. His heart beat rapidly, unable to contain his excitement, at the thought of starting anew at the factory in the village. The sublime natural landscape gave him hope and joy, but it was evident that Sun Hee was the real source of his passion and his uncontrollable emotions.

Seok Chun went down to the factory and saw Sun Hee in her dark uniform, working by the friction press. When she saw Seok Chun, she asked if he had slept well with the tender smile and beautiful tone of voice from yesterday. Seok Chun answered but then realized that the brevity of his response left no room for the conversation to continue. So he helped her lift some metal parts to the worktable to give her the impression that he was not here only to see her. He asked about the machine's performance and other inconsequential matters.

When the other workers saw Seok Chun, they knew that he did these things only because he fancied Sun Hee. Despite what others said behind his back, Seok Chun continued to help Sun Hee every chance he got. Even while assembling his own equipment, he would glance over in the direction of the friction press, hoping to catch a glimpse of Sun Hee.

Amid the noise of all the running machines, Seok Chun was able to distinguish the sound of the friction press that Sun Hee operated. He could see drops of sweat rolling down her forehead, around her lustrous eyes, and down her white cheeks as she arduously worked the press. Such images of Sun Hee occupied Seok Chun's thoughts and enlivened his soul.

A month had passed. Seok Chun yearned for Sun Hee, suffered at the very thought of her. He suffered because he loved her. He loved her with all the more passion because he loved her innocently. He paced frantically in his dormitory room, trying to find the means to express his indescribable feelings for her. At that moment, he allowed the purest of the reveries that filled his mind to fall upon a piece of paper. He sprawled on the floor and wrote with intensity, transcribing the ecstasy of his soul. His pen could not keep up with the pace of his thoughts. He crossed out words or ripped up the entire letter and began again. He wrote deep into the night without fatigue. He had written many pages, but none was to his liking. He reread his letter to see if he had made any grammatical errors or if the letter conveyed his feelings properly. He omitted phrases that made him sound utterly desperate or too ravenous for her love while still attempting to reveal his honest feelings for her without any reservations. In the end, he had written a corny love letter very much like something one would find in a cheap romance novel. But he did not want the letter to be a love letter, even though he knew it could not be anything other than a love letter. He did not want Sun Hee to think of him as a deluded romantic. When he realized that his letter was nothing but a love letter, he threw it away in frustration.

Early the next morning at the factory, Seok Chun asked the repairman in the next room, who worked closely with Sun Hee, to pass her a note requesting that she meet him by the willow trees near the riverbank in the evening.

That night, the moon hid behind a thick veil of dark clouds, and the stars that had twinkled momentarily disappeared without a trace into the opaque sky. As the low clouds rolled in, the night grew darker. The air was still and humid.

Seok Chun had been waiting an hour with his back against the willow tree. There was no sign of Sun Hee. In front of Sun Hee's dormitory, tall streetlights lined the road. The brilliance of the lights reached the riverbank where Seok Chun was standing. A few workers passed by, but none who resembled Sun Hee.

Clouds formed and raindrops began to fall. A few negligible drops at first, but then the rain began to beat on the leaves and bushes. Seok Chun became irritated, and then he felt lonely. Myriad thoughts crossed his mind.

*Did I invite her out too late in the evening? She probably doesn't even care about me.*

He began to regret the time he had spent around the friction press, helping her load and unload heavy equipment. He was annoyed with himself. At the same time, he wondered why she had treated him so kindly if she had not even a hint of affection for him.

The rain fell heavily. Seok Chun tried to avoid getting wet by standing under a willow tree, but it was futile. His clothes were soaked. He felt that the rain had found a way through the willow tree to mock him for behaving foolishly. But he also felt that the rain was helping him wash away all the feelings he had for Sun Hee—all those sleepless nights of thinking of her when she did not even care for him.

It had gotten later in the evening. The lights in the dormitory rooms began to turn off one by one. Seok Chun, who had been picking off flower petals, threw the stem away in disdain and left. The rain poured down mercilessly on him. His shoes and socks were drenched from stepping in muddy puddles, which intensified his frustration. To avoid the puddles, he decided to walk across the field of tall grass. Seok Chun meandered as though intoxicated and, struggling to keep his balance, proceeded in despair. Suddenly he fell into a ditch, a booby trap set by the neighborhood kids. Covered in mud, he wiped his hands on the wet grass to get some of the mud off, but instead he felt only a prickly sensation, as he was rubbing his hands on thorny weeds.

At that moment, he heard rapid footsteps coming toward him. Then they stopped. Seok Chun lifted his head and saw on the path the silhouette of a woman holding an umbrella against the dim dormitory lights. In her other hand was a second umbrella. Seok Chun approached the woman as though he were being pulled in her direction. The woman did not appear to be frightened; she did not step aside. In the shadow of the umbrella, Seok Chun saw the face of Sun Hee.

Sun Hee, with her hair disheveled from running and wet from the rain, appeared more attractive than ever.

Breathing heavily, Sun Hee asked, "Have you been waiting long?"

Even though Seok Chun perceived that she was apologetic for her tardiness, he asked curtly, "Did you have any intention of coming out tonight?"

Sun Hee handed the second umbrella to Seok Chun without responding.

He did not reach for the umbrella and instead remained upright, like a wooden post, with no life or expression. He then realized that she had brought him the umbrella out of pity, that had it not been for the rain, she would not have come out. As shame and regret combined with his damaged pride and frustration, he nearly burst like a pressurized smokestack and wanted to shout, *Do I look pitiful to you?* But he repressed his anger and, without a word, walked past Sun Hee.

"Take the umbrella. Your clothes are going to get wet."

"I'm already wet," barked Seok Chun. He then sneered, "Why don't you use the other one yourself?"

It was a derisive response. He knew that it would be silly for her to use two umbrellas, so he snickered. Then he thought that if Sun Hee had come out with the intention of meeting him, his behavior tonight would appear despicable. Nonetheless, he did not slow down and kept walking toward his dormitory. He did not hear footsteps following him, so he assumed Sun Hee remained standing where he had left her. Though he wanted to, he did not look back, instead forcing himself to keep his head still. He thought that even the slightest glance would betray weakness, so he pressed on to his room.

Seok Chun had once had uncontainable feelings for the village, the countryside, the warm sun, the cool air, and the lush hills. But now, none of his surroundings satisfied him as he trudged along the muddy path. He regretted ever coming here. By tomorrow, his duties here would be completed, and he would return to his hometown. With all these complicated thoughts whirling in his head, he proceeded to walk with determination, resolved to abandon all the feelings he had had for Sun Hee.

That was last night. And now the woman Seok Chun wanted to forget was approaching him onstage with a bundle of flowers. Seok Chun tried to ignore her and solemnly looked at the audience. But he could not remain calm and stole glances at Sun Hee from the corner of his eye. He felt nervous, and his heart raced like the heart of someone who had committed a crime, anxious and deeply distressed. He had no means of escaping from Sun Hee's presence. When he saw Sun Hee in the traditional Korean dress and with flowers in her arms approaching him, he felt his knees buckle. Seok Chun was not able to subdue his impassioned emotions. He felt as if he were caught up in a whirlpool, his senses thrown into disarray. This was because Seok Chun truly longed for Sun Hee. He wanted her to forgive him for his inappropriate behavior the other night.

Sun Hee approached Seok Chun, who was third in line.

"You've really worked tirelessly for us," whispered Sun Hee with a coy smile.

Sun Hee acted as if nothing had happened between them the night before and presented the bundle of flowers to Seok Chun with both hands. This time, it was not an umbrella but flowers. He was intoxicated by her perfume, and his distraught emotions dissipated. Seok Chun's heart melted with delight at the sound of Sun Hee's tender voice.

After the ceremony thanking the three men and the technicians, there was a performance by the Factory Arts Committee. It was a simple performance, amateur at best.

However, when Sun Hee got up onstage, the ordinary became extraordinary. Members of the audience applauded loudly, expressing their pride at having a worker with such talent at their factory. Sun Hee clasped her hands together and sang in a sweet lyrical tone, projecting the calm of a seasoned professional.

Seok Chun realized that Sun Hee was beyond his reach, an angel who dwelled in the celestial world who would never embrace, adore, or cherish an unsophisticated man like himself. The thought of his love being forever unrequited brought pain to his heart, his entire being. His body felt feeble at the very thought of having to dismiss his love for her. He felt a despairing certainty, which he had resisted, but, in the end, needed to accept.

While Sun Hee lured the audience into the sublime world of music, Seok Chun watched from a reserved distance. He could not participate in the festivities. He became more and more forlorn, overwhelmed with melancholy. He recalled the determination that he had made the night before in the rain while trudging home and recognized that it was the correct decision and that he must carry it out. He realized that a duck and a swan swimming in the same pond could not overcome the most apparent obstacle of their intrinsic difference. The duck would never be the swan's mate, as their different lives would lead to different destinies. He could not listen to the rest of the song, so he abruptly got up and left the hall.

It was a bright moonlit evening. He walked past the courtyard in front of the meeting hall and headed toward the small park surrounded by tall, dense willow trees. Seok Chun entered the darkness cast by the shadows of the trees. The moonlight could penetrate neither the park nor the solitude of Seok Chun's soul. He sat on a rock, which was still warm from baking in the sun all afternoon. He felt dejected, like a man who has lost his will to live. He was angry with himself and also sorry for himself. Why was he agonizing over a childish infatuation, over a woman who was beyond his reach? He had determined to forget about Sun Hee, but he deeply wanted his feelings for her to persist. He regretted his foolish behavior of the night before, when his words, which he had intended to use to express his love for her, had instead been cynical, deriving from his frustration and embarrassment. Yet he loved her, he still desired her. He felt that he had neither the strength nor the courage to control his emotions.

He decided to leave at dawn without anyone knowing, without a word, while the villagers were still asleep. He thought that if he left, his love for Sun Hee would subside, gradually fading into oblivion, and then his troubled heart would be able to find solace and regain its peace in solitude. Yet he could not forget the factory, to which he had grown attached. He did not want to leave because of Sun Hee. His heart would not find peace in an abrupt departure. He tried to convince himself that if he spent his energy solely on working on the lathe and living among the noble factory workers and adopting their humble lifestyle, then thoughts of Sun Hee, his love for her and everything that concerned her very existence would fade away. Seok Chun could never forget the lathe work that had become a part of his identity along with the smell of greased steel, the sharp steel rods, the admirable workers and their quiet ambitions, and the humorous stories the factory workers told. These were the elements that shaped his life, that gave passion to his creativity and aspirations. Just thinking of leaving this village, he already longed for the smell of the countryside, the beautiful landscape, and the people with whom he had worked for the past month.

Then the door to the meeting hall was flung open, and people poured out. People passed the courtyard and took the path next to the small park to go home. The night was terrifyingly dark, with no streetlights to guide them. Yet laughter, boisterous voices, coughing, someone calling for someone else, parents concerned about their children's whereabouts, and other loud voices reverberated in the darkness. There was the sound of a young boy trying to frighten a young girl, and the laughter that ensued. Flashlights and cigarette lighters flickered all around like fireflies flitting through a field. The night was dark but full of life.

Soon, silence fell and dampened any remnants of the festive sounds. But then, from the courtyard, Seok Chun heard footsteps approaching him.

*Someone must've just woken up in the concert hall and realized that everyone had gone home. Why doesn't he go toward the noise? Why does he have to come this way?*

The person approached with caution and then halted behind Seok Chun. There was silence for a moment, an awkward hesitancy that held Seok Chun back from stirring, talking, or turning around. And then a woman's soft voice called his name.

"Comrade Seok Chun?"

When Seok Chun heard that voice, it was as if he had touched an electric current that stunned his body. He rose slowly, trembling with anticipation. Seok Chun blushed in the presence of Sun Hee's angelic radiance. He gazed at Sun Hee with the desire and excitement of starting anew. Their eyes conducted a passionate dialogue. In moments such as these, words may fail to express one's feelings, but eyes can speak ineffable emotions. Seok Chun managed to stand up, but he did not know how to behave or read Sun Hee's expression. He had already forgotten about last night's humiliating incident, how he had worried over her and then had determined to forget about her. Although she was the source of all his anguish, he wanted to welcome her into his heart again.

"Why are you sitting here alone?" she asked.

Seok Chun had no words to respond.

"I saw you leave during my song," added Sun Hee.

He was surprised and relieved that she had noticed his absence.

*So, she did see me leaving while she was singing her song! She even found me sitting here at the small park!*

He wondered if this gesture was her way of expressing interest in him. He did not think she was taking pity on him, but he still could not shake off suspicion of her overt generosity. It could have been simply goodwill, but it could not be love, he thought.

"Would you care to join me for a walk?" asked Sun Hee softly.

Without answering her, Seok Chun started walking.

They walked in the park without exchanging any words. The village was quiet that evening. A light, warm breeze shook the persimmon-shaped lightbulbs that had been hung between the willow trees throughout the park.

"How did you find me?" asked Seok Chun, breaking the silence. He spoke carefully. He did not want to sound desperate or appear as if Sun Hee was the only thing on his mind. He was a proud man.

Sun Hee peered into Seok Chun's eyes as if she were trying to read his thoughts. The moonlight was reflected in her eyes, illuminating them with a bright glow.

"I just wanted to see you," responded Sun Hee. "That's why I came looking for you."

There was an impenetrable stillness between the two. The insects that danced around the lightbulbs were livelier.

After quite some time, Seok Chun said, "I'm sorry about what happened last night."

"Me, too. But let's not talk about that anymore."

Seok Chun was enamored with Sun Hee's breezy personality, which cleared away the stagnant air of uncertainty and embarrassment between the two.

But then, Seok Chun had to inform Sun Hee of the bad news. "I was thinking . . . either tomorrow or the next day . . . of going home as soon as the machine gets assembled."

"Why?" Sun Hee exclaimed impetuously. She looked shocked and stopped in midstep.

"Well, I think I will get lonely if I stay here. And besides, what else is there for me to do?"

"You promised to teach the factory workers how to operate the new machine, didn't you?"

"I did at first."

"Then you have to keep your promise. It's your responsibility, as someone from a larger factory, to assist people like us from a smaller factory, even if you don't think much of us."

Seok Chun was at a loss for words.

"I can't believe this," continued Sun Hee. "You promised." She paused. Then her eyes lit up as though she realized something. "Comrade Seok Chun, won't you teach me how to operate the lathe machine?"

Seok Chun looked at Sun Hee in delighted disbelief.

"Comrade Sun Hee, a lathe machine is nothing like a friction press."

"Yes, but, you see, my work is repetitive and monotonous. I want change, something new."

Seok Chun restrained himself from revealing his joy in having found a new excuse to stay.

"By the way, Comrade Sun Hee, you sing really well."

Sun Hee guffawed, "That's belated applause. It seemed like you left because you couldn't stand it."

"No. It was because I was moved," insisted Seok Chun.

"Liar," whispered Sun Hee teasingly.

Sun Hee's response was affectionate, a sign she was growing more comfortable with Seok Chun. This pleased him immensely.

Seok Chun stopped walking and turned to face Sun Hee. His abrupt movement caused his chest to bump into the curve of her shoulder. Sun Hee was startled at this sudden movement. She felt a strange sensation running through her, as if her body had become sensitive to even the slightest contact.

In the bright moonlight, Seok Chun could see her timid eyes, her long thick eyelashes, the blush on her cheeks, and the contours of her lips. His eyes followed her long neck, curved shoulders, and lingered on the swell of her breasts.

At that moment, Seok Chun was so driven by impulse that he reached out and grabbed Sun Hee's hands. Her hands were small, firm, and warm. She felt shy, but she cautiously allowed him to hold her hands.

Seok Chun hastily whispered, "Comrade Sun Hee, do you love me?"

Sun Hee, with her hands still in his, turned her head to the side.

"Huh? Tell me please."

The intervals between Seok Chun's breaths became shorter.

"Please don't do this," Sun Hee whispered apprehensively. Sun Hee freed her hands from Seok Chun's and lightly slapped his chest. Seok Chun did not budge.

"You love me, right?" he asked loudly.

"Shh! Someone might hear you!" Sun Hee cried, surveying her surroundings.

She slapped his chest harder.

"Please, tell me," begged Seok Chun.

"Let's just meet again tomorrow."

Sun Hee retreated with playful eyes. Seok Chun let out a robust laugh, pregnant with his burning passion for Sun Hee. She responded with a coy smile.

"Would you allow me to escort you to your dormitory?" he asked.

"No need. It's right there," Sun Hee said. "You should go. Your roommates must be wondering where you are."

Sun Hee walked away and soon disappeared into the dark night, while Seok Chun gazed fixedly after her.

Thereafter, Seok Chun did not return to his home in the city. Even after his two friends had left the village, Seok Chun postponed his return for another ten days or so, teaching the local factory workers methods for operating the new machines.

On the night before Seok Chun had to leave, a crescent moon dimly illuminated the vast sky. Seok Chun and Sun Hee met at their regular place, the riverbank near the willow trees.

Silver fog quietly descended from the majestic mountains and veiled the landscape. From the dim mountains beyond the hills rushed a strong river, gushing along its wide path with enough force to cut deeply into the earth, rumbling and crashing, washing over rocks and boulders, until it reached the lower rapids. The branches of the willow trees by the riverbank swayed, and the leaves fluttered with life. Pebbles covered the bank, and rocks glistened in the moonlight. Two large boulders leaned close together as though they, too, had come out to share their love for each other. It was a sublime sight, lyrical music, composed on nature's instruments.

Across from the rapids, somewhere in the hills, a cuckoo cried a melancholy song. Legend has it that a poor old woman died and then turned into a cuckoo, which cried for her abandoned children. However, tonight, even the cuckoo's sorrowful cries sounded affectionate to the two lovers.

Seok Chun sat on a rock, placing a guitar borrowed from a young man from his dormitory on his lap, and began to strum. He was not trying to demonstrate his guitar skills to Sun Hee, who already had musical talent and artistic sensitivity well beyond his capacity. Instead, he wanted to show her the tender side of his brusque personality. He did not consider this behavior foolish or arrogant but a genuine display of sentiment that emerged from the simplicity and innocence of his love for her. However, his guitar skills fell short of his desire to express his feelings—his fingers stumbled around the neck of the guitar and produced stubbed sounds.

After a few more attempts, Seok Chun sighed with disappointment and set the guitar down. The hollow body gave out a loud, resonant sound. Sun Hee encouraged him with a quiet sensibility. "There is too much ambient noise around the riverbank. A guitar should be played indoors, where there are better acoustics, for it to produce its true sound."

Seok Chun was grateful. He knew that these words conveyed Sun Hee's love for him. Strolling together by the river in the late evening, breathing in the fragrance of the evening mist, hiding in sheds to avoid getting wetter from the rain were unforgettable moments of their budding love affair. What else would these moments be other than love? He loved her, and Sun Hee loved him back. He looked at Sun Hee with soulful, passionate eyes.

Sun Hee coyly played with a string that hung from the front part of her dress. She appeared more attractive tonight than ever before.

The rapids released a cool, refreshing scent as they flowed forcefully down the valley. Foam from the tides and the small waves shimmered in the moonlight. Larger waves crashed and spread over the bank, momentarily dissipating the reflection from the moonlight, and then proceeded to flow in tranquil bliss. Another set of waves washed up along the riverbank and withdrew, and then another, over and over again.

"Comrade Sun Hee, the rapids also seem to have life. The river sounds like it has a thousand emotions."

"Ever since I was a young child, I've loved the sound of the river rapids," Sun Hee said.

"I wish I could play nature's deep and profound melodies with my guitar."

"Try it. You can do it," encouraged Sun Hee.

"No, I can't. I don't have the talent," Seok Chun confessed.

He stared at the river, immersed in deep thought.

"However, I have a passion that is better than my musical talents," said Seok Chun, reassuring himself. "Being a lathe operator. It's truly rewarding, and like the sound of the rapids, it, too, has a melodic tune. I just need someone who will play that tune with me. Comrade, do you know what I'm talking about?"

"I do."

"Sun Hee, will you come with me on that journey?"

"Yes, I will."

"So, you will marry me?"

"Yes." Sun Hee nodded her head. She answered as if she had already been thinking about this matter for some time. Seok Chun's soul was filled with ecstasy.

"Thank you!" he shouted.

He grabbed her shoulders and looked into her eyes. The crescent moon was not bright enough for him to see its reflection in her eyes, but he realized that her eyes this evening glowed brighter than before, different from the timid eyes he had seen many nights ago. Her soft eyes indicated a quiet promise of love and hope for the coming days.

"We got married two months later," said Seok Chun. He tried to smoke his cigarette, but it had already been snuffed out.

Judge Jeong Jin Wu lit a match. Though it was a long story, it was engaging, not quite what he had expected. Jeong Jin Wu had never planned on writing down the entire story on the divorce petition; he simply wanted to know the couple's past in order to explain their current life, emotions, behavior, and opinions of each other.

Seok Chun lit another cigarette and smoked it out of distress. He unconsciously let the cigarette burn to the filter before putting it out.

"Our married life was happy, like other newlyweds," continued Seok Chun.

No words could express Seok Chun's elation. He arranged a place in the city where he and Sun Hee could start their new lives as a married couple. He helped Sun Hee land a job as a lathe operator among the thousands of workers at his factory in Gang An. Rumors of Sun Hee spread throughout the factory. Seok Chun was unabashedly proud of his beautiful and talented wife.

Not long after she settled into her new surroundings, Sun Hee joined the Factory Arts Troupe, which desperately needed a talented singer. Whenever she finished rehearsing for upcoming performances and returned to the factory for the night shift, her coworkers would tell her to go home and rest. She had become the pride of the factory, and they thought it was more important that she sing than operate the lathe.

The days had passed like the cool rapids.

A son was born after they had been married two years.

One evening, Sun Hee returned from work with signs of irritation and dissatisfaction on her face. The couple sat across from each other at the dinner table in utter silence.

Seok Chun perceived that something was troubling his wife, but he did not inquire into the matter. He knew, after two years of being married to her, that Sun Hee was a strong-willed woman, insistent on resolving her own problems. She hardly ever spoke about her troubles or turned to him for help.

In the course of several months, the couple's conversations had become more infrequent, but Seok Chun could not identify the source of Sun Hee's change in attitude. He decided to wait for her to open up to him and initiate a conversation. Besides, he did not think much of it nor consider the possibility of marital problems between the two of them because Sun Hee continued doing the things she had been doing—washing his clothes, ironing his trousers, selecting his clothes every morning, and even tying his necktie for him. She did these not because they were the mandated duties of a housewife but because she had a quiet ambition to make her husband stand out, appear dignified, be respected among the ordinary factory workers. While Seok Chun appreciated her efforts, he preferred to live a simpler life, devoid of pretension and snobbery.

After dinner, Sun Hee put little Ho Nam to bed and then studied her new music sheets.

Seok Chun retired to his desk in the master bedroom to review the blueprints that he had started at work. It was not an actual blueprint but a sketch of his new lathe machine that was clumsily drawn on drafting paper. The other technicians and engineers at the factory had expressed difficulty understanding his sketches because the inconsistent configurations, proportions and scales, axes, and symmetry failed to conform to basic principles of engineering and design. Only Seok Chun understood his diagrams. He had never received proper training or education in engineering; experience was his teacher.

Sun Hee put her music sheets down for the evening and got ready for bed. She loosened her hair, which had been tied up all day, and curled up underneath the blanket.

"Um, honey," Sun Hee called, breaking the silence.

Sun Hee didn't speak, instead counting the ticks of the clock that hung on the wall. Seok Chun was pleased to hear Sun Hee taking the initiative in starting a conversation with him, something that had been lacking between the two for many days. And yet, Seok Chun's brusque personality overpowered his intention to respond gently.

"Well, hurry up and speak," urged Seok Chun without lifting his eyes from his sketches.

"Um, don't you think it's strange that both of us work in the same department?"

"What do you mean?"

"I mean . . ."

"Did someone say something to you?"

"No, I was just thinking to myself how strange it is," muttered Sun Hee.

Seok Chun sensed that something had been bothering her and that she had been thinking about this issue for quite some time.

Seok Chun asked, "So what's really on your mind?"

"I . . . thought about . . . quitting the lathe," stuttered Sun Hee.

"Is it difficult?"

"That, too. But I really want to be a singer . . ."

"You already sing for the Factory Arts Troupe. Isn't that enough?"

Seok Chun spat out his words without thinking and realized that he may have been insensitive to Sun Hee's concerns, especially when a moment like this was rare between them. He knew that she had always wanted to be a professional singer and that they would talk about this matter one day, but he did not expect this discussion to come so soon, particularly when she had worked at the factory for only a couple of years.

Seok Chun tossed and turned in bed that night, thinking about what she had said and even feeling a little sorry for her. He had often worried about Sun Hee having to work alongside other men on the lathe machine day after day, night after night. He realized he had not considered her aspirations and the opportunities that awaited her. He had been complacent because she sang for an amateur group. After all, he thought, she was already doing something she liked to do, and he further rationalized that people did not attain their dreams just because they had them. But he also thought that a professional singing career at the Provincial Performing Arts Company would be an admirable occupation, a real dream come true for her.

Fortunately, Seok Chun no longer had to worry about Sun Hee's occupational problem; officials at the factory took the initiative to recommend her to the Provincial Performing Arts Company. They felt she was better suited to the performing world than the industrial world.

Seok Chun was overjoyed for her, not only because she had achieved her desires but also because he hoped her exhilaration would rekindle the fading embers of their love and restore the family stability of the early days of their marriage.

As soon as Sun Hee started working at the Provincial Performing Arts Company, her face glowed with happiness as she ascended from misery to ecstasy. When she returned home from work, she would bring up conversational topics with Seok Chun that she would not have broached before—asking about his new project, the people she had worked with at the factory, and other trivial matters. Seok Chun was happy for Sun Hee and pleased with the restored harmony at home.

Sun Hee was quicker at honing her skills than her colleagues, and within a year, she became the lead mezzo-soprano in the province. Her innate talent for singing coupled with her insatiable ambition and hard work made her successful and immensely popular. She had become a celebrity and basked in the spotlight, receiving standing ovations and bundles of flowers, signing autographs, being recognized on the street or in other public spaces, and receiving fan mail.

Sun Hee was overjoyed and grateful for the opportunity to sing professionally. There was nothing that excited her more than performing onstage in front of thousands of people, touring the province, and greeting her fans. Singing was her passion, and being a celebrity had become her life.

Months had passed, and Sun Hee's jubilation waned. One evening, she returned from work, stood aloof from Seok Chun and her child, gazed at the living room, her living situation, and felt that her life, like a circle, had returned to the familiar place of emptiness and monotony.

Sun Hee did not discuss her emotions with Seok Chun, but he sensed that her dissatisfaction and frustrations were aimed at him. Despite the unnerving atmosphere, Seok Chun continued to do what he had been doing for Sun Hee. After work, he would pick up Ho Nam from the nursery, prepare dinner, put Ho Nam to bed, and then wait for Sun Hee to come home, hoping to move her, or at the very least, show her that he was supportive. None of these gestures pleased her anymore.

It appeared that Sun Hee was not satisfied with married life. She refrained from speaking much at home other than a few necessary words to her son. Toward Seok Chun, Sun Hee seemed to have closed her heart, locking her emotions in an impenetrable vault. She was certainly not trying to exhibit her strong-willed, independent personality to Seok Chun by maintaining her silence at home. It was clear to Seok Chun that she was frustrated with him. Although he did not know the exact reason, he had his suspicions. As much as he wanted to discuss the unsettling issue with Sun Hee, he waited patiently for an opportune moment. Meanwhile, Seok Chun scrupulously helped with the chores around the house, thinking Sun Hee would appreciate his efforts at trying to restore their deteriorating marriage.

One evening, Seok Chun finished the chores, prepared dinner, and sat with his son on his lap, waiting for Sun Hee to return from the theater.

When Sun Hee came home, she brought with her an air of irritation. If not for their son sitting in the room, the atmosphere would have been intolerably dismal. After glancing at the dinner that Seok Chun had prepared, Sun Hee became more vexed and complained, "I don't feel any better when you do this."

"I know you're tired, so I wanted to help you," responded Seok Chun.

"Look. I don't appreciate your cooking for me like this. Besides, it's the woman's responsibility," retorted Sun Hee. "And even if I'm tired, I can still make dinner for us. Is it a big deal if we eat later? You should not be wasting your time cooking, but studying. You should be studying."

"Here we go again," Seok Chun muttered, rolling his eyes.

Seok Chun had suspected that Sun Hee's frustration with him concerned his unwillingness to pursue higher education. She had brought up this matter for many years, and tonight was no exception.

"Don't sit around like this," Sun Hee persisted. "You should enroll in the Engineering College and do something with your life."

Seok Chun, a bit annoyed, raised his voice. "You want me to waste five years of my life in a classroom?"

"It could help you," Sun Hee countered.

"How can a name on a stupid diploma help me?"

"It's not the diploma. It's a degree in engineering. With it, you can be the top engineer at your factory."

"Have you forgotten that I am the top lathe operator?" yelled Seok Chun, flustered. "I am perfectly satisfied as an operator without a diploma. I go to the factory and I turn the lathe. I like living a simple life."

"You promised to follow your dreams when we got married," Sun Hee cried.

"I did," Seok Chun retorted. "What do you think I've been doing at work all these years?"

"All you do is turn the lathe. It's a mindless job! Anyone can do that."

"But not as well as I can."

"It's not innovative," Sun Hee argued.

"I come up with new machines!"

"How? With those childish drawings of yours? No wonder you've been struggling with your projects."

"So you think I'm stupid? You think I've been wasting my time?"

"Isn't it obvious? You haven't been productive with your work at all. With an engineering degree, you could've been a supervisor or an executive by now."

"A supervisor? An executive?" Seok Chun was flabbergasted. "What has gotten into you? You married me for who I am, but you've changed over the years."

She was at a loss for words, not because she had nothing to say but because there were too many things she wanted to say. Instead, she turned her head away from him.

The dinner on the table was left untouched.

Seok Chun tried to understand Sun Hee's point of view but could not find any fault in himself. He felt he had done nothing wrong—he worked diligently at the factory, took care of the chores, and genuinely supported his wife's celebrity lifestyle.

However, compassion for Sun Hee withered in Seok Chun's heart, and instead resistance surged. Seok Chun believed Sun Hee had forgotten about her humble beginnings and exuded pride and vanity as a celebrity. He did not feel the need to advance his career just to please Sun Hee. He no longer cared what she had to say about him, and he decided to live the way he wanted to and let her live the way she wanted. Sun Hee's nagging had slowly eroded his pride over the years, and it was now irreparably damaged.

After that tumultuous evening, Seok Chun never made dinner for Sun Hee again. After work, he would stop by the factory recreation center and play chess with other comrades or work on his sketches for his new machine at the factory. To others, Seok Chun seemed to have control over his life, passion for his work, and a plan that was being fulfilled; they were not aware of his decaying marriage.

One afternoon, Sun Hee was hand-washing Seok Chun's clothes in the bathroom. She pursed her lips and scrubbed the grease stains with all her might, but it appeared that the stains were the least of her concerns. She wiped the sweat off her forehead with her forearm, straightened her back, and then resumed her crouching position to scrub the clothes. Seok Chun was in his room, transcribing his ideas into his sketchbook. He glanced over at Sun Hee and noticed that she was violently scrubbing his pants on the washboard. She was so engulfed in her thoughts that she did not even respond to her son's call. She stopped scrubbing the clothes, placed her soapy hands on her knees, and called out to Seok Chun.

"How much longer do you need to work on your new machine?"

"Just a little bit more," he replied.

Shaking her head, she muttered, "It's always the same answer. You said that two months ago, last year, and the year before that."

"I've done a lot since then. I'm really certain about this one."

"Last time you compensated the factory for the wasted alloy. What next? The electric lamps?"

"Why are you bringing that up again?"

"Because I heard that the Materials Committee recently held a meeting to, perhaps, exempt you from having to pay for all those wasted parts? But, no," said Sun Hee in a bitter tone, "you had to insist on paying for everything."

"It's absolutely my responsibility to pay for the parts I misused."

"Forget about the money; your reputation is at stake. It's embarrassing to hear others talk about your ineptitude. It's your job, and you can't even do it right."

Sun Hee's acerbic words lacerated Seok Chun's pride, deepening the wound. He tried to suppress his fit of anger, as he came close to striking her with his fist.

Sun Hee perceived a violent atmosphere and tried to refrain from making any more critical remarks. But she could not remain silent about the issue; she felt the urge to say one more thing. She disposed of the soapy water and took another shot at Seok Chun.

"I don't know what you're drawing over there, but whatever it is, you know it's not going to work."

Seok Chun glared at Sun Hee and responded resolutely, "I don't care what you have to say."

Sun Hee shook her head in disdain. "You're really something, you know that? You have no ambition to go to college. Your project shows no sign of progress. You turned down a position as a supervisor at your factory. I don't know anymore. You tell me what's going on in that head of yours."

Seok Chun raised his voice, "All you do is insult me! That's all you're capable of."

He slammed his fist on the desk. "I am a lathe operator, and a proud one. Didn't you marry me knowing that?"

Sun Hee yelled back in a shrill, piercing voice. "What does our past have anything to do with what we're talking about now? Who cares what we did in the past? I care about how we live today and how we're going to live tomorrow!"

They glared at each other with menacing rage. Seok Chun could not think of a coherent response to counter Sun Hee. Resentment pervaded the chilly atmosphere between the two, and after a seemingly intolerable moment of silence, Sun Hee spoke.

"How can we live like this? There needs to be some kind of change in our life." She sighed grievously. "Our future looks bleak. Do whatever you want, but just know that you need to change your life so that our lives can improve."

"Do you really think that?" Seok Chun asked suspiciously.

"Yes," Sun Hee said adamantly. "You've walled yourself, Ho Nam, and me up in this . . . this impenetrable prison. Why can't you see that?"

"What? So you think it's my fault? Is that what it is?"

"How else can you see it?"

"What about you?"

"What about me?"

"Can't you see that you're a bitch!"

Sun Hee was flabbergasted by Seok Chun.

Silence ended their argument.

Out of spite, Sun Hee stopped tending to Seok Chun's needs. She felt that washing his clothes and ironing his pants were unnecessary. *He's just going to the factory to turn the lathe; he doesn't need clean clothes,* she thought. Sun Hee also stopped doing some of the other household chores that she used to do. She did not want to be burdened by those menial tasks anymore. They were meaningless to her, and, more importantly, she did not care.

Based on their outward appearance, others believed the family to be harmonious, unperturbed by marital problems. However, Seok Chun worked late nights at the factory and Sun Hee came home late because of back-to-back performances. The two avoided each other, but they also neglected their son. There were days, of course, when they would not argue and not get under each other's skin. Yet they still harbored bitterness toward each other, maintaining the abyss between them.

On the day of their son's birthday, Seok Chun brought home an apprentice and an elderly equipment manager from the factory. Upon entering the living room, they saw there were already two of Sun Hee's guests sitting on the floor. Sun Hee was cooking in the kitchen.

It had been a while since the house was filled with laughter and chatter. Delicious dishes decorated the table and were certainly reflective of a grand party. Dark red wine and cold beer filled the glasses to the brim. They raised their drinks to wish Ho Nam the best as the future of the nation and immediately downed them.

The equipment manager from the factory asked Seok Chun to play something on the guitar for them.

Seok Chun took out the guitar and sat in the corner of the room. He placed the guitar on his lap the way a girlfriend would sit on her boyfriend's lap and began to strum the guitar with his stubby fingers. Although he stumbled around on the guitar, his emotions had gone to a far distant place, where the sound of the roaring rapids rushed down the river and peace reigned. At times, he played the wrong chords, but it was still an emotional performance.

Sun Hee looked annoyed at her husband. "Please stop," she interjected. "Oldies are goodies, but inappropriate here. Besides, you can't even play them properly—"

"What's the matter with you?" scolded the equipment manager, who had been immersed in the music. Seok Chun was about to set the guitar down, but the equipment manager encouraged him to continue playing. "Ah, come on. Play one more."

"Then give the guitar to this comrade," said Sun Hee, turning to her colleague. "He's a professional guitarist from our music department."

The equipment manager looked at the young talent who had combed his hair back with mousse and wore a fashionable suit and tie. After regarding the young man with discontent, the equipment manager spoke calmly. "We will listen to your performance when you are onstage, all right, young man? Don't take it the wrong way, all right?"

"You're absolutely right, sir. At a time like this, the host should perform," said the young talent with a nervous laugh, recognizing the precariousness of the situation.

The equipment manager nodded at Seok Chun and said, "Keep playing. This time, play the one that you played at your wedding.

My goodness, what was the name of that song? It was such a good song. Ah! Sun Hee would know. Remember the song that Seok Chun sang for you?"

When Seok Chun remembered the song, his heart writhed in pain. Sun Hee started without Seok Chun's accompaniment.

> I love my fatherland where I was born and raised,
> The mountains and the blue sky . . .

Seok Chun struggled to keep up with Sun Hee, but since she sang beautifully, her voice counterbalanced Seok Chun's ineptitude. Unwittingly, each verse and each note of the song unlocked a blissful memory that had been locked away for so long, a memory that freed him from his present troubles with Sun Hee, a memory that allowed him to experience happiness once again. He was inebriated from the alcohol, the music, and his memories.

The guests swayed and clapped along with the music till their hands were red, and they even requested an encore. Sun Hee sang another song.

The second song also struck a chord with Seok Chun and took him further into the depths of his memory. He remembered their wedding night, when he sang this song for her, and they were standing next to each other with affection that seemed everlasting. She acted coy that night and blushed whenever another song was requested. She looked at the wedding guests and, most importantly, at Seok Chun with loving, tender eyes.

But tonight, the mood had changed since their wedding night. Sun Hee's voice irritated Seok Chun, and his bitterness toward her resurfaced. Those fond memories were adrift in the vast schism between the couple's separate lives.

Seok Chun could not contain himself any longer and suddenly stopped playing and set the guitar down. He stood up and glared at Sun Hee. It was a bitter stare. The guests held their breath, bewildered by Seok Chun's impetuous gesture. Silence fell on the room, and what was only momentary felt like an eternity.

Seok Chun went over to the equipment manager and said loudly, "Would you care for seconds?" He spoke with vigor in order to conceal his embarrassment.

The equipment manager lowered his eyes and replied quietly, "No, I'm fine. I ate plenty."

"Would *anyone* care for seconds?" yelled Seok Chun in one last desperate attempt to free himself from embarrassment.

The festive atmosphere quickly dissipated, and an uneasy feeling gripped the room. The wine and beer could not keep the guests inebriated any longer. When Seok Chun realized that he had ushered in the sober mood, he refrained from speaking any further. The guests stole glances at one another, anticipating the next appropriate move.

The equipment manager invited Ho Nam, who had been sitting in the corner eating crackers and witnessing the whole thing, to come and sit on his lap.

"Do you want me to give you something nice?" asked the equipment manager.

He pulled a shiny toy car made of stainless steel from his pocket. He had engraved Ho Nam's name and birthdate on the license plate. The car also had real wheel bearings and a man in the driver's seat. It was truly an elaborate toy car.

All eyes were fixed on the toy as the equipment manager wound up the car and released it on the living room floor. The toy car raced across the floor, making a lively chirping sound like crickets in a field.

Ho Nam, bursting with excitement, grabbed hold of the car. But the car had so much force and power that it escaped the boy's grip and went in another direction. The guests learned that this was not simply a toy but a miniature prototype of new machinery that the factory was planning to produce in the future.

The laughter and wonderment of the adults revived the somber atmosphere.

The equipment manager was the best technician at the factory, and it was evident that he had put all his time and energy into making this toy. Seok Chun knew that the toy car was not simply another toy for Ho Nam to play with; it represented the old technician's genuine desire for his family to be harmonious. This alone moved Seok Chun to tears.

While the other guests were still lounging around, the equipment manager got up and put on his red cap.

Sun Hee was surprised and asked, "Why don't you stay a bit longer?"

"I'm sorry, but I should be going now," said the equipment manager. "Mrs. Chae, take good care of Ho Nam. He is the future of our lathe factory. When he grows up, he will become an outstanding technician."

The equipment manager went over to Ho Nam and reached out his calloused hand for a handshake. The child stuck out his right hand like an adult. The equipment manager shook the child's small hand as if he were transferring his spirit and passion for working with steel to Ho Nam.

The others came out to bid him farewell. While they were standing in the front yard, the equipment manager put his hand on Seok Chun's shoulders and whispered, "Hey, what happened back there? Huh?"

Seok Chun knew that this solemn question was a rebuke. The evening was dark, but the equipment manager clearly read Seok Chun's face. He knew that the equipment manager worried for his family. Ashamed to look at him, Seok Chun lowered his eyes. After some time, the manager patted Seok Chun's shoulders in a gesture of encouragement.

"Don't be too distressed. It must be lovers' quarrels. They're soon forgotten. Besides, your wife was also once a lathe operator. Don't let her forget that."

Seok Chun walked the equipment manager out of the house, but he could not free himself from the agonizing torment of his distress.

It was true that his wife had been a lathe operator at one point. The night that the cuckoo sang its melody, silver fog covered the hillside with the rapids crashing along the riverbank. Although he stumbled around with the guitar, Sun Hee still gazed at him with loving and gentle eyes. But all that had vanished now, washed away by the tides of oblivion.

The other guests left, and Ho Nam fell fast asleep with the toy car cuddled in his arms.

Sun Hee stared out the window into the melancholy night and said quietly but sternly, "I don't think we're right for each other. We are not on the same rhythm."

"I think you're right. Rhythm. You've used the perfect analogy."

"So, what do we do about it?" asked Sun Hee.

"You do whatever you want to do. You don't have to ask for my opinion. I'm so busy with work, I don't have time to argue with you anymore."

Seok Chun went to the master bedroom and closed the sliding door.

Their domestic problems soon leaked out to others, becoming fodder for gossip. Even though the community tried to help the couple with their marriage with collective advice, they could not heal the wound. The wound grew wider and deeper and festered more and more, leaving a horrible scar that determined once and for all that the relationship could not be repaired.

Seok Chun went to work in the morning earlier than he had before and returned later in the evening. Sometimes he slept at the factory. He buried his troubles in work.

"And that is how our marriage deteriorated. Comrade Judge, I'm not trying to make excuses for our marital problems. But I cannot bear to live with her anymore. You must divorce us. I really think that we're not on the same rhythm anymore."

"So, did you eventually complete your project?"

"Yes. Last month I presented it to the Provincial Science and Technology Fair."

"So, you've succeeded," cried Jeong Jin Wu in a celebratory way. "How many years did it take you to make it?"

"Five years or so."

"It must've taken a toll on you. It's not easy to invent a new machine."

Jeong Jin Wu smoked a cigarette and sank deeper into his thoughts.

*It seems like the usage of "not on the same rhythm" may have hit the nail on the head. Whose fault was it, then? After his invention, their problems with their marriage seem to have worsened. Since he succeeded in inventing a new machine, he should've been able to save face and win his wife's approval. But is there something else that he isn't telling me?*

Ho Nam mumbled something in his sleep and then smiled, revealing his dimples.

Seok Chun leaned toward Ho Nam and wiped the perspiration off his feverish forehead.

"Wake him up. It looks like his fever has gone down. Besides, we need to eat dinner," said Jeong Jin Wu as he got up to prepare dinner.

"You don't have to do this. I will carry him home," replied Seok Chun.

Seok Chun tried to get up, but Jeong Jin Wu pushed down on Seok Chun's shoulders.

"My wife is away on a research trip, so I haven't made anything fancy. It's no problem."

"I came to pick up my son and discuss my marital problems. How can I stay for dinner?"

Seok Chun got up, feeling ashamed.

"My house is not a courtroom. So please sit down and relax. Don't get me upset, now."

There was a faint knock at the front door. Jeong Jin Wu rushed over and opened the door. Sun Hee was standing there, fatigued and soaked from the rain. In one hand, she was holding a bag, and in the other was a flower-print umbrella with water dripping from it.

Sun Hee trembled, "Comrade Judge, is my son—"

She had been running from the kindergarten to her house, and then to her theater and back to her house in the rain. The thought of Ho Nam missing frightened her. When she had finally encountered the young woman in her neighborhood and found out that her son was at the judge's house, she raced over to Jeong Jin Wu's apartment.

"Why are you standing there like that? Come in," invited Jeong Jin Wu.

When she realized that her son had really been at the judge's house all along, she was relieved, and life returned to her face. She squeezed the ends of her drenched dress outside the door and followed the judge into his apartment.

"Comrade Seok Chun, look who's here. She's been wandering around in the rain looking for you and your son. The whole family is together now. Wait a second, I should prepare a better dinner for this joyous event."

The judge tried to be humorous, but it did not seem to break the austere atmosphere in the room. Jeong Jin Wu took the apron down from the wall and wrapped it around himself.

Seok Chun, motionless and irresolute, did not know what to do or say. Sun Hee sat beside Ho Nam and began to change him into the dry clothes that she had brought with her in the bag.

She struggled to put his shirt on. Ho Nam's head jostled inside the shirt, trying to find its way out. Then she struggled to pull his arms out through the sleeves. When Seok Chun squatted to hold the child, Sun Hee swatted his hands away with a ferocity reflective of the couple's relationship.

When she finally managed to put the clothes on Ho Nam, he opened his haggard eyes. He glanced at his parents and then looked at Jeong Jin Wu. He remembered what had happened, and his eyes regained their luster.

As soon as Sun Hee grabbed Ho Nam and pulled him into her arms, Judge Jeong Jin Wu reprimanded her in the same way he had at his office.

"Comrade Sun Hee, let the child go. Take him home after he has eaten."

She realized that the law supported her son's welfare more than hers, and she cowered before the judge's sharp words.

Jeong Jin Wu prepared dinner for the blameless child of the contentious couple.

Ho Nam looked to his parents for permission to eat, but they were motionless. He then looked at Jeong Jin Wu, the gray-haired man who had carried him to this place on his back and had shown his generous nature. That very man was kindly urging him to eat. Ho Nam began to devour his dinner like a child starved for food and affection. When he saw tears rolling down his mother's face and his father's misty eyes, he put his spoon down gently. "I'm full. Thank you for dinner, mister," Ho Nam said.

"Thank you very much," said Sun Hee to Jeong Jin Wu, as she rose from the floor.

*Was it about her son, or something else?* thought the judge.

Sun Hee went to her son, but Seok Chun grabbed him first.

Ho Nam appeared to be accustomed to this kind of behavior from his parents. He did not say anything and hopped on his father's back.

The judge was not a relative or a friend, and it was out of the ordinary to invite the family over to his house and offer this kind of hospitality. The three left the judge's apartment. Jeong Jin Wu went downstairs to the first floor to bid them farewell.

Ho Nam waved goodbye to Jeong Jin Wu. Seok Chun mumbled something to Ho Nam, but Jeong Jin Wu could not make out what he was saying because of the rain gushing down the apartment drainpipes.

The family faded into the dark, rainy void. Indistinctly, Jeong Jin Wu saw Sun Hee holding her umbrella over her son and her husband. It was most likely to prevent Ho Nam from getting wet again, but in any case, the family was walking together under one umbrella.

The rain continued to pour down. A cold gust of wind suddenly blew rain into Jeong Jin Wu's face.

Jeong Jin Wu stared solemnly into the empty night. Seok Chun and his marital problems left a grim cloud behind. Jeong Jin Wu felt like the cold rain was afflicting his soul. Although the three were walking under one umbrella in the rain, they still got wet. Jeong Jin Wu could not ignore the haunting concern he had for the couple.

In the apartment building across the street, myriad lights shone through the windows. Jeong Jin Wu imagined that a husband, just returned home from work, was probably greeting his wife, and the children were probably throwing themselves at their father. A family should at the very least live like that, conversing with one another and sharing their emotions affectionately together like a peaceful stream flowing with no obstacles in its way.

The rain came down harder. The water from the drainpipes beat on the metal sheets, making a noise that hurt his ears.

The rain rolled down his face, dripped down his neck and into his shirt.

The weather was getting chillier as a cold front was coming in from China.

Jeong Jin Wu remembered his wife.

*It must be hailing or snowing in the high altitudes of Yeonsudeok. The ground might have thawed out during the day, but it will freeze again by dawn. She took only a light sweater. She really didn't have to go. The farmers there are more than capable of taking care of the vegetables.*

Suddenly, Jeong Jin Wu felt the presence of another person. He turned around.

By the stairs, a woman with a thick old sweater lingered with an umbrella in her hand. It was the wife of the coal miner who lived on the second floor. She was well into her forties but looked younger. She was a schoolteacher at the local middle school, and everyone in the apartment complex called her by her occupation.

She would always wait for her husband by the front gate of the apartment building at this time of the evening. She would wait to greet her husband, but there were plenty of times when her husband would enter the apartment building through the back gate without her knowing. Her husband enjoyed drinking. He would drink either at the local bar or at a friend's house. When he would get drunk, he would not cause a ruckus or do anything else to disturb the neighbors. He would go to sleep quietly without saying a word. He truly loved his wife and never fought with her at home. They appeared to be happily married, but the wife worried about his addiction to alcohol, while he cared little for his deteriorating health.

The schoolteacher had many other things to worry about and mounds of work to do for the school. Updating and preparing for her lessons and proctoring students' math diagnostic tests were some of her responsibilities along with being a homeroom teacher, modeling good behavior, grading, and disciplining the students. There were so many things that added to her daily duties as a teacher, but at the end of the day, she would treat her husband as tenderly as she did her students. No, she probably loved her students more than her husband. The schoolteacher was still as pure-hearted as she had been before she got married.

\*      \*      \*

The schoolteacher spent her energy on her students, which did not allow her any time to experience the wonderment of falling in love. She never had a chance to receive the kind of love a child in a normal family would receive because her parents had been killed by the Americans during the Korean War. At a young age, she was deprived of the love of her parents and engulfed by the cruelty and terror of the world. She had no family, no relatives, no friends to whom she could turn. Solitude, fear, and melancholy were her only friends. She had been naked to the bitter wind of misfortune, but when she was brought to an orphanage, she was clothed with love and care. She learned that collectivity supersedes individual desire and ambition. The notion of "self," or "my future," or "my ambitions" did not exist in her life.

She became a schoolteacher at the age of twenty, and since then, she had devoted her life to the country that had raised her. She found a new identity in her occupation, and she made her classroom her new home. She considered her students' future as her future, which was to become loyal citizens of the country. She used every cent of her salary for her students, for her teaching materials, and even for her sick students who could not afford to buy medication.

When the schoolteacher turned twenty-nine, someone introduced her to a coal miner. They met only a couple of times. She did not pry too much into the coal miner's past or his upbringing. She only desired a husband who would understand her passion for teaching. The coal miner promised that she could continue working as a teacher, which pleased her greatly. They got married soon thereafter.

On that first night in bed together, she placed her head on the coal miner's firm chest and wept inconsolably like a young child. She recalled the dreary nights of waking up to desolate darkness, absolute solitude in the absence of her parents. It was a terrifying experience for any child to endure. Sadder still, her parents could not attend their daughter's wedding. They could not witness how their daughter had grown up to become a respectable woman. A sudden indescribable fear seized her as the possibility of forgetting tonight's happiness clouded her thoughts. But what she feared most was that she would lose her love for teaching. She wept fearful tears; she sobbed through the night.

As for her personal belongings, she had only a small chest, a desk, and some books. However, on her wedding day, the neighbors, comrades, students, and the students' parents showered her with gifts, which filled her small room. Some students and their parents from ten years ago somehow had heard about her wedding and attended. The town had never before seen such a large wedding ceremony. The coal miner thought that his bride had always lived in solitude. But, when he saw the entire town showering her with gifts and love, he was bewildered and delighted at the same time. He was deeply moved by the impression his wife had made on the townspeople, and so he loved her and respected her all the more. When he would return home from work and hear her talking with her students, he would close the door, go downstairs, and smoke a cigarette until she was done. He would go up only after the students finished talking with their teacher. The coal miner had maintained his commitment and loyalty to his wife all these years as if they were still newlyweds.

Jeong Jin Wu stepped aside from the front gate of the apartment.

The schoolteacher ducked past Jeong Jin Wu as if she were sorry about something. She unfolded the umbrella and stood in the rain waiting for her husband.

Jeong Jin Wu turned and slowly climbed the stairs back to his home, dragging his heavy feet up the endless flight into the void. He knew that even if he went home, there would be no one to greet him. He felt utterly desolate and frustrated with his wife.

She had been away twenty days this month, the month of April. It had not even been a week since she returned from her laboratory before she left again. He considered his life no different from that of a widower. He resented his wife and her research.

As he approached the second floor, he heard the sound of wet shoes, muffled voices, and the folding of an umbrella downstairs.

"Why did you wait for me in the rain?" asked the coal miner. "Didn't think I would come home?" It was always the same brusque greeting coupled with frivolity.

"Why are you so late?" asked his concerned wife.

"You see, I was installing a crane. And it got late. Everybody had already gone home, you see, so I had to do it all by myself. Ah, my back is killing me."

"And you didn't just happen to pass by the bar."

The coal miner guffawed. "Do I smell like alcohol? I quit drinking, honey!"

"Since when? Tonight?"

"Of course!"

"Would a ten-year drinking habit stop overnight?"

"It's going to be overnight."

"Really? You promise?"

By the time Jeong Jin Wu reached the third floor, he could barely make out what the two were saying. The coal miner's and schoolteacher's voices faded away as they entered their apartment.

"Honey, do you need more of that crochet thingy?" asked the coal miner.

"Why do you ask?"

"I was thinking of getting more for you at the store."

"The store at this hour? Don't try to be sneaky. You want to go out and drink some more, don't you?"

"How in the world did you know that?"

"You're very easy to read. In any case, I don't need more."

"That's too bad. You see, honey, the weather's getting colder. Do we still have some of that juice left inside the closet?"

"It's been three minutes since you quit."

"Come on, just one glass. I can't divorce alcohol. I fell in love with her long before I met you," said the coal miner laughing.

The teacher quietly shook her head.

Jeong Jin Wu thought that perhaps his son had sent a letter, so he checked the mailbox again even though he had checked it earlier that day. It was an excuse to put off entering his desolate apartment.

When he entered, he was greeted by frigid air. He shivered.

He remembered the small greenhouse in the master bedroom. When he went there, the ventilation window was wide open, letting in the cold air. The leaves of the peanut plant were trembling because of the brisk wind coming in. He quickly closed the ventilation window and looked at the thermometer. Fortunately, the temperature had not dropped too much. Although he was worried about some of the young plants, he thought that they ought to learn how to adapt to the cold climate.

Jeong Jin Wu watered the young seedlings. A variety of plants had begun to sprout and showed signs of blooming soon. Peppers, tomatoes, cabbages, radishes, and other plants were awakening from their deep slumber.

Nearly all the plants were products of his wife's green thumb. Some of these seeds had been discarded by her laboratory because they were not suitable for the soil in Yeonsudeok. But she brought them home and provided them with a new living environment. She considered each seed to be precious and life-giving. She also took these vegetable seeds and planted them in a plantation field and in her laboratory. She hoped these plants would yield two-fold so that the field size and labor required would be reduced by half. She envisioned the people of this mountainous region relishing the plentiful vegetables she cultivated.

However, just as vegetable farming was contingent on seasonal changes and climate fluctuations, her research on her vegetables also required time to adjust to these natural occurrences. She had to repeat the experiment countless times. It was not going to be easy to make the seeds cooperate with her plan, especially when there had already been thousands of years of agricultural experience and revolution in human history.

*How would she feel about giving up her research? It's been proved fruitless so far. Besides, there are so many happy families that live ordinary lives with ordinary occupations.*

Jeong Jin Wu thought about the long and difficult path ahead of his wife as he succumbed to regret and disappointment.

Before they were married, he had never imagined that she would embark on this kind of fruitless journey.

# 4

One autumn day twenty years ago, Jeong Jin Wu prepared to present his senior thesis before his fellow students and respected professors. He worked on the paper during his fifth and final year as a law major and titled it "A Legal Study on Divorce in Human History."

The topic was too broad for a short presentation. If he had used historical and sociological material to do an in-depth study on the topic, it would have been worthy of a multivolume book. But the hastily written essay for his department fell short of that. Jeong Jin Wu based his thesis on dialectical materialism applied to the concept of divorce, an approach that had not been explored by his predecessors. That was why his comrades from his dormitory agreed that this paper was worthy of being presented and thought it would be well received as a university student's senior thesis.

Jeong Jin Wu approached the podium with an air of pride and confidence. The students in the conference hall were mostly undergraduate and graduate students from the law school, along with some who had already graduated but maintained an interest in academic goings-on. There were also a number of students from other departments. Whenever a paper was presented at the university, the title, name of the presenter, and date appeared in the school newspaper and were posted on campus. Students were more inclined to attend a discussion on law than any other department presentations.

Yun Hee, a fellow law school student and Jeong Jin Wu's friend from his hometown, entered the hall with an unfamiliar female student. Yun Hee's nickname was "Bee Sting" for her sharp wit and critical remarks, and she inspired wary discomfort in her peers whenever she spoke. She sat in the front row with her friend and, arms crossed, smirked presumptuously at Jeong Jin Wu. Yun Hee was prepared to criticize and attack him for any minute flaw. Even if the presentation turned out well, she would find some way to criticize it. In contrast to Yun Hee, the unfamiliar female student was looking at Jeong Jin Wu with soft eyes, which drew his attention to her. Her warm eyes encouraged him, and after glancing at her one last time, he lowered his head and began reading from his paper.

"In the infancy of human civilization . . ."

Jeong Jin Wu paused for a moment to survey the conference hall and wait for the noise to subside. He continued with a stronger cadence. His deep voice resounded with authority.

"In the infancy of human civilization, primitive people lived in groups in tropical and subtropical jungles and caves. Fruits, edible plants, and hunting weak animals were important sources of food for survival. The Paleolithic Era can be divided into several periods. If we're going to examine the origins of the division of labor, then we're going to have to journey back to a period before the Paleolithic Era. Man evolved from higher animal species and began to walk on two legs. And he lived in this way for thousands of years before he discovered the use of a stick and a rock-ax.

"The first form of marriage that humanity managed during this era was a form of communal marriage. Because of the unpredictable nature of wild beasts and the limited amount of food, primitive people, who lacked a great deal of ethical judgment, needed to live in groups. Very much like the basic instinct of animals (to eat and survive), these people did not have a mind-set capable of determining their goals, and therefore, communal marriages were ethically natural for them. They did not feel the need to regulate and control their system of communal marriage. This type of marital system continued for some time.

"The type of man that advanced from these primitive stages discovered tools made of wood and rocks, fire, fishing, the invention of the bow and arrow, agriculture, etc. Then, man entered the Paleolithic Era. Man, who had once been a savage, developed the concepts of family and clan. Clans were originally established to be matriarchal. Since it was a polygamous society, or one that engaged in group/communal marriage, children followed only their mothers.

"There was no sense of distinguishing generation from generation or kinship through bloodlines. Violence, resentments, and other types of emotions slowly emerged from the frail consciousness of early man. The scope of this disorderly society was limited. Therefore, great progress developed from the subsequent matriarchal society. From this disorderly society, they decided to organize a generational system, in which the notion of siblings was born. Siblings got married to one another. This type of marriage is called 'endogamy.' This system started in the mid-Paleolithic Era and continued throughout the Neolithic Era.

"The production of the primitive family-economy advanced as population density increased, and polygamy continued to be the organizing principle of society. However, this caused women great difficulties as it produced economic problems. Women wanted to flee from social oppression. They wanted to show that they were productive on their own and thus began to establish ethical and sexual principles. The process of establishing this new social creed was not without its problems. There were efforts to get rid of old-fashioned traditions and customs and attempts to change the beliefs of the men who still considered polygamy to be beneficial. After several thousand years of battling polygamy, women were finally able to overthrow this outdated ideology and establish a new form of marriage that went beyond 'family relations' and marriage with other families: exogamy. Exogamy was based on one man and one woman outside the family unit. The man continued to wield authority, while the woman took care of the children. Although polygamy was not completely eliminated, exogamy was viewed as a 'legal' victory for women in the history of humanity.

"The process of changing from exogamy to monogamy happened from the mid-Neolithic Era to the Bronze Age. During this era, society developed into an agrarian and livestock-based system. Great agricultural advancements occurred, and the domestication of animals progressed. Men decided to abandon exogamy and adhere strictly to monogamy by taking a single woman to wife. From this point, the notions of kinship and a genealogical system were established. This was because man needed his children to inherit his possessions . . ."

Jeong Jin Wu wanted to know if the audience was listening attentively to his presentation, but he did not have the opportunity to steal a glance. So he stopped reading altogether and looked up. After a moment, he proceeded.

"The division of the maternal clan and the paternal clan, the development of products during the Iron Age, division of labor, surplus production, private consumption, material production, exchange, exploitation, class division . . ."

Jeong Jin Wu described the historical development of socioeconomic levels through the characteristics of a family based on monogamy. His objective in describing the historical development of marriage was to draw the interest of his law school colleagues and others sitting in the audience. However, he felt that some portions of the legal analysis contained his personal opinions on the matter.

"Nations were established on the basis of a hierarchical system that derived from class division. The resultant bureaucratic system served to increase the profits of personal gain. New sets of laws were created to benefit and increase profits for the exploiters who oppressed the workers. Nations, which supported the exploiters, and the national system of law, which was used as a weapon against the workers, were fundamentally different from the clan system of the primitive era that had maintained customs, traditions, and communalism.

"The ancient Sumer civilization in 1600 BC and the Babylonian civilization had laws that regulated people and marriages. They did not establish these laws with the objective of getting rid of prostitution or adultery but for the regulation of personal property that would be passed down according to genealogy. The accumulation of personal property in the family strengthened the man's authority and subjugated the woman as a mere economic commodity. As a result, women were deprived of any political power and were enslaved by men.

"As man entered the feudal era, a married woman was considered the property of a man and was forced to be submissive to her husband. This allowed women to develop an awareness of their human emotions and human rights that was beneficial to them. In the Goryeo dynasty, the first legal codes were called 'Sang jeong rye mun,' and in the Joseon dynasty they were called 'Gyeong guk dae jeon' . . ."

Jeong Jin Wu took a sip of water to quench his dry mouth. The audience in the conference hall remained still and attentive. It seemed as though the audience members were entranced by Jeong Jin Wu's academic essay.

Jeong Jin Wu looked at Bee Sting sitting in the front row. Yun Hee shifted her position in her seat and faced the podium with an expression of wonder. Her arrogant smirk had vanished from her face. She had always thought of Jeong Jin Wu as a good-looking but only mildly intelligent student and had doubted whether he would be able to deliver a worthy essay, but after listening to his comprehensive research, she changed her opinion. In contrast, the unfamiliar female student sitting next to Yun Hee no longer gazed at Jeong Jin Wu with soft eyes but rather with a serious expression, stern and focused.

Jeong Jin Wu thought that Yun Hee and her friend were taking his presentation unnecessarily seriously. He fanned out the pages of his essay, proceeded again with an authoritative voice, and managed to return to the mental state of academia. Jeong Jin Wu's topic was so specialized that he was not able to explore areas beyond marriage laws and funeral rites in history. He felt as if a white fog covered the podium, causing him to lose focus on his paper. The audience was traveling with Jeong Jin Wu through the long history of marriage. None of the heroes in his talk were alive, but they were the ones who had changed the face of history and society's outlook on marriage.

As soon as Jeong Jin Wu finished reading from his essay, the audience applauded in sincere appreciation for his hard work in preparing this talk. He stepped down from the podium like a professional with experience giving talks at these types of colloquia. His heart beat rapidly, and he could not seem to contain his elation.

The audience members exited the conference hall like a herd of cattle.

Jeong Jin Wu was overwhelmed with joy and could not come down from his state of excitement. As he remained standing on the stage, the two women approached him. Yun Hee smiled brightly at Jeong Jin Wu.

"Congratulations on presenting your senior thesis," said Yun Hee.

"Don't spare me your criticisms. Hit me directly and quickly," said Jeong Jin Wu.

"There's nowhere to hit. I honestly learned something from your talk," Yun Hee said. "Oh, I almost forgot to introduce you two. This is my comrade Han Eun Ok."

Jeong Jin Wu greeted Eun Ok and gazed into her eyes.

Yoon Hee continued, "Comrade Eun Ok is majoring in biology through the long-distance education program. She's here for only a couple of days. She came up from her hometown in Yeonsudeok."

"Is that right?" said Jeong Jin Wu with keen interest. "You've come a long way to be here. Yeonsudeok is about, what, seventy miles away, right?"

Yun Hee bemusedly stared at Jeong Jin Wu, who was acting overtly genteel toward Eun Ok.

"But you know," Yun Hee interrupted, "Comrade Eun Ok has a few remarks about your thesis, Comrade Jin Wu."

"Oh, does she? Please, tell me," said Jeong Jin Wu.

Eun Ok blushed. She looked at Jeong Jin Wu and then quickly averted her eyes.

"No," said Eun Ok. "I really don't have an opinion. Comrade Yun Hee is just—"

"They say if you have any advice to give, don't withhold it," interrupted Jeong Jin Wu.

"I think your thesis was well written," Eun Ok said reassuringly.

Yun Hee grabbed her friend's arm and said, "My goodness, dear. You were muttering something during the talk. If you have nothing to say, then let's go."

"I'm sorry," Eun Ok replied, directed at both Yun Hee and Jeong Jin Wu.

The two women walked out of the conference hall.

Jeong Jin Wu did not have a moment to think about Eun Ok that evening. After his talk, he had to attend a meeting to discuss and evaluate another comrade's thesis. However, the next day at the University Park, Jeong Jin Wu inadvertently ran into Eun Ok.

It was a brisk autumn morning. Jeong Jin Wu was taking a stroll on the University Park trail. He enjoyed the serenity of the park and the refreshing air. He had come out of his dormitory with a book under his arm, but he was so captivated by the morning atmosphere that he tilted his head back and walked leisurely, appreciating the simple wonders of nature.

As the fog hidden among the trees slowly dissipated, a ray of morning sunlight traversed the vast forest of tall deciduous trees and verdurous pine trees. The kaleidoscopic hues of the luminous autumn leaves were sublime. In the stillness, the sound of falling leaves resembled a fledgling spreading its wings in preparation for an ascent. A thick blanket of golden leaves covered the trail. A rich, natural aroma from foliage steeped in the damp soil and the fragrance of dried leaves permeated the entire park. A young bird woke from its sleep, flew over Jeong Jin Wu's head, and then vanished beyond the tree line.

Jeong Jin Wu saw Eun Ok sitting on a bench under a large oak tree. She was reading a book and scrupulously underlining in it, absorbed in her own world and oblivious to her natural surroundings.

Jeong Jin Wu approached her without even thinking about whether he would be intruding on her reading.

Eun Ok lifted her head and was alarmed by the presence of another person. As soon as Eun Ok realized it was Jeong Jin Wu, she blushed. But the surprise in her eyes was mixed with a warm invitation.

"May I sit?"

"Please," responded Eun Ok. She tried to clear some of the leaves off the bench, but Jeong Jin Wu sat down without wasting a moment.

The two hesitated, and instead of speaking, listened to the ambient sounds of the park.

Jeong Jin Wu broke the silence. "Yesterday, you had some remarks about my thesis, right? Would you share them with me?"

Eun Ok did not respond and tried to keep her eyes from meeting Jeong Jin Wu's.

"Please, anything," Jeong Jin Wu urged.

"What can a biology student say about a legal thesis?"

Eun Ok was no longer blushing and returned to the serious expression she had worn during the talk.

"In any event, I want to hear what you have to say," said Jeong Jin Wu in a modest but obstinate manner.

Eun Ok put her book down and twirled a leaf that had just fallen from the tree. Innumerable golden leaves sprinkled the landscape as the wind blew them off their swaying branches. Birds that had woken up from their deep slumber chirped lazily. In the misty maroon morning, golden rays of sunlight penetrated between the tree branches, and the silver fog that had covered the trees slowly crawled up to the treetops and vanished in the blue sky.

Eun Ok finally gave in and spoke. "My father was a member of the People's Justice Association, so I read many of his books at home out of sheer interest. I just read whatever I could get a hold of in his library, which would explain my limited knowledge of the law. So there's really nothing that I can say about your talk."

Eun Ok looked at Jeong Jin Wu and smiled like a schoolgirl, coy and innocent. "But if you insist. After listening to your senior thesis—"

Her voice became incrementally more serious and contemplative. "I guess I don't have to tell you about how well you did, based on the thunderous applause that you received last night. What I wanted to add was that your thesis was not filled with legal jargon, but you tried to reveal some of the historical problems that we need to be aware of. I learned a lot from you. It may have been better, though, if you accentuated its relation to law a bit more."

Eun Ok continued by saying that historians had already researched the general idea of marriage in relation to the problem of the family in the past century, particularly regarding the social aspects of reproduction, changes in economics, and marriage. She suggested that a study of the ethical relationship between psychological and historical aspects would have made Jeong Jin Wu's argument stronger. Eun Ok added that by trying to reveal all the problems in human history, Jeong Jin Wu's analysis was a simple generalization. Instead of reiterating past contradictory problems and discussing issues beyond the relationship between ethics and morals, a psychological analysis of married couples would encourage the people of this nation to improve and strengthen their own marriages and families.

"Since you're considering the history of marriage from the point of view of the law, don't you think it's that much more important to examine it from the psychoanalytical perspective? Don't you think it's the people's ceaseless renewal of the mind, effort, and struggle that create tradition, lifestyle, and customs, the things that the law cannot disregard?" Eun Ok stopped, fearing she had spoken too honestly about his paper.

Jeong Jin Wu was pleasantly shocked by her critical response and could not keep his eyes off her.

The mild glow of the morning sunlight reflected off Eun Ok's deep eyes. It was as if her entire body exuded the fragrance of the autumn forest.

Jeong Jin Wu had first thought of Eun Ok as quite ordinary, but her acute intelligence and angelic face made him more attracted to her.

"Although I want to offer my rebuttal to your argument, I can't. Your theoretical thoughts have given me a fresh perspective," said Jeong Jin Wu.

"You don't have to take my comments seriously," added Eun Ok.

"No, you're absolutely right," Jeong Jin Wu corrected. "It's clear you are well-read, and I truly admire that."

Eun Ok humbly remained silent.

That afternoon, Jeong Jin Wu spent many hours in the corner of the library revising his thesis by including an appendix that Eun Ok had recommended.

"... The accomplishments of humanity, high productive capacity, and economic progress became the foundation of man's ethical progress, and this advanced the noble human emotions. Although the primitive age had a lower form of human emotions, such as love, responsibility, respect, anxiety, humiliation, fear, conscience, virtue, etc., these ethical concepts began to flourish beginning in that era. Maternal instincts are considered a higher grade of emotion and could have caused clans to evolve in a progressive direction. But when man dominated the family and demanded certain emotional responses from his children, the communal marriage system could not progress. The need to pass down property to their progeny occupied and dominated the ethics of that era. However, this was based on a 'life or death' system of ethics, which reveals the psychological instincts of even men. The transformation of this form of man into a loving father to his children with developed paternal instincts required thousands of years. During the long passage of time, all kinds of ethical reasoning and sentiments occurred, and as they became clearly divided and subdivided, humanity's psychological life increased. This was one of the determining factors in a marriage. That is why exogamous and monogamous relationships were no longer seen as relationships meant only for survival or economics but for ethicality ... However, the process of developing human psychology did not always progress so smoothly. Since the ancient past, man's conflicts, contradictions, and solutions ..."

Jeong Jin Wu could not develop the scope of the topic for his thesis any further. He included the legal study of marriage relations and the first half of the psychoanalytical problem with the development of ethics and morals. He did not realize that his appendix could not substantiate a strong argument and that it was turning into an abstract theory. Researching the wider scope of historical and social materials and analyzing the law would require a tremendous amount of time and effort. He tried to rewrite the appendix in excellent penmanship because he realized that in order to present a scientific and theoretical argument, the story of the development of the consciousness of marriage relations needed to be written with patience. But Jeong Jin Wu rewrote the appendix hastily so that Eun Ok could read his revision. He could not suppress his desire to see her one last time.

Jeong Jin Wu quickly gathered his thesis along with the appendix and went toward Eun Ok's dormitory, where he ran into Yun Hee. She could not contain her curiosity and noticed that he was carrying his senior thesis and some other essay. Yun Hee perceived that Jeong Jin Wu was more interested in seeing Eun Ok than discussing his paper with her. She gave him the unfortunate news that Eun Ok had left for the station to take the late afternoon train back to her hometown. Jeong Jin Wu had only thirty minutes to make it to the station.

He immediately hopped on a bus that was heading in that direction. As soon as he got off the bus, he raced to the turnstile, only to be met by a long line of travelers. The train howled as it approached the station. Jeong Jin Wu grew impatient and restless.

Jeong Jin Wu searched frantically for Eun Ok amid the crowd on the platform. He identified her in a plain, dark gray fall suit. She had her luggage on one side and three flowerpots on the other. He shouted her name several times, hoping she would glance in his direction. Confused, Eun Ok turned and saw Jeong Jin Wu standing by the turnstile waving at her. She was shocked and hesitated to respond. Jeong Jin Wu then hopped over the turnstile and swiftly maneuvered his way through the crowd.

Eun Ok asked warmly, "Did you come to meet someone?"

"I came to see you, comrade," responded Jeong Jin Wu excitedly.

"Me?"

"I revised my senior thesis, and I wanted you to take a look at it."

"What, now?"

"That's why I'm here!"

Jeong Jin Wu knew that he was being dishonest with her. He blushed and rolled up his thesis.

Eun Ok was taken aback. "You took my comments seriously? I don't think I'm in any position to read your thesis. Besides—"

Eun Ok could not find the words to complete her sentence, and as she strained to come up with an excuse, the screeching wheels of the incoming train defused the awkward moment. She stood aloof, trying to avoid looking at Jeong Jin Wu. The train shook the platform and brought with it a gush of wind. Eun Ok brushed her hair back in place and grabbed her luggage. With her left hand, she reached for the three flowerpots.

Jeong Jin Wu sensed that Eun Ok knew that he had not come to the station just to show her his revised thesis but that he had come to see her. He was ashamed of bringing his thesis to her, so he put it in his back pocket and grabbed the flowerpots for her.

She tried to prevent him from helping her. "No, I'm fine. I was going to put my luggage on board and come back for these."

"Comrade Eun Ok, it's no trouble at all. Do you not like it when someone helps you?"

Eun Ok could not respond to that statement and turned her eyes away.

Jeong Jin Wu asked an ignorant question to clear the air.

"What kinds of flowers are in these pots?"

"They're actually vegetables."

"Really?" asked Jeong Jin Wu, closely examining the soil in the pots. "So why are you taking vegetables back home?"

"My hometown is Yeonsudeok, and, at the vegetable research institute, we're conducting research on a new breed that can grow in high and unforgiving altitudes."

Jeong Jin Wu was secretly moved by Eun Ok's noble research. He carried the flowerpots for her and followed behind her. He boarded the train and placed the flowerpots in the compartment above the seats.

"Thank you," said Eun Ok.

"Please have a safe trip."

With those words, Jeong Jin Wu did not know whether to shake her hand as a customary farewell gesture between comrades. He did not want to appear too forward, so he waited for Eun Ok to make the first move. After an intolerable moment of uncomfortable silence, he realized that nothing was going to happen, so he hurriedly deboarded the train. He waved at Eun Ok from the platform, reassuring himself that it was an innocent and less awkward gesture. But to make matters worse, the train did not leave just yet. Jeong Jin Wu found himself waving more than he should have, so he disguised his embarrassment by burying his hands deep in his pockets and looking beyond the roof of the train to the distant clouds in the sky.

An inexplicable impulse of anxiety surged from within Jeong Jin Wu. He felt as though someone precious was about to slip away, and the intensity of the pain was past enduring. But he didn't know what to do; he felt utterly unfulfilled.

As the train slowly departed, he looked at the window where he could see Eun Ok. She was not sitting in her seat but standing by the flowerpots. As the train passed Jeong Jin Wu, Eun Ok waved her hands but quickly lowered them so it wouldn't seem like a departing gesture between lovers. She turned her head away. The train faded into the distance, but Jeong Jin Wu could not keep his eyes off the parallel tracks that stretched into the horizon.

Deep in Jeong Jin Wu's heart was the lasting image of beautiful Eun Ok. He could not forget her genuine, tenderhearted, and reticent personality. Jeong Jin Wu considered her disposition and her efforts toward her research to be more attractive than her eyes and rosy cheeks.

About a year and a half later, Jeong Jin Wu was assigned to his hometown to preside over the Superior Court as the People's Judge. He settled down in his new office and grew acquainted with his colleagues. Meanwhile, Jeong Jin Wu discovered that Eun Ok was working at a vegetable research facility in a suburb near the city. He decided to pay her a visit.

Eun Ok received the news that Jeong Jin Wu was there to see her. She paused, hesitated for a moment, delighted and yet troubled at the same time. She plucked an unripe pear from one of the trees and went to the front entrance of the facility with a welcoming expression. She offered Jeong Jin Wu the pear, which was evidently hard and sour.

Jeong Jin Wu proudly explained that he now worked as the People's Judge at the Superior Court and attempted to keep the conversation light. He tried to avoid revealing the real reason for his visit and to prolong the transient moment he had with Eun Ok. But he grew impatient. It was not easy for Jeong Jin Wu to articulate his impassioned feelings for Eun Ok. Nonetheless, he took this opportunity to explain his feelings logically and rationally, like a veteran judge of the legal world.

Eun Ok was surprised, not because she had not expected this from Jeong Jin Wu all along but because of his unabashed forwardness. She blushed, flashed a timid smile, and remained utterly speechless and motionless. Jeong Jin Wu invited her to watch a movie with him, but she kindly declined. He then asked if she would join him on an evening walk, but she declined that as well. Eun Ok scurried to find an excuse to return to the lab and left Jeong Jin Wu in unexpected stupefaction. First the shock, and then numbness spread across his body. He felt his legs go limp and searched for something to keep himself from falling. Jeong Jin Wu needed a moment to regain his breath, his senses, and his composure. He felt utterly dejected but resolute.

Jeong Jin Wu returned to the research lab a couple of days later, persistent in expressing his affection for Eun Ok.

However, Eun Ok was not there. She had left for a field farther away at a much higher altitude. A young woman at the front desk recognized Jeong Jin Wu and handed him an envelope. It was a letter from Eun Ok.

Jeong Jin Wu was impatient to read it, but he opened it with caution, hoping not to see the contents that would confirm his fears. She began with an apology for not speaking to Jeong Jin Wu in person and for expressing herself so bluntly. She proceeded to write about how flattered and overwhelmed she was to know that he loved her (if one could call that "love") and that she did not know how to accept his feelings for her. She wrote that someone as ordinary as she, researching vegetables in a region with harsh conditions, does not deserve such love. The next few lines were sharp and cutting. She wrote that Jeong Jin Wu was wasting his time, particularly in the first few weeks of starting a new job, and that he should be more focused on his work instead of her.

The letter was not even a page long, but it moved Jeong Jin Wu. Eun Ok considered Jeong Jin Wu's love for her to be affectionless and a mere infatuation. Her insistence on ending all relations with him made him want her even more. Eun Ok was Jeong Jin Wu's first love, a love that was pure and innocent. Days and months would pass before she finally opened her heart to him.

Just days before they got married, Jeong Jin Wu and Eun Ok took a morning stroll in the suburbs of his hometown. The remnants of the long and blustery winter persisted in March.

Eun Ok wore a thick wool overcoat and a scarf wrapped around her neck. With her leather boots, she walked delicately on the snowy path. Some of the long frills from her scarf rested on her shoulders, while others fell over her back and some on her chest.

There were traces, myriad indistinguishable footprints, of people having walked on this snowy path. On some parts of the path, the snow had been trampled. On other parts of the path, the snow had melted and refrozen, making it shiny and slippery, like glass.

Eun Ok walked beside Jeong Jin Wu with an arm wrapped tightly around his.

She was jubilant, her face gleaming like majestic snowcapped mountains. Simply gazing at Eun Ok's radiant face and lustrous eyes made Jeong Jin Wu ecstatic.

The ice crunched under the feet of the two lovers treading on the snowy path.

The brisk morning breeze had become calm, and the sky was clear. The silver clouds receded from the snowcapped mountains into the far distance.

Next to the path were residential houses with hanging icicles, sparkling like crystals as the sunlight reflected off them. And when the fragile icicles shattered on the ground, Eun Ok would cry happily, "Oh my!" and press her body closer to Jeong Jin Wu.

A plush layer of cottony snow had covered the entire area—streets, houses, and rows of trees—and the lovers were captivated by the pristine, abundant silvery scenery. The grandeur of the natural landscape surrounded the lovers, painting the canvas with beautiful, light, soft snow, as if to bless them on their new journey of happiness. The white guests had visited all night, creating a vast sea of snow. The brisk, fresh aroma of spring embraced the lovers with affection.

Like little schoolchildren, the two held hands and slid down a slippery path by the riverbank. A thin layer of snow coated the limbs of the pine trees that lined the riverbank, snow that had been there since the festivities of the New Year. The pine trees had inevitably welcomed the wintry snow in their arms and were looking forward to summer, but for now, they affectionately welcomed the two lovers in spring.

A couple of silver-blue silk-clothed, red-capped woodpeckers flew past the lovers and rested on the pine trees. Using their stethoscope-like sensors, the woodpeckers diagnosed the thick, leathery bark and identified the insects that had burrowed their way into the tree to escape the cold winter. They began pecking at the bark with their sharp beaks and used their long tongues like surgical tools to penetrate the bark and find the insects.

The thick layer of snow that covered the river looked like crumble cake, but it could not mute the sweet, angelic sound of the flowing water.

A light breeze gently brushed across the willow trees, causing the powdery snow to sprinkle the ground.

The sun climbed higher in the sky, allowing Jeong Jin Wu and Eun Ok to bask in its warmth.

The lifeless branches recognized the scent of spring and lifted their limbs toward the sky. The willow trees began to dust off the thick layer of snow and swayed in the sun. Nature was opening her eyes from a deep wintry slumber.

"Comrade Jin Wu, come look at this. Magpies! They're trying to grab twigs," said Eun Ok, pointing to a tree on the riverbank. "I think they're trying to make a nest."

"I think you're right," confirmed Jeong Jin Wu.

"With their black suits and white dress shirts, they look like newlyweds," Eun Ok added.

At that statement, Jeong Jin Wu looked fondly at Eun Ok.

The two magpies did not leave each other but instead stuck out their chests and fluttered their wings. As soon as they grabbed hold of the twigs, they flew toward the top of the poplar tree.

"Eun Ok, should we sit over there?"

"Sure."

Jeong Jin Wu and Eun Ok brushed the snow off a tree stump and sat next to each other. The tree stump had endured the rain and snow and was frozen, but the two lovers did not feel the iciness. The two were slightly exhausted from their morning hike and sat on the tree stump without saying anything to each other, only looking at the splendor of the snow-covered mountains in the distance.

Jeong Jin Wu gently placed his hands on Eun Ok's hands.

"Your hands are cold," he said.

With her hands secured in his, Eun Ok opened her heart to Jeong Jin Wu and looked at him with loving eyes.

"So are yours, comrade," replied Eun Ok.

Their passion for each other emanated from the surface of their cold hands.

"Comrade Jin Wu, will you love me like this even after we get married?"

"Of course I will."

"For the rest of your life?"

Instead of answering, Jeong Jin Wu gripped Eun Ok's soft hands tightly. He felt the impulse to pull her into his arms, if only she would permit it, and embrace her, promising her that he would love her eternally.

Eun Ok quietly spoke. "At times, I'm afraid of you."

"Why?"

"Because you're a judge."

"Didn't you study a bit of law yourself?" reminded Jeong Jin Wu.

"What good is that? It was just a hobby for me. But you, you're an actual judge. I'm afraid that you'll treat our family like defendants, prosecuting us with the law." Eun Ok then imitated the gestures and tone of a judge, "'According to the code of civil procedure, on page so-and-so in paragraph so-and-so, a complaining wife is as the following.'" Eun Ok giggled vivaciously.

Jeong Jin Wu did not appear to share her sentiment and stated sternly, "No matter how much I love you, if you break the law, I will prosecute you."

"Oh dear!" Eun Ok gasped with slight trepidation.

His mischievous eyes smiled. They burst out laughing again.

The two magpies descended from the poplar tree and landed not far from where the two lovers were sitting. The magpies looked at the couple with vigilant eyes, but recognizing no immediate threat, they began to pull out the dead grass. The March sun melted away the snow and revealed the barren land. Clumps of snow that had accumulated on the trees fell to the ground. And the bit of snow that was on the couple's shoes melted as well.

"Eun Ok, what are you thinking about right now?" asked Jeong Jin Wu. "You haven't said much."

"I'm sorry. I was thinking about my hometown, Yeonsudeok. I can't seem to stop thinking about it . . . the house I grew up in, my friends, neighbors . . ."

Eun Ok's hands became warmer as she fell into a meditative mood. She rested her head on Jeong Jin Wu's shoulder and recalled the painful memories of her village.

"Comrade Jin Wu, there was a time when you told me about your hometown, and how it was a little town in the foothills. And how there were so many trees in the vast landscape with fresh water from the river. In my hometown in Yeonsudeok, there is no river, no brook, no fresh water. It's just a vast empty field. Vegetables can't grow there. There is a large spring, though. It is the life of our village. We called it the 'drinking fountain.' In the summer, there were water plants and weeds growing along the edge of it. There were lively swallows, red silk worms, and all kinds of insects. Whenever the cold front came in from China, the spring would freeze. Every morning, the men would have to come out and break the ice. The women would collect the ice chunks and boil them on the fire. That is how we survived the winter. There was no holiday for us. About twenty miles away from our village was a river. Sometimes everyone in our village would trek to the river to collect water. That was our holiday."

Jeong Jin Wu felt Eun Ok's soft hair on his neck and cheek as she pressed closer to him.

"After the war, Yeonsudeok became a collectivized farm. The state contributed a lot of funds toward paving a channel that would bring the river to our village. From that point onward, our village lived like the other large towns. We harvested abundant potatoes, oats, and barley. Then we exchanged those for rice, and we were able to eat white rice for the very first time. We also raised a lot of cows, sheep, and goats. But vegetables still did not grow so well. There were many researchers and scientists who came up from the city to study the quality of our land. They really put in a lot of effort."

Eun Ok's voice choked, and her eyes became despondent.

"But there still aren't any promising results from all those experiments. We still eat vegetables brought in from towns located at a lower altitude. They say that Yeonsudeok is a region that will never produce vegetables, and the researchers and scientists are slowly giving up."

Tears filled Eun Ok's eyes, preventing her from speaking any further.

Jeong Jin Wu was moved by Eun Ok's love for her hometown and her insatiable desire to continue working at the vegetable research institute for the sake of increasing the probability of success. He was moved by how she thought of her hometown and how she longed to be with the villagers even with her wedding day ahead of her.

Their wedding took place on a mild March afternoon. Jeong Jin Wu's single-story house was located in the suburbs of the mountainous region. And it was there that his parents and friends celebrated the couple and feasted on a plentiful dinner. This was the first time in his life that dinner had been so wonderfully prepared.

A large decorative Korean folding partition—handed down for many generations and discolored with age but still exhibiting its classical artistry—stood behind the couple. The two lovers basked in their ineffable happiness on this joyous occasion.

The food was neither exquisite nor extravagant, but it reflected the indigenous customs and traditions of the northern region, showing the simplicity and genuineness of the people who live there.

The combination of a fading traditional marriage ceremony and a modern ceremony mixed well, creating a formal but entertaining atmosphere.

Jeong Jin Wu was so preoccupied with the thought of getting married that he was unable to think or observe everything that was going on. He did not even have the courage to look his guests straight in the eye. He could only savor this formal yet joyous moment.

The room was silent, a sublime silence in which one could not even hear children rustling. Jeong Jin Wu's colleague from law school stood up and began to read a congratulatory speech.

People were absorbed in the stillness. As the colleague spoke, the elderly people began to recall the bright and youthful days of their own wedding ceremonies, as if they were experiencing that joyous time all over again.

The children were hungry and restless but were forced to listen to the speech. The expressions on their faces reflected their grudging feelings toward the lengthy speech. They just wanted to devour the food, drink, play, and sing.

"And that is why—" continued the colleague in a resounding voice.

The colleague's voice sounded as if he wanted to make it clear that the newly married couple ought not to forget the significance of marriage and this historic moment in their lives.

"The bride and groom, in the presence of their parents, relatives, comrades, friends, the older generation and the younger generation, the Party, and the country, have wedded on this day to form a family. Never forget that a family is the basic unit of our society, and your harmonious relationship reflects that. You must help and serve each other till the day your hair turns silver, and you must devote your lives to serving our country's prosperity. You must live faithful lives . . ."

The speech echoed as it would in the mountains, inspiring the people in the room.

While the room was still quiet, Jeong Jin Wu and Eun Ok poured wine into glasses and offered it to their parents and elders.

The guests received the bride and groom's wine with care and respect. As they looked at the clear wine, their eyes sparkled with satisfaction. The wine embodied the overwhelming joy of marriage, gratitude toward the Party for bringing the couple to the zenith of their happiness, respect for elders and comrades, and the eternal covenant between the newlyweds.

The guests lifted their glasses, congratulated the couple, and emptied them without leaving a single drop. The wine that the couple had poured for them was special, so the guests knew they had to drink all of it.

As soon as the formal ceremony was finished, Jeong Jin Wu's university friend sat down in a corner of the room and pressed the keys of the accordion, as the guests sat around the dinner tables. The music was delicate, but also full of life and hope. Jeong Jin Wu looked at his friend with admiration. The friend, on behalf of the other colleagues, had come a long way to attend the wedding. Teenagers, men and women from the vegetable research institute, Eun Ok's father's coworkers, and children sang along with the accordion.

At the people's request, Jeong Jin Wu and Eun Ok sang a duet.

It was a night full of celebration—songs, laughter, stories, and delicious food.

The popping sound of beer bottles being opened and the foam that overflowed the glasses all blessed the newlyweds' future.

As the hours passed, the topic of the bride and groom slowly faded, and the elderly people sitting around the tables began to share their personal stories of women, love, and marriage. Vulgar words were exchanged among the elders, whose experiences in life provided deep and honest lessons for one another.

"I don't care what other people say, the woman needs to be strong in a family," began one elderly woman.

"That's right. You know my husband?" added another woman, "Don't even get me started. I married him because he was big, thinking that he had something great in him. But I realized that he's a good-for-nothing."

Then another woman joined the conversation, "As the old saying goes, 'If you want to pick a husband, then think like a farmer who goes out to the marketplace to buy a cow that can plow his field.'"

"Yeah, but that was in the good old days. These days, youngsters go for good looks first."

The diffusion of the sounds of spoons and chopsticks, wine glasses, and people chattering made it difficult to distinguish one speaker from another.

"Hey, don't worry about your daughter being ugly now," said yet another woman. "Young women are like flowers. Just wait till she's in her mid-twenties. She may not be a rose, but certainly a morning glory or a pumpkin flower. Then, the bees and butterflies will swarm around her to taste a bit of her sweet stuff!"

The elderly women burst into laughter.

"I'm so frustrated with my eldest daughter. She has a bitchy temper, and she is well beyond her ripe age. These days, they say that women who are twenty-six years old are over the hill. But she thinks that getting married is child's play, like playing house. She doesn't look at men and isn't even remotely feminine. I was so frustrated with her the other day I yelled at her, saying, 'Hey, tough girl! This is why men don't come on to you. Why don't you change your tomboyish appearance and try to look more attractive? If you bring home a man tomorrow, I'll do whatever it takes to set up a wedding, even if it means I have to yank the head off a chicken!'"

"Youngsters these days don't mature until they're in their late twenties. They're so content with life right now that they don't know why they have to get married."

After a while, a more rational voice was heard.

"Last year at our factory, our boss, 'Tiger,' his wife passed away. But these days, his face is awfully bright. He married a widow with a round face and a voluptuous figure. Whenever our boss returns from his business trips, she puts on makeup and dresses well for him. She even goes to the train station to greet him. She holds his bag and walks close to him. I think *we're* benefiting from her. He used to be the kind of guy that blew up at us during the factory meetings about increasing production, but now he's a completely new person. He has become gentler, and he speaks kindly now. He has completely changed, and production has increased!"

The bride and groom were forgotten as the guests conversed on various topics.

The night grew deeper.

The guests slowly started leaving after a delightful night of food, alcohol, and amusing conversations.

Jeong Jin Wu shook hands with every guest.

With a beautiful flower in her hair, Eun Ok bowed to her guests and went out to see them off. The cold air from outside rushed into the house, which was filled with cigarette smoke mixed with the smells of food and alcohol.

Once the guests had all gone home, the two sat quietly in the master bedroom with the lights off. Jeong Jin Wu's mother had prepared a soft cotton blanket and a mattress for them to sleep on. The couple, still overwhelmed from their wedding ceremony, could not contain their excitement.

They looked at each other in silence, the kind of silence that had existed before the universe was formed.

The moonlight quietly peeked into their room.

Embroidered lovebirds decorated the pillows, and there were colorful birds and flowers on the blanket. In the moonlight, the birds and flowers appeared to have come alive and begun to move about.

All of a sudden, the sound of a shattering icicle broke the silence in the room. Even this late in the evening, nature did not sleep and kept the couple awake. The shrill sound of the icicle startled the couple, who were immersed in their world of happiness. However, what they quietly feared most was the future that lay ahead.

Jeong Jin Wu and Eun Ok approached the window.

The icicles hanging on the eaves sparkled in the moonlight. The couple saw houses across the street faintly through the snow-covered elm trees. The roofs looked like they were covered in a fluffy white blanket. Under the peaceful moonlight, all the houses were fast asleep. In the distance, there were silver hills, and at a further distance were snow-crowned mountains, stretching their regal summits into the limitless sky. Small houses were scattered along the feet of the mountains, appearing like mosaic pieces. In the moonlight, the snow shone like crystals, attesting to nature's true work of art. It was an enchanting sight on this frosty evening. Nature had never looked so splendid and sublime.

"It's a really beautiful night. The stars look like diamonds," uttered Jeong Jin Wu.

Eun Ok stood motionless.

"Our first night together will never be forgotten," continued Jeong Jin Wu.

Eun Ok gazed into the far distance.

"It will forever be a beautiful memory. Won't it? Eun Ok, what are you thinking about right now?"

"Comrade Jin Wu." Eun Ok hesitated for a moment before she said, "Beyond those mountains, where the three stars are, is Yeonsudeok."

They looked at the dark sky. It appeared as if one could grab any of the flickering stars from the peak of a mountain.

"I can't help but recall my childhood. I feel like I'm still in that place. It feels like some other woman got married and not me. I'm scared. I feel guilty for leaving Yeonsudeok over there and living over here. In that village, there are the old-timers and comrades whom I grew up with."

Jeong Jin Wu was moved.

Eun Ok looked ever so beautiful with the moonlight on her voluptuous body. Eun Ok's face glowed the way it had when he had seen her at his senior thesis presentation, in the early morning at the University Park, and on the train station platform. It made Jeong Jin Wu more attracted to her.

"Eun Ok, if it'll make you happy, cultivate the vegetables at Yeonsudeok. I will help you. As your husband, your comrade, and your friend."

Jeong Jin Wu promised Eun Ok to support her, thinking that her research project would take only a year or a couple of years at most. He had never imagined that her research would be indefinite; he certainly had not imagined that he would have to live a life that was very different from those of other families. He did not want to look that far ahead. The enchanting reverie of marriage veiled the reality of life. Jeong Jin Wu and Eun Ok were in their prime. From their perspective, any difficulty appeared easily overcome and any agony tolerable.

"Thank you very much," said Eun Ok softly.

In the vast, dark sky, a comet flew over the mountains and then disappeared. The moonlight cast a shadow of the two lovers embracing on the blankets.

"Comrade Jin Wu, when we receive our new home, I was planning on using the master bedroom as a greenhouse so that I can check on the plants when I return from the research lab. Would that be all right?"

"Of course it will. I will buy you all the flowerpots you need," said Jeong Jin Wu.

Eun Ok, completely moved by Jeong Jin Wu's commitment, gazed into his eyes and promised eternal love, a harmonious family, and positive results from the research lab.

Jeong Jin Wu perceived their wedding vows materializing in her eyes. He read his wife's heart with his. A week later, Eun Ok left for Yeonsudeok.

It was still too early to conclude that there would be, or hope for, any positive results from Eun Ok's research lab, but since it was nearing the end of March, she had to sow new seeds.

This was how their life began.

Jeong Jin Wu reminisced about the early, innocent, and passionate days of their marriage. And now, twenty years had passed.

Jeong Jin Wu felt utterly dejected.

*It was such a beautiful, elegant wedding. Those were good days, full of love and joy. But how could I have forgotten about all that just because time has passed?*

Time had passed. Marriage had not been an enchanting reverie but a harrowing reality.

Jeong Jin Wu had been burdened with his legal duties along with having to take care of the greenhouse in their apartment and other chores in Eun Ok's absence. He had bid farewell to her with their infant son on his back on countless occasions. He had raised his son from kindergarten to the day he left for compulsory military service because she was absent most of the time. Rather than being eventful, those days were hazy to Jeong Jin Wu. He had complied with every one of Eun Ok's requests and desires. He had done all this without complaining once.

Now he was frustrated with her and his family situation. He has become indignant about her research experiment. Where had his passion on their wedding night gone? What had happened to the covenant of faithfulness he had made at the altar? Had it, perhaps, passed along with time?

Jeong Jin Wu sank into a pensive mood as he looked at the flowerpots and the moss growing on them.

The rain continued to pour down, and the wind moaned.

*It must be snowing heavily in Yeonsudeok. And by tomorrow morning, the ground will have frozen. Eun Ok must be cold.*

# TWO LIVES

TWO LIVES

# 5

un Hee lay in bed with her eyes closed, listening to the rain beating on the roof tiles, flowing down the eaves, and splashing on the ground. The unpleasant sound irritated her and kept her awake. The heavy rain seemed to be an ominous sign. She thought that nature did not discriminate among people, but tonight, it seemed that nature was not going to free her from her misery.

During her carefree childhood days, her dream-filled teenage years, and her blossoming adulthood, nature had blessed her with warmth and beautiful memories. In her home village, the sound of the summer rain dripping from the eaves was an enchanting and vibrant song, a joyous and wonderful melody. Sun Hee thought that each drop of water contained the universe. Each drop of water that fell from the vast sky contained a power too great for the dark clouds to hold and, like the faint sound of a bell tolling in the distance, dropped to earth one by one. If she were to put her ear close to the ground and listen to the beating rain, she would be able to picture everything of interest that was happening at school, in the fields, and on the hillsides.

Sun Hee reached out her small hands and received the summer rain. The rain began to fill her cupped hands, and some drops bounced off her face. As the rain began to fall harder, a stream of water flowed from the tip of the roof tile into her hands. Drip, drop, drip, drop. The rain tickled her hands. At first, the dripping rain sounded like a stringed instrument. But soon it turned into the sound of a symphony orchestra, producing harmonious melodies as it fell on pear tree leaves, barn roof tiles, wooden fences, flower gardens, clay pots, and the dirt path. The rain allowed her to experience something entirely new and musical. It rolled down her face and down her shirt. It seemed like the neighborhood children, who were also listening to the sound of the falling rain, were soon going to congregate at Sun Hee's house to appreciate nature's symphony. Children sang and danced to the rhythm of the rain. Sun Hee, full of vibrant energy, joined the neighborhood children. The falling rain, the sound of children laughing and chattering . . .

"Mom?"

What a familiar voice. That voice was now pulling at her shirt, dragging her away from her memories of her youth.

"Mom?"

Sun Hee was tossing and turning in her bed as she returned to reality, leaving her youthful days with the neighborhood children in her ephemeral dreams.

"Are you asleep?"

"No, dear . . ."

Sun Hee shuddered at the sound of reality. It was her son, Ho Nam. He was sitting by the sliding door between the two rooms. She was able to make out the silhouette of her son fearfully hugging a pillow in the dark. Ho Nam had been sitting there because he had not decided which room to sleep in. His father was sleeping in the main room and his mother in the other room. The two rooms, which were separated by only a sliding door, appeared to be worlds apart. They had turned off the lights to go to sleep many hours ago, but Ho Nam sat between his parents, between the two rooms, amid the tense atmosphere, completely alone and dejected. Sun Hee recognized Seok Chun's stubbornness in Ho Nam, a resemblance that displeased her greatly. However, she could not suppress her motherly love.

"Come here, sweetheart."

Ho Nam stood up with his pillow clutched to his heart. As he moved toward his mother, he banged his knee on the dinner table that Sun Hee had prepared for Seok Chun. Neither she nor her husband had eaten that night. So the dinner was untouched, and the dinner table remained in the room as evidence of their lack of concern for each other. Ho Nam crawled into the blankets next to his mother. He turned his back to her and got into a fetal position. He did not sink into his mother's arms like he used to. Even though he snuggled next to his mother, he had his back to her and his face to his father in the other room.

Sun Hee tried to make her son look at her by turning his body. Ho Nam obediently went into his mother's arms, fondled her breast, and fell asleep. His deep breathing was a telling sign that he had been upset over his parents' quarreling for quite some time. The dark sky wept through the night like Ho Nam's dejected spirit, beating the earth, trying to keep the boy awake with its irritating noise. The boy slept, while Sun Hee lay awake in fear that the rain would wash her precious and beautiful childhood memories down the muddied gutters.

In the other room, Seok Chun rustled in bed. He finally sat up and lit a cigarette. Seok Chun sighed deeply as the smoke clouded the room. He, too, could not fall asleep, knowing his marriage was nearing its end. He no longer felt like a member of his own family, but like a stranger to his wife and a mere acquaintance to his son. Although he was still considered a husband and a father socially and legally, he had relinquished those responsibilities.

Seok Chun did not eat the dinner Sun Hee had prepared, but she did not care. He decided to sleep in the other room by himself, but she did not care about that either. This had become a nightly occurrence, the physical realization of their isolation and scarred emotions.

Sun Hee recalled the judge's countenance when he had escorted her out the door at the courthouse. She recalled his deep-set but soft eyes and his authoritative voice. Sun Hee knew that Judge Jeong Jin Wu was the only one who could legally put an end to her marital problems and her inexplicable misery. She regretted not convincing the judge to allow her to divorce Seok Chun. When the judge inquired about the marriage, all she did was brood over their personality conflict, her future, her occupation, speaking in nonsensical abstract metaphors like "not on the same rhythm." Like a child, frustrated with things not going her way, she had rambled on and on to the judge without making a clear case for herself. She sighed with regret . . .

# 6

Jeong Jin Wu woke up at dawn, disturbed by the sound of the moaning wind and rustling tree branches.

A ray of moonlight and the dim glow of the streetlights penetrated the curtains, casting a gloomy shadow over the room. The furniture and other household objects were consumed by the darkness, but the large shadows on the ceiling and walls seemed to come to life, roaming about the desolate room like nocturnal creatures, whispering to one another.

Soon the wind subsided, and Jeong Jin Wu felt calmer. Like a child, he did not want to get out from under his warm covers. The heated floor was at just the right temperature, and he was cozy inside the silky, fluffy blanket his wife had made. He wanted to fall back asleep and imagine the sound of his wife preparing breakfast in the kitchen. However, there was no sound coming from the kitchen, and his room was the only place alive in the apartment, with the animated shadows dancing on the walls.

Convoluted thoughts troubled Jeong Jin Wu, and he felt confined and trapped. Was it because he had not slept well last night? Or was it perhaps because he had to return to the many marital problems waiting in his office at the courthouse? Civil suits were not serious problems compared to the criminal trial that would be held that morning.

The director of the City Electricity Distribution Company had designed an electric blanket for personal use and had been using it without permission from the government. This was considered a felony, as the entire country was trying to conserve energy. He was not an ordinary citizen, but the director of the very institution whose priority was the conservation of energy. For this reason, he was going to receive a severe sentence. It was not simply a crime of wasting energy, but a crime of selfishness and greed. Electricity was more precious than money or any other commodity because it was the property of the nation.

Jeong Jin Wu expected a large turnout at this hearing. The sentence was to be stern in order to prevent anyone from thinking that wasting electricity was a negligible offense. Representatives from local institutions, industrial complexes, and factories were expected to attend. Before the senior judge left on a business trip, he had ordered the district judges to give the director a harsh sentence and had told Jeong Jin Wu to oversee the entire hearing so that there would be no errors.

Jeong Jin Wu finally forced himself out of bed and did some chores around the house. He was worried about the vegetables in the greenhouse, so he took a closer look at each one and recorded the changes in humidity level and temperature that had occurred during the night.

The world outside Jeong Jin Wu's apartment was still dark. There was no light in the sky. Across the street, there were only a few apartments with lights on as diligent housewives prepared for the new day and husbands dressed to go to work. The other apartments still had not woken from their peace and comfort, their dark windows obscuring a dormant hope for a new day coupled with anticipation for new challenges. One by one, the lights went on. Joy, hope, curiosity, and love of life woke up to face the new dawn. More lights were turned on, and soon, a new determination for a new day emanated from all the apartment windows.

*Are Lee Seok Chun's lights on at this hour? The couple could not have had a good night's sleep. Without a doubt, Sun Hee must have slept with Ho Nam in the other room, while Seok Chun slept alone. It must have been a cold and lonely night for the family,* thought Jeong Jin Wu.

The sun, too, woke from its slumber and brightened the morning sky.

Jeong Jin Wu completed the chores and prepared to go to work. He paid closer attention to his shirt, suit, and tie than usual because today was no ordinary day but the day of a big trial. After one last glance in the mirror, he grabbed his briefcase and left his apartment.

By coincidence, Jeong Jin Wu saw Seok Chun and Sun Hee on his way to work that morning.

The two were walking in the same direction, but at a distance from each other, with Sun Hee in front. She wore a fancy feathered brooch on her bright two-piece suit, and she had her hair and expensive makeup done like a true celebrity. She was easily identifiable in the crowd of other women. This was how she normally dressed, and she always carried herself with confidence. It would be hard for anyone to believe she was miserable just by looking at her appearance. She had taken extra measures to hide her despondency from the locals of the Gang An District out of pride.

Sun Hee turned and gestured at Ho Nam to catch up to her.

Despite his mother's urgency, Ho Nam kept his distance. Then he stopped and stood by some trees on the side of the road. The distance between him and his mother increased, but he did not care. He kept looking back.

Behind him was his father, dragging his feet with his head lowered. Seok Chun's disheveled hair fell forward and covered his forehead. He kept his head down and looked at the small pebbles on the road.

Seok Chun's countenance was utterly wretched. Although he had on a nice dark-blue suit, it looked as if he had not ironed it. His white dress shirt was covered in yellowish grease stains. It was evident that Sun Hee had not washed his clothes for quite some time. His shoes were dirty and worn, as though they had not been shined. Those shoes were lugging around a heavy and depressed pair of legs. He did not even realize that he had just passed his son.

"Dad!" cried Ho Nam.

Seok Chun stopped. As soon as he looked at his son standing by the trees, Seok Chun's face turned bright and full of life.

"Hey, you! Why are you standing here?" Seok Chun knew why, but for the sake of Ho Nam, he said, "Why don't you follow your mom? You'll be late for kindergarten."

"I don't want to go."

"What? Where do you want to go then?"

"To your factory!"

"You know you can't do that," corrected Seok Chun.

Seok Chun fixed Ho Nam's collar and buttoned his sweater.

"Now go on to school, and watch out when you cross the street," said Seok Chun softly, patting Ho Nam's head.

Ho Nam nodded reluctantly.

Sun Hee turned around, looking for her son. When she spotted him, she unconsciously raised her hand, but when she saw her husband, she quickly lowered it and looked the other way. She felt bitter with embarrassment, as if someone had thrown cold water on her face.

Judge Jeong Jin Wu observed this on his way to the courthouse and was deeply concerned for the couple. His determination to resolve their marital problems began precisely at this moment, on this road.

The couple's attitude and behavior in public made it clear what happened behind closed doors at home every night. It seemed that their strife had worsened. Sun Hee and Seok Chun probably thought that there was no way to cure this disease between them, that their marriage had reached its end, and that the only solution was to begin anew without each other. Most couples perceived the law as something that resolved their marital problems once and for all, without any compromises. That was why couples would act as if they were strangers after filing for a divorce. Any iota of caring or regret was thrown out the window, and it was common for couples to feel only cold and embittered loathing toward their partners.

Some students raced toward Jeong Jin Wu from the opposite direction and shoved him aside as they passed, nearly causing him to fall. One student looked back apologetically, but then he continued on his way with the others. Normally, such disrespectful behavior would have angered Jeong Jin Wu, but today, rather than feeling indignant, he felt that the students were driving a stake deep into his heart, a stake that urged him to work on Seok Chun and Sun Hee's divorce case. He was determined to restore harmony to this family, but he had an important trial waiting for him. He looked at his watch and picked up his pace to the courthouse.

Sun Hee stopped walking to wait for Ho Nam.

From a small path between the apartment buildings, Sun Hee's colleague Eun Mi walked out with her daughter and husband. The daughter was about Ho Nam's age. She held both her parents' hands and fluttered like a baby bird. She looked up at her father and mother and grinned, a radiant smile that was as bright as the pink hairband on her head. The child's gaiety lit up her parents' faces.

Eun Mi's husband worked at the Gang An Machine Factory as a cannery supervisor. He had graduated from an industrial college and was now a respected supervisor among his peers and community. He wore a heavily starched suit and a classy necktie.

His hair was neatly combed back and styled with mousse. He did not look like someone who was going to work at a factory but like someone who was going to give a lecture or some kind of important presentation. His appearance gave the impression of a dignified intellectual of the nation.

Sun Hee thought that a person who was ambitious, like Eun Mi's husband, required only a little support from his wife to excel and achieve his goals. Sun Hee envied Eun Mi because she was also a great singer and dearly loved her husband with the kind of innocence that had not yet seen the harrowing reality of married life. The couple's intimacy was evident, and harmony dwelled in Eun Mi's family. Sun Hee felt empty and bitter. She walked ahead to be apart from her husband and son, but Eun Mi walked alongside her husband and daughter. This sight was too much for Sun Hee to bear, so she picked up her pace to avoid running into her.

However, Eun Mi called out Sun Hee's name and ran toward her. When Eun Mi examined Sun Hee's gloomy face, she said in a quiet, nearly reproachful tone, "You're walking alone *again*."

Sun Hee did not respond.

Eun Mi said, "I was about to congratulate you on something, but it doesn't seem like you're up for it."

"On what?"

"On Seok Chun's getting third place at the Provincial Science and Technology Fair."

"Whatever."

"Oh no, did you two fight again?"

Sun Hee continued walking without saying anything. She had always known that Eun Mi had a caring disposition. Eun Mi looked out for Sun Hee's best interests, but this morning Sun Hee couldn't deal with Eun Mi's advice. Word about Sun Hee's marital problems had spread like wildfire among the other singers. While the others had grown distant, Eun Mi stood by Sun Hee, attesting to their true friendship. Eun Mi had known about Sun Hee's marital problems, but she never shared them with others and kept her silence on the matter. However, Eun Mi did not know that Sun Hee had gone to the courthouse to file for a divorce. Sun Hee wanted to tell Eun Mi about it and get her advice, but she thought that Eun Mi would immediately reproach her and force her to retract the divorce petition.

After walking in silence for some time, Eun Mi spoke. "Sun Hee, it's about time you let it go. You can't perform under these circumstances."

"I know. That's why I'm thinking of quitting. I heard that our deputy director is also thinking the same thing."

"Get out of here! Where did you hear that?" asked Eun Mi. "It's just a rumor."

"Not from what I heard."

"No, it's not true. It's because you act like you don't care about singing anymore and because you avoid everyone."

Sun Hee did not care for Eun Mi's attempt to come up with excuses.

"Talk to me and get it all off your chest. I hope you're not looking down on Seok Chun just because he's a lathe operator, right? And you feel superior just because you're a celebrity singer, right? Because if that's what it is, then you're wrong. It's wrong to think like that. Sun Hee, it's not that, right? It's because he yells at you and insults you, right?"

Sun Hee did not respond. Eun Mi's words were plain and simple, but they somehow stung Sun Hee's conscience. Sun Hee began to question whether she had been belittling her husband because of her superior occupation. But she shook head. No. Had she not been supportive of her husband for the past ten years? It was not due to a pompous attitude. What right did a singer have to belittle a factory worker? And what was the point of doing that now, anyway? Sun Hee quickly dismissed all those thoughts. But then again, she could not convince herself that she had never had such thoughts either.

"Just give in to him, for Ho Nam's sake. Did you know that my husband thinks highly of Seok Chun?"

"You've said that before," replied Sun Hee indifferently.

"Well, listen to me again. You will never fully know your husband even if you live under the same roof." Eun Mi wanted to continue, but she realized she was lecturing Sun Hee. "All right, I'll stop since it's not right to talk about someone else's husband."

Eun Mi lifted her eyes and saw her husband approaching from a distance with their daughter. She turned to Sun Hee and said, "Do you think that my husband is always charming and respectful when he comes home from work? When things don't go well at the factory, or when I make a mistake, or when things just don't go his way, he throws a fit. He shouts till the house comes down. He throws tantrums and yells at me when he's had a few drinks. When he's like that, I just shut my mouth, keep my thoughts to myself, and continue doing whatever I was doing. Sure, I want to yell back at him, but I just take it all in. There's no point in arguing with the sky for sending a thunderstorm. But when I give him some alone time, he eventually calms down. And then the house becomes peaceful again. After a few days, we talk to each other about the issue. Now, we don't fight anymore. I'm not trying to brag or anything. But I was hoping that it would help you because your situation seems to be getting worse."

"You have no idea."

Sun Hee said the words without thinking, but her heart was still bitter. She envied Eun Mi's simple marital problems, which Sun Hee did not even consider real problems. Arguments between partners who still have feelings for each other are like spring showers, a welcome visit after a long wintry season. What Eun Mi had never experienced was the kind of argument that would lacerate her heart, the ice-cold words that would paralyze and suffocate her to the point of excruciating death.

Around eleven o'clock that morning, the trial against the director of the electrical plant ended. Those who had attended the trial flooded out the door of the courtroom. The mood in the hallway was austere. The law did not forgive or compromise with the criminal. The cross-examination, accusations, and harsh sentence instilled fear in the attendees. As they walked out, no one made a sound. Only nervous coughing and footsteps echoed in the hallway.

Judge Jeong Jin Wu secured all the legal documents under his arm and walked back to his office. As soon as he sat down, someone opened the door.

"I'm from the Provincial Industrial Technology Commission Board," said the man in a coarse voice. He was obese, but he entered the office with easy nimbleness.

Though Jeong Jin Wu was exhausted from the morning trial, he got up from his seat and stuck out his hand.

"Hello, I'm Judge Jeong Jin Wu."

"I'm Chae Rim."

Jeong Jin Wu glanced at the man again and was relieved that his guest was not the man whom he had divorced six years ago. It was just a coincidence that they had identical names. If the man whom he had divorced six years ago came to see him today, it would have been most unpleasant for Jeong Jin Wu.

Chae Rim's heavy body fit snugly in the armchair. He unbuttoned the blazer that was wrapped tightly around his body and loosened his brown necktie. He rubbed his heavy chin as he surveyed the office. It was a condescending look from a man full of arrogance. He did not have many wrinkles on his face despite his age, and his complexion was smooth and bright, evidence of his concern for his appearance. He had a large square forehead and a tasteful hairstyle, meticulously combed to one side. Chae Rim's imperious demeanor told of his satisfaction with his wealth and accomplishment. Nothing seemed to worry him. This speculation arose from Jeong Jin Wu's many years in his profession.

When Chae Rim realized that the judge was waiting for him to explain his visit, his face took on a solemn cast.

"The reason I'm here, and I'm not trying to interfere with your work—"

Chae Rim bore in mind his telephone conversation with the judge the other day and proceeded cautiously.

"I came to ask you for a reasonable favor. I feel as if I'm representing the divorcée."

"Comrade Chairman, are you related to Chae Sun Hee?"

"Yes, she's my second cousin. I know it's not the closest of family relations, but she has no other family in this city. She just calls me 'cousin' to keep it simple. However, I've been so busy with work that I haven't been able to look after her. Even though I knew she'd been fighting with her husband for some years now, I just thought that they would get over it someday . . ."

Chae Rim's words seem to drift off into a vast empty space. Jeong Jin Wu had no interest in this discussion and stared blankly at Chae Rim, focusing only on his moving lips. This was not the first time that a relative had come to him as an advocate for a member of a divorcing couple. An urgent curiosity, though, occupied Jeong Jin Wu. *Chae Rim.* Perhaps it was the identical name that continued to linger in his thoughts, the name of the man whom he had divorced six years ago.

*What kind of woman did Chae Rim marry after the divorce? His son must be much older by now. Probably around thirteen. If his stepmom had turned out to be a nice woman, then he surely hadn't had any problems growing up.*

"That's why," continued Chae Rim, "I've decided to roll up my sleeves and do something about Sun Hee's marital problems . . ."

Jeong Jin Wu remembered that day in the courtroom six years ago. Chae Rim's wife. The woman who wiped away the tears that were streaming down her freckled cheeks, the one who ardently cried out for someone to respect her dignity as a woman, the one who had lived in the deep mountains with her two children, the one who had planted trees to support her husband financially. Then there was the daughter, who refused to be separated from her younger brother and who requested to live with her mother. These were all matters that did not concern the law, but these thoughts distressed Jeong Jin Wu. He could not escape a haunting concern for that family. *Was it wrong for me to divorce them? Had there been a problem with the division of their property or with the child custody arrangements?*

Jeong Jin Wu was exasperated with Chae Rim's seemingly endless explanation. He sighed deeply and asked, "Comrade Chairman, you say that you know Sun Hee's marital problems well. What do you think? Who do you think is at fault?"

Jeong Jin Wu did not ask Chae Rim because he wanted legal advice but to get him to stop talking.

Chae Rim straightened his posture and smirked. "Comrade Judge, do you ever go to the theater?"

"Yes, every now and then."

"Then you must have seen Sun Hee's performances."

Jeong Jin Wu nodded and said, "She sings well."

"It's sublime!" corrected Chae Rim. "As a mezzo-soprano, her voice is bright and soft with depth and richness, very distinct from her colleagues. Whenever she sings about the nation, I, along with the rest of the audience, fall in love with our country all over again."

Chae Rim spoke as if he were a music connoisseur, gesticulating with his arms to the cadence of his excitement.

"Comrade Judge, don't you agree that the relationship between a family and the nation is interlinked? Think about it. Can a woman who sings so passionately about the nation be the source of her family's troubles? No, she can't. She would be a hypocrite, and we all know that a hypocrite cannot move her audience the way a genuine singer can. Sun Hee sings genuinely and, therefore, cannot be the cause of her failed marriage."

Jeong Jin Wu was impressed with Chae Rim's rational analysis and remained silent.

"Sun Hee is the kind of woman who lives her life as nobly as she sings. She has a bright future ahead of her. The problem is with that husband of hers, Seok Chun. He is the source of their marital problems. I've never seen anyone who lives as pathetically as he does. At my factory, we accept young, intelligent workers. But Seok Chun has no aspirations or ambitions. He just remains a lathe worker. He lives his life like a tree, stationed in one place with his roots deep down in the soil. He either stays home or by his wife's side. He's always so clingy and always nagging. How can a celebrity walk around town with an annoying man like that?"

Jeong Jin Wu withheld his thoughts until Chae Rim finished.

"Sun Hee just couldn't handle it anymore, so she suggested that he attend college and change his profession. She even tried to change his appearance, you know, make him look presentable. But then he would frown and yell at her, asking what was wrong with the way he dresses. He would mock her for this and that and yell at her for no reason. That imbecile screwed up his work and his family. He's a failure. Do you think it's right for him to talk back to his wife and flex his patriarchal muscles?"

Jeong Jin Wu sensed that Chae Rim's bias was getting out of hand and cut his words short. "I, too, have met with Comrade Seok Chun."

"Ah, really? Then he must've said some nonsense like how hard he's been trying to finish his project."

"That seemed to be the truth."

"Of course. He has to tell the truth. Who does he think he is? He has to tell the truth in front of a judge." Chae Rim uttered these words to gain Jeong Jin Wu's confidence, but he did not believe in those very words. Chae Rim adjusted his position and quietly asked, "So, did he request a divorce as well?" Chae Rim held his breath in anticipation, trying to read Jeong Jin Wu's eyes.

"Yes."

"That's a relief! I was a bit worried that he would back out."

Chae Rim took a Silver Bell cigarette pack from his pocket. He effortlessly peeled off the packaging, put a cigarette in his mouth, and offered one to the judge.

Jeong Jin Wu pushed an ashtray in front of Chae Rim without a word.

"Comrade Judge, since they both want a divorce, isn't it a simple case now?"

"I have to investigate Sun Hee's side of the story a bit further."

"Come now, you met with them. Is there a reason to make this so complicated? Let's just divorce them here and now. Just sign the papers."

"Comrade Chairman, please do not misunderstand me. The Superior Court does not divorce couples based on some legal documents or on advocates like yourself."

"Of course, I'm familiar with the procedures of the court."

"I'm not just referring to the procedures but more to the importance of the divorce issue. Comrade Chairman, I'm sure you know that when a man and a woman fall in love and decide to marry, it's their free decision. But they have to register for their marriage license. The law protects the entity of the family, as it is a component of society. It's not an easy matter to destroy a piece of the nation. Divorce disconnects the relationship between a husband and wife. It's not a personal matter or a matter that can be decided by executive administrators like you. The family's fate as a unit of society is intimately connected with the greater family of said society. As a result, the court will carefully assess the divorce case."

Chae Rim straightened up, as if he had heard enough, and raised his chin to tighten his necktie.

"Comrade Judge, I am *well* aware of the law."

Jeong Jin Wu also straightened up.

"Comrade Chairman, I'm sorry for lecturing you. Please don't be offended. Comrade Chairman, as someone who oversees one of the sectors in this province, I was hoping you would understand my position. Don't take Sun Hee's divorce case too personally."

Chae Rim guffawed cynically. "Do you think what Sun Hee has is a family? Let's look at the reality of her situation. If I may speak frankly, my cousin lives not in a family but more like in a boarding house. They share a single kitchen, but they sleep in separate rooms. It's really pathetic. Do you still think they are a family? Is that how a family of this great nation lives?"

Chae Rim glared at Jeong Jin Wu and said, "It would be in your best interest to divorce them quickly and quietly. I don't want their divorce to be fodder for gossip in this city and have it ruin Sun Hee's reputation or, certainly, mine. And you had better not come up with excuses to reject their divorce case. Just know that you're dealing with an explosive man here. That is, once I'm set off, there's no telling what will happen next."

"Are you threatening me? Or expecting me to guarantee their divorce?"

"Isn't it the job of the court to foresee future events and prepare necessary measures?"

"Don't borrow trouble. If there is enough evidence, then I will divorce them. Just wait patiently," said Judge Jeong Jin Wu.

Chae Rim stood up to button his suit and then reached out his hand to Jeong Jin Wu. It was not a gesture prescribed by etiquette but a sign that the conversation was over. As Chae Rim approached the door, he stopped. It appeared that he was unsatisfied with the result of his visit. He was disappointed that he was not able to bring the judge over to his point of view.

"Comrade Judge"—Chae Rim's voice was serious—"I'm asking as a favor. Please, handle this issue rationally and not only according to the strictures of the law."

Jeong Jin Wu cracked a smile at Chae Rim's comment, not because Chae Rim thought that rationality and the law were separate entities, but because Chae Rim thought that Sun Hee's divorce case was something exceptional.

Judge Jeong Jin Wu walked Chae Rim out to the front of the courthouse.

# 7

After Jeong Jin Wu paid a visit to the neighborhood leader of Sun Hee's residential area, he went to the Gang An Factory.

The musty air in the factory smelled of metal machinery and grease residue mixed with steam from the cooling water. Enormous green lathe machines occupied one side of the factory, while massive blue boring machines and planing machines lined the other side. If one did not have a good sense of direction, one was liable to get lost in the jungle of machines. The cleaning apparatus clanged, and the pressing machine stamped out huge metal sheets in a jarring rhythm.

A forklift carrying metal parts roared up behind Jeong Jin Wu. He stepped out of the way so it could pass. The female driver nodded a greeting at Jeong Jin Wu and made her way to the boring machines. A technician with blueprints under his arm hopped on the forklift for a free ride. The female driver nonchalantly raised the fork high, elevating the technician perilously close to the boring machine. The technician recognized the imminent danger and hopped off, waving a fist at her in anger. The female driver laughed.

Jeong Jin Wu could not help himself and laughed along. It was refreshing for him to leave his office with its piles of dull legal documents and come to an exuberant factory.

Judge Jeong Jin Wu met with Seok Chun's equipment manager.

The equipment manager was well over sixty, but he still looked strong and energetic. He stretched out his thick-veined calloused hand to Jeong Jin Wu. After shaking his hand, the equipment manager led him to a corner of the factory and pulled out some metal chairs. A ray of sunlight penetrated the windows, exposing dust particles lingering in the air and scraps of metal on the floor.

The equipment manager quietly smoked the cigarette that Jeong Jin Wu had offered him and sat silent, motionless, with his pensive eyes fixed on the ground. Jeong Jin Wu looked at the manager with respect and admiration. The equipment manager's leathered face and bent back told of years of work at the factory.

"Comrade Judge, you came all this way to see me, but there is not much I can say about this matter. I feel responsible and ashamed. I taught Seok Chun how to operate the lathe machine but neglected to teach him about family. I didn't tell him how to manage his family because I didn't want to poke my head into another man's personal life. Besides, I'm no family counselor."

"I see, sir."

Jeong Jin Wu was in his fifties, and for him to call the equipment manager "sir" was strange, but he did not feel he was worthy of calling him "comrade." He recalled the old equipment manager from Seok Chun's story, and even at this first meeting with the elderly man, Jeong Jin Wu deeply respected him and humbled himself before him.

"I didn't come here to ask you about your responsibility to Comrade Seok Chun's family or to make you feel guilty. I just want to know what you thought of their marital problems."

The two sat in silence. This was someone else's family problem, but they both handled it as if it were their own.

Jeong Jin Wu asked quietly, "Sir, what do you think about Comrade Seok Chun?"

"He's a genuine worker," the equipment manager said without skipping a beat. "I'm not saying that just because I trained him. If someone asked me to pick out the best workers, I would pick Seok Chun. Ever since he started working here, with peach fuzz under his nose, he worked on the lathe machine relentlessly. He works on the lathe as if it were his life and soul.

"Some workers start with the lathe, and later when it gets to be too difficult, they resort to learning less complicated machinery. Others consider the lathe a stepping-stone to joining the Party, and they eventually do work that doesn't require much physical labor. They think a promotion means they've succeeded. But I know what they're really thinking. They're lazy and have no conscience. They work at a factory for a few days and put down on their résumés that they've done something great, betraying the true workers of this nation who are here year in, year out. I've had to put so many of that kind of worker in their place. There was this one time when I reported them to the Factory Party Committee, saying that these boys should not be admitted to the Party unless they've worked here for more than ten years."

The equipment manager's aged eyes lit up as he spoke in the righteous tones of a true employee, as he, too, had labored at the factory for decades, finding his joy and life's worth among the machines.

"I somehow veered onto another topic. Pardon me. There are many employees who've worked here for ten, twenty years. There are many whom I've trained as my apprentice. But, shamefully, there are also troublemakers."

The equipment manager started to get flustered. However, he was not one to stray far from the topic like other old men. His words embodied his passion from all those years of hard work and his hope for the next generation of workers. He defied any sort of corruption and stood on the side of righteousness.

"If I can say something about Seok Chun . . ." began the equipment manager. But then he stood up quickly as if he remembered he had to do something. He walked over to the tool cabinet and opened it.

An oilcan, drill bits, and wrenches were among the many tools neatly organized inside the red tool cabinet. The tool cabinet was Seok Chun's hope, the source of his creative energy, and his pride as a worker. Anyone would be able to tell that these tools were emblems of diligence and dignity.

"Since Seok Chun was eighteen years old—so, basically, almost twenty years ago—this is the tool cabinet that he has been using ever since he started working here."

Jeong Jin Wu was shocked. He tried to mentally draw the face of Seok Chun, whom he had seen this morning walking to work— wrinkled suit, dirty dress shirt, worn-out shoes, gloomy countenance, disheveled hair. That image of Seok Chun presented a significant contrast with the neatly organized tool cabinet.

Jeong Jin Wu realized that Seok Chun had not lost his passion for his work as a lathe operator but that he struggled with his work because of his discordant marriage. *How could he work productively at the factory when his family situation is so stressful?* thought Jeong Jin Wu.

Seok Chun fell into a routine as he had been programmed to do all these years. No desire, no passion, no focus. He wanted to forget about all that was happening at home and vented his frustration on the lathe machine like a madman. He had been losing focus at the factory because of the conflict at home. He was now someone who had lost his passion for everything, as was evident when he had plodded to work this morning. Seok Chun had once cared about his work, but now he was desolate in his own barren world, dejected and utterly helpless.

"Comrade Judge, are you going to divorce Seok Chun and his wife?" asked the equipment manager, interrupting Jeong Jin Wu's thoughts.

"Well, we will have to see. I don't quite know for sure. That's why I'm here to see you," responded Jeong Jin Wu candidly.

The equipment manager stared at Jeong Jin Wu as if he were peering into the judge's soul.

"Actually, I know Seok Chun's wife quite well," the equipment manager started. "Before Sun Hee became a celebrity, she worked at our factory. She seemed like a sweet woman, and cheerful, but she was rather stubborn. She sang well, but she didn't work whole-heartedly. I perceived this and warned her about it, but she didn't take it to heart. It seemed like she didn't like me too much either, so I didn't interfere again. I didn't expect as much from her as I did from the male workers. Besides, she was the wife of Seok Chun, one of the best workers here. So I dropped it."

Jeong Jin Wu listened attentively.

"A few years later, I went over to their house on Ho Nam's birthday. But I felt something was wrong. If the air was that cold when guests were over, can you imagine how cold it must have been when they were alone? Without a doubt, the news of their marital problems came to me from their neighbors and coworkers. You know, people are often more interested in other people's problems than their own. It's rare to hear any unembellished gossip, though. So I filtered them out, and what I'm about to tell you are my personal thoughts from my own observations of the couple."

The equipment manager stared into the distance and explained Sun Hee's transformation from a humble lathe operator to a popular singer. He described how Sun Hee's vanity surged with her quick rise to stardom, as she started to receive compliments from everyone and was recognized on the street. He explained that she thought she had progressed while her husband was still an oil-stained factory worker. In the end, she would give him the cold shoulder in public and would not give in to him at home.

"But Seok Chun is not the type of guy to remain still," the equipment manager said. "He is stubborn and hot-tempered, and not willing to lose to his wife. From what I hear, he's hit her several times."

Jeong Jin Wu was speechless.

"A firm sense of principle," the equipment manager continued, "reflects the character of a true worker. Those lacking principles are prone to drift and veer from the right path, and they begin to manipulate others who are trying to live rightly. They also resort to belittling others. I'm not sure if Sun Hee fits into this category, but this is my opinion of her."

Judge Jeong Jin Wu listened carefully to every word the equipment manager said. He thought it was reasonable for the equipment manager to measure the value and principles of the couple based on his own work ethic.

However, Jeong Jin Wu did not want to nail Sun Hee's fault on vanity. Performing artists were different from other workers. Their special gift could cause them to be vainglorious. Hundreds of eyes focused on them each night, always having to have their makeup done just right, extravagant costumes, bright lights, the audience's thunderous applause, and receiving bundles of flowers—these things consumed the life of a celebrity. For Sun Hee to not be made vain by all this but to live a modest life would require her to be extremely self-disciplined. She was as much a part of her music as the music was a part of her. As an artist, she was responsible for moving the people of the nation through songs, lyrics, and her voice.

As Jeong Jin Wu thought about the relationship between nation and family, he recalled Chae Rim's remarks. Chae Rim might have had a point when he said that singing has absolute influence over the singer's emotional and ideological world.

If that were the case, then was Sun Hee's vanity really the problem? Jeong Jin Wu did not think she was complaining about her husband for being a lathe worker but rather for living a backward life without making any progress for the past ten years. It seemed as if Seok Chun's intellectual drive and idealistic passions had leveled off or even regressed since the day of his marriage. He had become complacent in his work, feeling more pride at being recognized as a humble worker than at actually completing his projects. He built a tight fence around himself under the cover of diligence and national duty, but in doing so, he excluded his wife and his son. This precise friction between the couple made Sun Hee react adversely, even imperiously, toward Seok Chun. His reluctance to fulfill his *true* national duty—the duty to progress and advance in his social position—thrust Sun Hee into despair. Jeong Jin Wu concluded that the source of the problem seemed to be with Seok Chun.

Seok Chun was in his thirties, a young age when hopes and dreams have not yet been extinguished. Unlike the equipment manager's generation, which was content with humble manual labor and a traditional wife who would be subservient to him for the rest of his life, Seok Chun's generation sought something different. A harmonious family may help one do well at work, but this alone was not enough. Compassion for others, particularly in the family, was still one of the foundations of society.

"All in all, the greatest loss is Seok Chun's talent," continued the equipment manager with a deep sigh of regret. "Since his wife behaves like that at home, his head must be overloaded, preventing him from being creative at work. That's okay for some, but a skilled worker must have a clear mind to produce good material, and invent things as well."

"Didn't Seok Chun succeed in inventing a multispindle machine?"

"You mean the one that won him third place? He went through a lot for that. Nearly five years to finish it. It seems like you know something about the *incident*?"

"Incident? No, I don't. All I know is that he was successful . . ."

"Then let's not talk about it. I get very frustrated just thinking about it."

"Why?"

"It's because the Provincial Industrial Technology Commission is completely corrupt," replied the manager angrily. He rubbed the cigarette butt out with his foot and changed the subject. "There's another machine he's been working on for some years now. It's a semiautomatic lathe machine."

The equipment manager led Jeong Jin Wu to the assembly sector.

A machine was buried in dust. It was Seok Chun's invention. It looked like a lathe machine, but half the body had been removed and dismantled, with rusty parts scattered around the station.

"A few days ago, I said something that must've hurt Seok Chun's feelings. I said, 'Don't walk around like a deadbeat and go complete your machine. Don't let the outcome of the contest stop you from your next project.'"

The equipment manager picked up a rag from the floor and began to wipe the machine.

Jeong Jin Wu also picked up a rag and began to wipe the machine. His hands were covered in machine lubricant, which soon brought on a cold and numbing sensation.

"Don't bother. Your clothes will get dirty," said the equipment manager, as though he was irritated with the judge for bringing up the past.

The equipment manager's tone did not bother Jeong Jin Wu. In fact, he was thankful to the equipment manager for allowing him to gain insight into Seok Chun's marital problems.

*What was the reason for the other argument between them when Seok Chun had completed his first invention?*

"Sir, please tell me. How did the Provincial Industrial Technology Commission Board evaluate Seok Chun's machine?"

The equipment manager glared at Jeong Jin Wu. The manager did not think that the evaluation of Seok Chun's new machine had anything to do with the divorce case.

"Please tell me," Jeong Jin Wu persisted.

The equipment manager relented when he realized that it might have everything to do with it. He wiped the grease off his hands with the rag and led Jeong Jin Wu to a corner.

"Comrade Judge, take a look at this first."

The equipment manager opened a large cabinet, three times the size of ordinary tool cabinets.

"The multispindle machine is still at the exhibition. But take a look at this, and you'll see the painstaking process that he went through. Our factory made this cabinet for him and put a plaque—'Inventor's Chest'—on it."

The cabinet had five shelves. On each shelf, there were used tools and machine parts in disorder, covered in grease and dirt.

The equipment manager reached for a pile of blueprints on the bottom shelf. Many of the small and large blueprints had oil stains on them and were faded, so the angles and measurements were difficult to make out.

"These are Seok Chun's that he's been working on for many years. The one that he recently finished is at the technician's lab. He would draw the plans over and over again. Then he would try to make the machine, and when that failed, he would go back to the drawing board. There's no telling how many times he repeated this routine. There must be hundreds of these blueprints on this shelf. Can you imagine the ones he's thrown away? He has also paid for all of the wasted materials and prints."

Jeong Jin Wu helped the equipment manager put the blueprints back on the bottom shelf. An indescribable feeling weighed down Jeong Jin Wu's heart. He could not ignore the blood, sweat, and tears Seok Chun had put into the hundreds of blueprints and wasted materials. For so many years, Seok Chun desired affection from Sun Hee, and for so many years, he had to endure his family discord, leaving evident traces of suffering on the broken machine parts. Who will ever truly understand the extent of Seok Chun's efforts, even with the copious blueprints?

"They say raindrops bore holes in stones, and needles are made from grinding metal. The harder the labor, the greater the reward. The multispindle, for Seok Chun, did its job and functioned well. I saw tears welling up in his eyes. I'm sure you know, but only the inventor can truly feel the joy of his work. The difference between an ordinary person off the street who sees a golden field of rice and the farmer who harvests the rice that he planted is immeasurable."

Jeong Jin Wu nodded his head in quiet acknowledgment.

"When I was younger," the equipment manager said, "I, too, invented a new machine. And let me tell you, there's no feeling quite like it. This one time, I was so overjoyed with my invention I went to my wife to tell her about it. She laughed and said, 'Could it possibly compare to the joy of giving birth?' I know that you can't compare a metal invention to the birth of a child. But let me tell you, my eyes welled up with tears."

Jeong Jin Wu stared at the ground with a pensive smile. He, too, remembered the joy of seeing his law essays published in prestigious legal journals.

"Comrade Judge, the multispindle is very energy-efficient with good speed and power, and it will increase the nation's production. It requires very little manpower, so it will cut down on labor. On top of that, it can be sold at a reasonable price. The technicians at the exhibition, however, questioned the engineering of the mechanisms and asked for the blueprints. And even after that, the Provincial Industrial Technology Commission Board—"

With a sigh of frustration, the equipment manager closed the door of the Inventor's Chest. His warm expression turned cold and rough. His wrinkles settled in deeply as he frowned, and his eyes reflected his vengeful thoughts.

"How could they do that to him? All they gave him was a vase and a plaque."

Jeong Jin Wu was confused and wanted to ask about it, but he let the manager explain.

"Seok Chun is so selfless and humble that he received those gifts as a sign of honor. I also saw the vase. It wasn't a special vase that was made particularly for the inventors or something that honored their hard work. It was bought at the local flower shop. It was something that anybody could go and buy anytime he wanted to. It was very condescending. I was absolutely livid, so I called the Provincial Industrial Technology Commission Board. This chairman or someone answered the phone and told me that everyone received a plaque equally without any partiality or discrimination, so I shouldn't complain about it. I was so enraged I just hung up the phone. Then Seok Chun confronted me and gave me a piece of his mind for calling the chairman. I'm sure he had his own reasons."

Jeong Jin Wu remained silent as myriad thoughts occupied his mind.

"It's really pathetic and humiliating. Comrade Judge, this incident doesn't just affect Seok Chun, but think about all the other factory workers and technicians who helped him with the machine parts and assisted him from the sidelines for so many years. Imagine how they all felt? The chairman said that the judges evaluated all the contestants from other factories the same way, so you can imagine how much it affected all the workers involved."

The equipment manager smoked a cigarette.

"I know that an inventor does not invent solely for the cash prize, but still. I've been here for many years, but I've never seen anything like this before. We have to respect the technicians and skilled laborers, the ones who produce materials for this country. We have to evaluate their labor and research, along with their character. Otherwise, there will be leeches that suck the life out of the ones who have labored earnestly. They're parasitic slackers, that's what they are, slackers who do not have the skills to invent new ideas for this country. They're lazy workers who care only about filling their stomachs, who will do anything to avoid working by coming up with all kinds of excuses not to work. Times have changed, and so have these slackers, who have found clever ways to avoid doing their jobs. We have to be wary of these slackers and differentiate them from the ones who are genuinely committed to their work. As you know, just because we're part of a collective does not mean that we're all the same. We have to weigh the work ethics of these workers on a scale."

The equipment manager's face was red with anger, and his face turned redder when he coughed harshly, making the veins on his temples bulge out. After rubbing his chest for a while, he calmed down.

"Comrade Judge, I think I've said some irrelevant things. I'm not good at getting to the point. I just speak according to how I feel. I don't think I was of much use to you."

"Not at all, sir. Your words moved me."

Judge Jeong Jin Wu looked respectfully at the equipment manager, who appeared to be self-conscious of his position before a judge. He considered the manager's wrinkles to be not simply vestiges of old age but rather evidence of backbreaking labor and undying loyalty to the country. The old man strove unremittingly to expose societal problems. This was the noble spirit of the people and the sentiment of the Party. It was this kind of person who maintained the moral principles of society and washed corrupt individuals out to sea. Parasites in disguise, chameleons, viral scum, slackers who have caused more harm than brought good to the nation and the collective would stand no longer. These corrupted seeds must be identified and exposed in order to prevent further impairment to society. In fact, these seeds might have already become tall trees with large branches that cast ominous shadows. Judge Jeong Jin Wu was reminded of this today and was determined to take action.

The state would never assess the inventors the way the judges from the Provincial Industrial Technology Commission Board did. Someone on the commission board was in the middle of this. Someone must have laundered the cash prize and used it elsewhere. This was indeed a felony. Jeong Jin Wu was prepared to charge and sentence the culprit for fraud and embezzlement of national funds. He knew that such people impeded the nation's progress.

Jeong Jin Wu stopped conjecturing because he did not have enough concrete evidence to prosecute anyone yet. He could not draw any conclusions based on the manager's words. He would have to talk with Seok Chun about this matter, meet with the Provincial Industrial Technology Commission Board members, and investigate the quality of the inventions, the production costs, and the net worth of these machines.

"Comrade Judge, you said that you have met with Seok Chun, right?" asked the equipment manager.

"Yes. But I need to see him again."

"Then let's go to the casting sector. Seok Chun is probably there working on a remote control."

They exited the building and walked around the premises on a thickly wooded path. From the opposite side of the narrow path, a young worker with his hat tilted and his hands deep in his pockets sauntered toward the manager and Jeong Jin Wu.

The equipment manager approached the young man and scolded him harshly, "Why are you always like this? Straighten your hat. Your face is caked with soot again! You act like you're the only one working hard around here!"

The young worker quickly straightened up without saying a word.

"Is Seok Chun over at the casting department?" asked the equipment manager.

"He was working with me in the morning, but then he went to another factory to get some casting sand."

"Did he say that the molding material was the source of the problem?"

"There were a couple of problems with the stork remote-control connection rod, and it started bubbling," replied the young worker respectfully.

The equipment manager looked at Jeong Jin Wu as a sign that he should ask the young worker something. Jeong Jin Wu told the young worker to tell Seok Chun to come by his office when he returned. Jeong Jin Wu thanked the equipment manager for his time and went back in the direction of the factory.

Judge Jeong Jin Wu was very busy that day. He came across a new lead on someone or some group embezzling national funds at the science fair. He had not expected illegal activities to be connected to the divorce case. He decided to look into it further, but he needed to be discreet and approach the members of the Provincial Industrial Technology Commission Board cautiously to find out about the distribution of the cash prize. He would then have to have the entire board audited for records from previous years as well. He could not probe around this issue like any other case; he had to be careful.

# 8

J udge Jeong Jin Wu went to the Provincial Industrial Technology Commission Board the next day and talked with the secretary and bookkeeper. He inquired about Chae Rim. The secretary told Jeong Jin Wu that Chae Rim was gone on a business trip and therefore could not meet with him. She also told him to come back when Chae Rim returned or she could have Chae Rim go to the court. Jeong Jin Wu had to wait to see any part of this investigation develop. He returned to his office later that afternoon.

He could begin the prosecution with the little evidence he had on the Provincial Industrial Technology Commission Board's mishandling of the evaluation process at the science fair. However, he needed to meet with Chae Rim, who had allegedly organized this fraudulent evaluation process, to get a clearer idea of the case.

*Did Chae Rim do it intentionally? Could it have been an innocent mistake? The equipment manager could have misunderstood the whole thing. Couldn't Chae Rim defend himself by saying that it wasn't embezzlement but a different fund that was meant to be distributed to the commission board, the local government, and the people? Then what happened to the cash prize? How should I proceed?*

Jeong Jin Wu recalled Chae Rim's visit a few days ago. He remembered that he had assessed Chae Rim's sensibility, rationality, and political discernment rather highly. Chae Rim had also graduated from a polytechnic university, so it was likely that he knew something about the quality of Seok Chun's machine. Jeong Jin Wu figured Chae Rim had known that the cash prize was intended for the inventors but went ahead and organized a fraudulent evaluation process. No excuses could exonerate him. Jeong Jin Wu was determined to prosecute Chae Rim.

Jeong Jin Wu rested his elbows on the desk and buried his face in his hands. His face was burning with indignation, a feeling of unrelenting anger toward the investigation. He was not able to meet Chae Rim and interrogate him on this matter, but Jeong Jin Wu believed—no, he was certain—that Chae Rim was responsible for the crime. Jeong Jin Wu had come to this conclusion based on the evidence and his intuition and legal experience. Punishing a corrupt official like Chae Rim would be gratifying to Jeong Jin Wu—he intended to summon Chae Rim to the court, make him confess his crime before the magistrates, and force him to resign from his official position.

Although he knew that working himself up like this, becoming emotionally involved, and rushing into a case were against the principles of a prudent judge, he could not control his feelings. Whenever he dug deep into an investigation and identified the truth of the crime, a yearning for justice for the people and the Party would surge within him. The law and Party doctrines were, of course, the correct guidelines for assessing a case, but at times the zealous application of these guidelines would overcome a judge's objective perspective, causing him to be overly dogmatic and abandon prudence.

Judge Jeong Jin Wu picked up the phone and dialed slowly.

"Is this the Provincial Performing Arts Company? How do you do? My name is Judge Jeong Jin Wu at the Superior Court."

"Hello, sir. I'm the deputy director."

The volume on the telephone handset was so loud that anyone sitting next to Jeong Jin Wu would have been able to hear the deputy clearly. Jeong Jin Wu arranged a meeting with the deputy director, who was acting as the interim chair of the performing arts company.

"Comrade Deputy Director, are you going to be at the theater this afternoon from three o'clock to four o'clock?"

"Yes. Is there a problem?"

"I want to talk to you about Chae Sun Hee."

"Ah, if that's the case, then you don't have to come by. I will come directly to the courthouse. I have some errands to do in that area anyway."

"Very well. I'll be waiting for you."

Jeong Jin Wu hung up the phone, feeling less burdened than before. He thought that the deputy director could persuade Sun Hee to not go through with the divorce, as it was customary for local officials to deal with individuals and their personal problems before the court got involved. Jeong Jin Wu closed Sun Hee's divorce file and decided to wait for the deputy director to speak with her first. He had not completed Sun Hee's divorce petition because he did not feel that he fully grasped her ideological disposition.

People needed to recognize the nobility of the law. For Jeong Jin Wu, the highest law was conscience, the sublime and wondrous court of human emotions, moral judgment, integrity, respect, and honor. Egotistical opinions, self-aggrandizing assertions needed to be silenced in order for one, particularly Sun Hee, to take heed of the quiet voice of compassion, which had been, for so long, locked somewhere in the depths of her embattled heart.

Someone knocked cautiously on the judge's door.

"Come in," Jeong Jin Wu said.

Seok Chun waited sheepishly at the threshold, fidgeting with his hat. He approached the desk only after Jeong Jin Wu welcomed him in. Seok Chun delicately placed his hat on the desk as if it were fragile and pulled out a chair.

"I know you must be very busy, so thanks for stopping by," Jeong Jin Wu said.

"It's not a problem," Seok Chun replied.

He sat with his eyes lowered in respectful solemnity. He felt awkward, tense, and even a bit embarrassed to be at the court, but he also showed his willingness to comply with Jeong Jin Wu's request.

"So, were you able to find good casting sand?" Jeong Jin Wu asked, engaging in a lighter topic of conversation before delving into the serious issue.

"I bought some from the other factory, but the quality isn't good."

"What about the sand from the riverbank? Won't that work?"

"Well, I'm not sure. It may be useful for other castings, but there are only a few places that have good-quality sand. Most of them are near the Eastern Sea."

"I see. That is a problem. By the way, what was that called? The storklike—"

Seok Chun cracked a smile and asked, "Are you talking about the remote-control connection rod?"

"That's right. Your equipment manager was also worried about finding the right sand. I'm not sure if you know, but the sand on the riverbank is of high quality."

"Comrade Judge, don't worry about it. I'll find a way to get the right casting sand."

"I like your determination. Anyway, don't lose your passion for inventing new machines. Keep at it. If you were to lose passion for your work, that would be a great loss."

Judge Jeong Jin Wu paused for a moment and then continued.

"I came by your factory this morning because I wanted to hear the rest of the story you began at my apartment that rainy evening. You may think that you've provided me with enough information, but by legal standards, I don't have enough. Of course, I was able to formulate an idea of your family problem based on what you told me. Your expectations for your invention, and Comrade Sun Hee's expectations for your success . . . the pain and suffering you two have had to endure all these years. What is this that I hear about you two having an argument about the prize? Did you really argue about the prize?"

Seok Chun sighed deeply.

"We had an argument. No, we fought. I brought home the vase and plaque that evening. Ho Nam was excited about my prize and told Sun Hee about it. She didn't say a word. The three of us sat around the dinner table without saying anything to one another."

After dinner, Ho Nam immediately fell asleep, exhausted from playing all day, and the couple remained silent, inviting the ever-so-familiar austere atmosphere back into the room. Seok Chun had been elated by the applause from the audience upon receiving the prize, but his elation was truncated by his wife's apathy. He had grown accustomed to not sharing his thoughts with Sun Hee, so he had no intention of sharing his excitement at winning the prize. Attempting to connect emotionally with Sun Hee was more difficult than inventing a new machine. He was not going to force himself to "fix" his marital problems because he did not see any purpose to it, and even if he tried, his marriage would never return to its original state. Although he would have to endure the pain and loneliness of a broken marriage, he thought that it would be best to remain silent until it was time for bed.

Seok Chun opened the *Handbook for Metal Cutters* and perused it. The figures, instructions, graphs, and diagrams on engineering in the book took him to a peaceful grassy field under the warmth of the sun. Seok Chun journeyed into his imagination, momentarily escaping the problems of his marriage. His love for engineering had filled the void in his heart where his love for his wife had once been. Solitude no longer frightened him; it became his companion, his friend, during those long, sleepless nights.

It appeared that Sun Hee had accepted that their nights were going to be spent in agonizing silence. Unlike other ordinary days, however, tonight she was determined to settle something. Sun Hee approached Seok Chun with her arms crossed. She picked up the plaque on the desk and read it aloud. And then she put it down. She smirked bitterly as she picked up the cheap vase and asked, "You went through all that trouble to receive *this*?" As she placed the vase back on the desk, it wobbled around a bit until it found its balance.

Seok Chun glared at Sun Hee and asked, "What, did you expect something grander?"

Sun Hee retorted, "Of all things, would the country really give you *this*? Why didn't you demand what's really due to you? And why do you just sit there like Buddha?"

"What would you have liked me to receive? A new suit? A television set?"

"At least some kind of medal or an article about you in the newspaper. Something more than *this*!"

Sun Hee's true desires seemed to be contained in this piece of sarcasm.

"You're living in a fantasy . . ." Seok Chun muttered.

With those words, he lit his cigarette.

Sun Hee stared at Seok Chun with inexpressible hatred as she recognized his embittered mockery. She raised her voice, "Is it really that bad to receive a cash prize and treat your friends to dinner and drinks? Ever since you didn't win first place, you've been depressed. Is it too much for me to ask you to really focus on your project and invent something that will get first place and win you some respect from others?"

"A housewife should not interfere in a man's work," Seok Chun retorted. "If my invention somehow advances technology, then what more can I ask for? Is it really that important to appear in a newspaper article or win a cash prize? You need to know that pride in one's work is far nobler than fame or fortune."

Sun Hee was momentarily seized with a shudder and could not respond. She only glared at Seok Chun with her mouth agape. She felt the enmity and resentment brewing inside her, and it was only a matter of time before she exploded. But somehow, she could not find the right words with which to respond, and that added to her frustration.

"Pathetic," Sun Hee said, which was about the only word she could think of.

"What did you just say?" Seok Chun shouted, as smoke from his cigarette filled the precarious space between the two. "You don't have the right to say that to me! You may insult me, but don't insult the fruit of my labor! Don't mock my sacred purpose!"

"Let's just stop," said Sun Hee exhausted. "I can't do this anymore. I can't live like this. I . . . I can't live with you anymore."

"Ah, you want to end this? I won't beg you to live with me. I don't need you! Get out of my sight, you filthy bitch!"

Seok Chun slammed his fist on the desk. The vase wobbled from the shock and rolled off the desk, shattering on the floor with a terrible sound. Ho Nam woke up frightened and began to weep.

"Comrade Judge, basically our arguments just repeat themselves. They escalated to this point. But that last argument was the *last* argument. I can't stand it anymore. Comrade Judge, I'm asking you as a favor."

Seok Chun clenched his hands tightly and cracked his knuckles. Very much like Sun Hee, he was desperate for a divorce.

Jeong Jin Wu spoke in a soft but stern voice.

"Your divorce case will be decided by the court. Since we don't have that much time, I'll ask you a few questions. You claim that Sun Hee has become vain and arrogant. You think that this is her fundamental flaw, and that is why you want a divorce. Can you provide me with a concrete example?"

Seok Chun was taken aback by the unexpected question. He wanted to provide the judge with all the instances that showed Sun Hee's vainglorious attitude toward him, but he was not certain if those would qualify as grounds for divorce.

Judge Jeong Jin Wu asked, "Do you want to divorce her because she walks around in lavish outfits and belittles you for dressing unfashionably? Does that even make sense to you?"

Seok Chun remained silent because he knew this would also not qualify as a reason.

Judge Jeong Jin Wu spoke sternly. "Did she ever discourage you from achieving a higher degree at the Engineering College?"

Seok Chun lowered his eyes in shame.

"Go home and think about it," instructed the judge. "Think about what your wife wants from you. Look at the bigger picture of what society demands from you and not just from your narrow perspective. You said that you haven't received sincere affection from Comrade Sun Hee. But her way of showing you affection was to encourage you to become more than a lathe operator. She loves you so much that she wants you to exceed your potential. How can that be a lack of affection?"

Seok Chun hung his head for a while and then straightened his body. He grabbed his hat from the desk and stood up. He waited for Jeong Jin Wu to give him permission to leave. Jeong Jin Wu stuck out his hand and shook Seok Chun's hand.

"I'll stop by your factory in a couple of days. Share your thoughts with me then."

# 9

Back at the theater, Sun Hee leaned against a pillar and stared out a tall window.

The theater hall was serene except for her comrades practicing on the second floor. The music irritated her, but it was inescapable as it resounded throughout the theater.

Sun Hee stared at the part of the outside world she could see through the window. Behind the theater was the kindergarten, and little children were kicking a ball in the adjacent open grassy field. They were about Ho Nam's age. Upon a closer look, she saw they were all familiar children. They were the older kids at Ho Nam's school. She assumed that school was out. The children were kicking a rubber ball around and swarmed to wherever the ball went. Sun Hee envied the children playing in the field, laughing and oblivious to misery and fright. Such children had no concerns about a troubled family life and likely had never experienced any such thing. Sun Hee then felt a pang of sorrow when she could not identify her son amid the children.

*Where could he be? He must no longer be playing with his comrades. Is he standing around somewhere by himself like I am right now? Did he walk home by himself again?*

For the past few weeks, Ho Nam hadn't thrown childish tantrums or performed his usual silly antics. He had hardly laughed or smiled, an evident indication of his miserable situation at home. Sun Hee was on the verge of bursting into tears at the thought of casting a dark shadow over Ho Nam and leaving an irreparable scar on his heart. Whenever she fought with her husband, she would tell Ho Nam to go outside and play by himself. Sun Hee was all the more frustrated with Ho Nam because he had Seok Chun's temperament and always sided with his father. She recognized that she had not been a good mother to her son. But after visiting the court, her maternal instincts surged with a desire to nurture him. It could have been from the thought of separating Ho Nam from his father.

All of a sudden, Sun Hee remembered the events of yesterday evening.

Sun Hee was anxious to find out if Chae Rim had settled anything with Judge Jeong Jin Wu, so she raced home with Ho Nam and discovered that Chae Rim had been waiting for her. She invited him into her house.

Chae Rim gave Ho Nam an eggbread with a red bean filling. As soon as Sun Hee walked into the living room, she collapsed on the floor from exhaustion.

Alarmed, Chae Rim said, "My goodness, you don't look well at all. How are you holding up?"

"I'm just tired," Sun Hee replied. "Any news?"

"Well, I went by the court the other day," Chae Rim said, as he was finding a place to sit.

"And, so what happened?" Sun Hee asked blankly.

"I found out that Seok Chun had finally gone to file for a divorce."

"I know."

"You do? Well, then it's settled! You should be divorced in no time."

"Yes, but . . ."

"Right. That judge looks to be an inflexible man. But don't you worry. I think I can pull some strings and make some calls. I'll make sure this divorce goes through."

Sun Hee sighed.

Chae Rim continued, "By the way, you look awful, like a wilted flower."

Sun Hee did not protest this description.

"I guess you must be under a lot of stress with the divorce," Chae Rim said.

"I feel so bad for Ho Nam. And—"

"And for *Seok Chun*?" Chae Rim interjected. "You couldn't file for divorce a few years ago because of that low-life, right? You have to be firm this time. How much longer are you going to live like this?"

Ho Nam was eating his bread and glared coldly at Chae Rim.

"You're going to ruin your life by prolonging the situation. He's an idiot. You're still very young and have lots to live for. Let's see the result of this divorce and prepare for a new beginning. After you get divorced, I will introduce you to a man who is a hundred times better than Seok Chun."

Ho Nam threw his bread at Chae Rim's feet. Some of the pieces crumbled upon impact and spread across the floor. Chae Rim was startled by Ho Nam's actions and momentarily forgot what he had been saying.

Ho Nam wiped the crumbs off his mouth and shouted at Chae Rim. "Don't talk about my dad like that! My dad's not a bad man!"

Chae Rim's cheeks reddened with embarrassment, but then he chuckled to lighten the awkward moment.

"You're quite a kid!" Chae Rim said, dusting off the crumbs. "What an insolent child."

"Honey, you shouldn't do things like that," admonished Sun Hee.

She felt sorry for Chae Rim, so she grabbed Ho Nam's wrist, but Ho Nam pulled away effortlessly.

"Go home! Take your bread with you," shouted Ho Nam.

"Have you no respect for family?"

"If you're family, then why are you telling my mom to leave my dad?"

"Well, that's because your mom and dad fight all the time," rationalized Chae Rim.

Ho Nam did not know what to say. Perhaps it was because he was frustrated or furious, but his eyes welled up with tears as he darted sullen and ferocious glances at Chae Rim. Ho Nam clenched his fists as if he were prepared to fight.

Chae Rim thought that he should not upset a child from a dysfunctional family, so he stood up slowly.

Sun Hee began to sob in front of her child, who had defended his father with all his might. She felt terrified at the thought of separating Ho Nam from his father after the divorce.

There will be no one to take Ho Nam fishing by the river, and no one to make him a rubber-band gun. When the neighborhood kids tease him for not having a father, he will surely blame her. The more Ho Nam becomes aware of not having a father around the house, the more he will become intimidated and introverted. It will alienate him from the other kids. A daughter would open herself up to her mother, but a son has problems talking to his mother about everything on his mind. Once the divorce is settled, she and her husband will become strangers, but there is no way to break the bond between father and son. No matter how much a mother cares for her son, she will never be a substitute for the child's father. This is because maternal love and paternal love serve different needs for the child.

That was last night.

*　　*　　*

Sun Hee heaved a sorrowful sigh. Seok Chun was a wretch to her, but he was a wonderful father to Ho Nam. She could not deny that fact.

Sun Hee wiped the tears off her face. She shook her head to cast away any doubts about the divorce. At the same time, she could not easily dispel the misfortune encroaching on her son. She brushed her hair behind her shoulders and touched up her face.

It took some time for her emotions to settle down. Sun Hee began to rebuke herself.

*How did you file for divorce with such a weak heart? Did you not anticipate this kind of heartache? Surely there's bound to be someone out there who will love Ho Nam like his own son?*

Sun Hee still did not see Ho Nam playing on the grassy area with the other kids. She began to worry as she had the day it had rained, when she had been looking everywhere for Ho Nam before she was told that he was at Judge Jeong Jin Wu's apartment. Sun Hee heard her comrades practicing on the second floor of the theater. They were preparing to perform in Seong Gan District this coming weekend, a tour that would carry on without her. She felt alienated from the music and the theater. She decided to leave.

Sun Hee calmly turned around at the sound of high heels running down the stairs. It was Eun Mi. She ran toward Sun Hee, who was on her way out of the theater.

"I've been looking for you. Had I known you'd be here . . ." said Eun Mi.

Sun Hee did not understand Eun Mi's statement.

"The deputy director is looking for you."

"Me? Why?"

"I don't know. But why aren't you rehearsing with the other vocalists?"

"Uh . . . I needed to take a break, and . . . I . . . I decided to practice on my own."

"Or is it because you're avoiding them?"

"Eun Mi, please, not you, too."

"They need you."

"You know perfectly well that those comrades don't like me."

"No, that's where you're wrong. You've really become sensitive these days, haven't you? Ok Hee says that you've been avoiding them, not coming to rehearsals, and when you do come, you don't sing like you used to."

Sun Hee listened indifferently.

"You know you shouldn't act like this."

Sun Hee was irritated with Eun Mi's admonitions, despite her good intentions.

"Your personal issues should not interfere with your work," Eun Mi continued. "You shouldn't give your comrades the cold shoulder. What will happen to our troupe if you don't do your job?"

Sun Hee hissed, "Stop it!" unable to contain her frustration any longer. She did not want others to hear her, so she kept her voice to an angry whisper. "That's enough! You sound just like the deputy director. I thought that you, of all people, would understand."

Sun Hee glared at Eun Mi with tears welling up in her eyes, tears from feeling betrayed by the only true friend she had at the performing arts company. She walked past Eun Mi, who seemed to be nailed to the floor, rendered speechless by Sun Hee's violent reaction.

The deputy director was standing at the top of the stairs looking down on the two. In a fit of urgency, he slammed his hands on the handrail and shouted, "Comrade Sun Hee, how dare you leave without my permission! Get back here."

Sun Hee turned her head away. The deputy director descended the stairs and confronted her forcefully. Eun Mi, anticipating an upsetting altercation, refrained from interfering with the two and kept her distance.

"You're an embarrassment to the company—an embarrassment!" The deputy director tsk-tsked and shook his head in disdain.

Sun Hee bit her lip to suppress her irritation.

The deputy director pointed at her and said, "You better get your act together, or else I'm going to have to—"

"Fine!" Sun Hee said boldly. "If you feel that I'm an embarrassment to the company, then I'll quit."

"What? You're going to quit?" the deputy director retorted, aghast. "Is giving up your answer to everything? You only care about yourself!"

Sun Hee had nothing further to say.

"I have an appointment at the courthouse now, but when I return, we're going to get to the bottom of this."

The deputy director raced past Sun Hee, grunting and mumbling indecisively. She stood resolutely, to give the impression that she was really determined to quit, but then she began to lose courage and felt the terrifying weight of regret on her shoulders. She felt her soul was being wrung out of her body, and numbness started spreading up her legs. Dizzy, short of breath, and on the verge of collapsing, she held on to the handrail.

Fear gripped her. She felt that her best friend, her company, and her only son—all that was precious to her—were abandoning her. No, she was certain that they had abandoned her. She realized that divorce was not simply a legal process concluded in the privacy of the courtroom but a public matter with her entire community involved. She felt as if she were being weighed on an ethics scale, naked and vulnerable in the critical eyes of the disapproving public.

Divorce was the only option for her.

She realized that to go through with the divorce, she would have to persist and endure public humiliation, sacrifice her fame and status as a celebrity, and be ostracized from the large family called "society." The divorce would be a detriment to her livelihood, an inestimable, insurmountable blow to her career.

Yet she was going to have to accept her wretched destiny if divorce was going to be a reality, which caused her distress. Her hands were clammy, she was nervous, she felt she had committed a crime against her community.

A strange uncertainty flickered in her heart, momentarily suspending her decision.

Would she have to remain married to her husband in order to save face in public?

Sun Hee shook her head. She convinced herself that these terrifying thoughts derived from her anxiety over the whole matter, and that she was the victim in this marriage, not the perpetrator. She was certain of this, but she could not allay her fears.

# 10

The Provincial Performing Arts Company's deputy director paid a visit to Judge Jeong Jin Wu. He sat on the edge of his seat, upright and dignified, exuding the air of a veteran performer.

He was a skinny, pallid man with a receding hairline, a beaky nose, and small eyes. Above all, Jeong Jin Wu was amused by the deputy director's high-pitched, nasal voice and its contrast with his distinguished demeanor.

"Comrade Judge, I don't know what to say. I'm ashamed of myself for allowing Sun Hee's problems to get to this point. I had no idea she had filed for a divorce. Perhaps I've been treating her too . . ."

The deputy director did not complete his comment and furrowed his brow in deep contemplation, as though he were the one who had instigated the divorce.

"How is Comrade Sun Hee doing at the theater?" Jeong Jin Wu asked.

"Well, she was quite introverted when she first started but began to open up to her comrades after a few years. She then became arrogant and extremely high-strung, sensitive to every word or gesture. Her fame probably had something to do with it.

Some of the members of the troupe dislike her, talk behind her back. They don't like the fact that a once humble factory worker is now the lead soloist. But she sings so well that they have to overlook that part."

"How much do you know about her marital problems?"

"Quite honestly? Not much. There are rumors that her husband has a bad temper and that he cares only about his work. I've also heard that he complains about her lavish outfits. Despite all that, she should still try to repress her indignation and work things out with him. But Comrade Sun Hee is not that kind of person."

The deputy director continued in his high-pitched voice. "I've told her many times to get her marital problems sorted out."

"Many times?" Jeong Jin Wu asked.

"Perhaps not many, but certainly a couple of times," the deputy director replied.

"How did you instruct her to sort things out?" Jeong Jin Wu probed.

"Well, she hasn't been practicing with her team for some time now, and so I pulled her off the performance roster. We're going to Seong Gan District this weekend, and I'm thinking of pulling her again. If she doesn't change her attitude, then I'm thinking of letting her go altogether."

"What do you mean, her attitude?"

"Her indifferent attitude toward her comrades, toward me, and her bad attitude from her marriage."

"Do you think letting Comrade Sun Hee go will benefit her and the company?"

"Of course not! We need Sun Hee. She's one of our main attractions. Once she gets a divorce, I will consider letting her rejoin the company."

The deputy director provided plenty of information in a short span of time, speaking like a doctor diagnosing a patient's health.

At this point, Judge Jeong Jin Wu sided with Sun Hee and disagreed with the deputy director. It appeared the deputy director also secretly wanted the couple to divorce so that Sun Hee could free herself from the bondage of despair. This was not because the deputy director cared about Sun Hee but because he wanted her to return to the company and perform the way she used to. Jeong Jin Wu knew that if Sun Hee returned to work for the sake of working, then she would have the wrong idea of what was expected of a national singer.

After tapping on the desk for a while, Jeong Jin Wu spoke in a heavy tone.

"I don't think you've done your best."

Judge Jeong Jin Wu's decisive statement startled the deputy director.

"At first," Judge Jeong Jin Wu continued, "you accepted her with open arms because of her talent, and now you want to let her go because of her attitude problem and her marital difficulties. Deputy Director, what do you think? Don't you think it's a bit unfair?

The deputy director's large forehead turned bright red.

Jeong Jin Wu continued.

"I don't think Comrade Sun Hee's personal problems and flaws affect her as a singer. People may not know the dark side of her personal life, but they do enjoy her singing. If you take Comrade Sun Hee's love for music away from her, then not only will you be depriving the people of the music they love but you will also cause Sun Hee greater despair. If you don't allow her to participate in the Seong Gan tour, and if you dismiss her from the company, then what will become of Sun Hee?"

The deputy director pulled out his handkerchief and wiped the sweat off his forehead.

"Comrade Sun Hee's aspirations are noble," Jeong Jin Wu continued. "Life's true meaning is swimming upstream, is it not? It's not right to make matters worse just because of her marital problems. A person's talents are one of the most important elements that build her character. The law does not permit anyone to prevent the development of another's talents.

"Comrade Deputy Director, your group should be more patient and try its best to sympathize with Comrade Sun Hee at a time like this. The way I see it, Comrade Sun Hee has had high expectations of her relationship with her husband. However, she was unable to make that her top priority because of her duties as a national singer. I believe she has many talents and expresses them well. However, these things conflict with her personal ideology and her goals."

"Comrade Judge, thank you very much. In truth, I, not very long ago, should've gone to Sun Hee's house and encouraged her . . ."

The deputy director looked at Jeong Jin Wu with self-reproachful eyes as he explained his shortcomings.

# 11

I t was a sunny afternoon. The warm sunlight awoke the trees, flowers, and grass from their wintry slumber. The soil was still damp from the rainstorm of a few days ago, and the strong winds set the dark clouds adrift beyond the horizon in the vast sky. The spring air was fresh, and the muddied river had cleared.

Sun Hee brought laundry from her house to wash by the river.

She had to wash Ho Nam's dirty clothes before she went on the tour to Seong Gan with her troupe. She could have washed the clothes at the neighborhood laundry center, but she didn't want to encounter any of the neighborhood women or hear any of their comments on her marital problems. The river was frigid from the melting ice somewhere upstream, but the riverbank was her safe haven, a remote place where Sun Hee could find peace in solitude.

She scrubbed the stains off the clothes and repeatedly rubbed her numbed hands. She clasped her hands tightly and stared blankly at the clothes. She fell into deep thought.

She had told her deputy director that she would quit and waited anxiously for his response, but for some reason, he didn't bring it up again. After the deputy director came back from the courthouse, he didn't hassle Sun Hee for more information about her marital problems. He simply told her to prepare for the upcoming tour. He also suggested that she should practice more and gave her some time off to catch up on her housework. Sun Hee was grateful to the deputy director for not adding more work problems to her marital problems.

She felt as though some of her burden had been lifted and continued washing the clothes. Her fingers had become stiff and numb from the icy water, so she rubbed her hands fiercely and blew on them. When her hands regained life, she picked up the clothes and started to head home.

Just then, Sun Hee identified a man with a bucket and a shovel hobbling along the upper section of the riverbank.

It was unmistakably Judge Jeong Jin Wu. He was shoveling some sand by the riverbank and tossing it behind him. He then took off his shoes and rolled up his pants.

When Sun Hee saw the judge step into the river in his bare feet, it gave her a cold sensation. She assumed the judge was planning to use the sand to fix his furnace. She was bemused to see a respectable judge slogging through the freezing water to collect sand. Jeong Jin Wu appeared helpless and pathetic. *He could have called his apartment maintenance man and had him send some workers to fix the furnace for him,* Sun Hee thought. But she also concluded that the judge was something of a handyman and liked to solve his own problems.

Although Sun Hee tried to mind her own business and return home, she felt sorry for him. She kept glancing over her shoulder to see the judge shoveling laboriously in the icy river.

It was not long after Judge Jeong Jin Wu rolled up his pants and entered the river that his feet and ankles started to sting from the cold water. Despite the pain in his feet, he continued to dig with his shovel. Soon, his feet became entirely numb.

He dug up a big clump of sand and took it out of the river. On examining it more closely, he was not pleased with the quality of the sand and knew that it was not going to work as casting sand. He slumped with disappointment and stared at the flowing river in defeat.

Many years ago, when he and his son had come to this river to rinse salt out of seaweed, he had seen an area in the middle of the river that had superb sand.

*But*, he thought to himself, *if the sand is truly superb, then why hasn't the factory already taken it?*

Jeong Jin Wu stood still to let his feet regain feeling, but he did not want to waste too much time. He was intent on going into the deep section of the river, near the huge boulders. This time, he took off his trousers and thermal underwear.

Passersby saw Jeong Jin Wu in his underwear nearly waist-deep in the freezing river. They stopped to watch this unusual spectacle. Some muttered jokingly that he was out to catch the enormous legendary fish that dwelled in the depths of the river.

The water had come up to his waist. He huffed and puffed each time he took another step into the river. His teeth chattered uncontrollably, and his entire body became paralyzed with numbness. He gently lowered the shovel to the floor of the river and took a scoop of the sand from between the boulders. Carefully, he lifted the sample out of the water without dropping it back to the bottom.

As soon as he examined the clump of sand, he shouted with joy. The sand was translucent, fine, and firm, the same sand he had seen many years ago with his son.

As he waddled back to the riverbank, Jeong Jin Wu seemed to have forgotten about his frozen limbs. He pulled a long stick from the bucket, which looked like a fisherman's bait container, and a rope from his backpack. He then tied the rope onto the bucket and hung it around his neck.

From the other side of the river, he heard women giggling.

Jeong Jin Wu looked at the path where people were standing and then boldly went back into the river. The icy water did not bother him as it had before. His body had become used to it by now.

He dug up the sand and placed it in the bucket. It took some time to fill it halfway. He came out of the water and placed a large plastic bag on the ground. He then poured the sand into the bag. He rubbed his legs to get his blood flowing again and then returned to the river. He repeated this a few more times and collected enough sand to fill the bag. He then put the bag in his backpack.

The people standing by the road, curious at first, decided Jeong Jin Wu was an eccentric. They shook their heads in disdain and went about their business. They did not understand why he had to go so deep into the freezing river when there was abundant sand on the riverbank.

Jeong Jin Wu quickly put on his pants and threw the heavy backpack over his shoulders. He put the stick back into the bucket and held the shovel in his other hand. The backpack was filled with wet sand, which made it extremely heavy. He started to feel the weight of the sand on his lower back. As he walked down the path, he felt the backpack weighing down his shoulders, causing him to drag his feet.

He had done this to help Seok Chun, but he was having second thoughts, wondering if all this trouble was absolutely necessary. Judge Son had once complimented Jeong Jin Wu for going out of his way to do things for others. He could not accept that kind of compliment from Judge Son. If he could prevent a divorce and regenerate the couple's lost love, then going out of his way for them was no trouble. How wonderful would it be for Seok Chun to appreciate what he had done for him, and for him to complete the new machine with this sand? Seok Chun would be able to complete the remote control, improve the multispindle machine, and come home with a sense of accomplishment. Seok Chun would then be able to spend more quality time at home with his family. Family and work may appear to be different at times, but affection was the thread that held the two together. Therefore, the duty of the law lay in restoring dysfunctional families and not only in arresting criminals. That was why, even though the backpack was burdensome, he continued trudging along the path.

Jeong Jin Wu stopped by a tree on the side of the road to rest. He put the heavy backpack down and leaned the shovel against the tree. Without the weight of the backpack, his shoulders felt as if they were going to float toward the sky. He pulled out a cigarette, took a deep drag, and blew out the smoke. He felt his frigid body warming up.

On the pathway, a woman was walking with a book under her arm, completely preoccupied with her thoughts. It was the coal miner's wife, the schoolteacher, who lived on the second floor of his apartment building. She had committed her life to helping her students and had always worried about her husband's addiction to alcohol. She was wearing the same old sweater that she had worn on that rainy night when Jeong Jin Wu saw her waiting for her husband to return from work.

When she saw Jeong Jin Wu, she smiled. Then she stopped, utterly perplexed.

"My friend needed sand, so . . ." explained Jeong Jin Wu, pointing to his wet pants.

The schoolteacher tried hard not to look at Jeong Jin Wu, and tried harder not to look at his pants.

"Has your wife returned from her field research?" asked the schoolteacher, searching for another topic of discussion.

"I imagine she will come back when the weather gets warmer up there. By the way, are you just coming back from a student's house?" Jeong Jin Wu asked.

"Comrade Judge, you make it sound like you were following me."

"I even know what you were thinking as you were walking back."

The schoolteacher peered at him with curiosity and kept her eyes from glancing at his wet pants.

"You were thinking about how to punish the students who didn't come to school today, right? Am I right?" Jeong Jin Wu chuckled.

Jeong Jin Wu put on the backpack again. The schoolteacher missed her opportunity to assist him.

"We're going in the same direction. Can I help you with anything?" asked the schoolteacher.

She picked up the bucket and shovel for the judge. Jeong Jin Wu tried to stop her, but she had already begun walking ahead.

They had been walking without saying a word to each other for a while when the schoolteacher broke the silence. "Actually, I *was* thinking something along those lines." She spoke in a soft voice. "It's probably a coincidence to run into you like this, but every time I come back from this student's house, I always feel a bit annoyed with the court for divorcing his parents."

The mention of court jolted Jeong Jin Wu's attention. He was at a loss for words and listened carefully to the schoolteacher, who appeared to be speaking about something that had been troubling her for quite some time.

The schoolteacher continued, "One of my students, Chae Yeong Il, has been living with his stepmother for—"

"Wait a minute!" Jeong Jin Wu interrupted. "Chae Yeong Il? How old is he?"

"I believe he's . . . uh . . . thirteen years old."

"Thirteen? Who's his father?" Jeong Jin Wu asked impatiently.

"His father is the sales manager at the electric power plant . . . uh . . . Comrade Chae Rim. Why, do you know him?"

Jeong Jin Wu adjusted his backpack and avoided looking at the schoolteacher. How could he *not* know the sales manager? The memory of that day in court six years ago was coming back to him.

*That woman, who was living in the mountains with her children. The one who dreamed of raising a harmonious family. The one whose tears rolled down her freckled face in court. The one who pleaded with her husband to acknowledge her and respect her dignity. The children who were separated because of the divorce. The frightened seven-year-old boy, Chae Yeong Il.*

"I know a little bit about him. I met him a few years ago," said Jeong Jin Wu.

He made it sound like a casual remark, but he was perturbed at the very thought of the child. An unsettling memory of Chae Rim and his children, which had been buried in his mind, was haunting him again. It had haunted him a few days ago in his office, and it was haunting him now. Even so, he turned his attention to the schoolteacher's words like a magnet to metal as she described Yeong Il's stepmother.

Chae Rim remarried soon after the divorce. His new wife was ten years younger than he, a young woman for whom raising someone else's child was not a priority. Like most stepmothers, she cared little for her stepson. She would wash his clothes but never buy him new ones. She would prepare food for him, but never the dishes he liked. She would scowl at him in the absence of his father, but in his father's presence, she would coddle him and shower him with affection. Her orders to him to clean his room extended to the living room, the bathroom, and even the kitchen, while she rested. Chae Rim was Yeong Il's father, but his stepmother was his master. Yeong Il dared not complain about his stepmother to his father lest he be forced to endure harsher mistreatment from her in his father's absence. She cared very little for his well-being, much less his education.

Her only aim was for Yeong Il to graduate from secondary school and find work in another town, away from home, out of her sight. She wanted him out of the house as quickly as possible and wondered if secondary school could be accelerated. But she would have to wait five more years for her desires to come to fruition. This irritated her, and the irritation was made known to Yeong Il every day. Maternal love had been replaced with moral apathy, and his happiness had been extinguished by her tyranny. Yeong Il had been living in fear and oppression for the past six years, suffering in the grip of his stepmother. He was an unhappy child in dire need of parental love, in desperate need of the simplest love from anyone who would offer it.

Fear had made him an introverted student. He would sit quietly in class, aloof from the rest of his rambunctious classmates. He had no friends, and no one wanted to be his friend. His teachers had attempted to help him socialize with the other students, but by the end of the day, he would walk home by himself.

One day during the art lesson, the art teacher taught the class about the anatomy of a grasshopper so that the students could draw one. The next day, Yeong Il brought to class a wooden grasshopper, which he had carved at home, and shared it with his peers. The wooden grasshopper also jumped because Yeong Il had attached a small spring to it. The result was more than an art project; it was a piece of clever engineering.

The schoolteacher recalled that day and said, "Students like him are rare. If we guide him to the right path, then he could be a great engineer someday."

She paused for a moment before continuing.

"But ever since last year, he has become more and more of a problem. He skips school on a regular basis and fights with his classmates. The other parents complain to me about him. He seems to cause trouble every other day. I just don't know what to do with him."

Jeong Jin Wu empathized with the schoolteacher's disappointment.

"Comrade Judge, truthfully, I thought that I had done my best as his homeroom teacher. But I can't neglect all the other students for Yeong Il's sake."

Self-reproach and sorrow cast a shadow over the schoolteacher's face.

"Last Sunday, our school went on a spring picnic trip. The students had fun doing a treasure hunt, catching insects, and picking leaves and flowers. At lunchtime, I sat with my class, and we all opened our lunchboxes to eat. Just then, I realized that Yeong Il wasn't sitting with us, so I looked around for him. *I thought I saw him sitting here a moment ago . . .* So I went looking for him around the entire park until I came upon a huge boulder next to a small brook. Yeong Il was sitting there!"

The schoolteacher took a moment to regain her composure before proceeding with the story.

She quietly approached the boulder and noticed that Yeong Il was sitting with his sister, Yeong Sun. They were sharing their lunches. Although they lived in different homes, they had been going to the same school, seeing each other every day but forced to act as strangers. Yeong Sun kept giving Yeong Il food that their mother had made for her. Rice cakes, fried vegetables, stir-fried beef, and bean sprouts. Their mother had prepared more food than Yeong Sun could eat. Yeong Il was on the verge of crying and could not control his chopsticks. Next to him was his lunch box, untouched, unopened. His stepmother had packed just rice and boiled spinach. Tears streamed down the schoolteacher's face. She left the siblings and sat by the brook. Many thoughts raced through her mind. She realized that no matter how devoted a teacher was to her students and would, therefore, do whatever it took to help them succeed, that devotion waned in significance compared to the love between siblings. She realized that the parents had deprived the siblings of their love for each other and the siblings were the ones who suffered the most from their parents' divorce.

"You may have used your best judgment in divorcing the parents, but I feel that separating these children was a crime. Comrade Judge, why did the court permit the divorce? Was it for the adults' new life, their newfound happiness? Can there be happiness for parents who deprive their children of happiness?"

The backpack full of sand pressed down on Judge Jeong Jin Wu's shoulders. He felt chills run down his back, a feeling colder than that of the river.

*Did I give the wrong verdict that day? Is that why these memories keep haunting me? What if I hadn't divorced the couple? The children may have been better off than they are now, but the wife, who was working in the mountains with her children in agony, would have had to live with Chae Rim. She wouldn't want that. He had disrespected her, belittled her, and exploited her like a housemaid. For ten years, she had sacrificed her health and her youth for her husband. She had lost all sense of self-worth and, needless to say, her pride. After enduring her husband's betrayal for all those years, she was not willing to forgive him.*

Jeong Jin Wu had not regretted divorcing Chae Rim and his wife six years ago. Yet the schoolteacher was telling the truth about how the children had become the victims of the divorce, and that alone stung his conscience. The verdict was the correct one, but there was still a lingering concern that he could not get past. It was more than a legal matter; it was a societal problem. Although finding happiness in a new family and the son's healthy development were problems that existed outside the court, he felt deeply responsible. This was also the responsibility of Chae Rim and his ex-wife, and he felt that he needed to reprimand the parents, who still caused problems for the family. He was distressed by the thought that there might be other divorced couples out there who had not completely settled this issue about the welfare of their children. But what made him even sadder was the fact that many of these divorce cases repeated themselves under the same pretenses—irreconcilable differences.

He began to think, not about Yeong Il, but about Ho Nam—the child who had been soaking in the rain, crouched in a fetal position, coughing frightfully as he waited for his parents to come home; the child who got on Jeong Jin Wu's back with a high fever; the child who felt embarrassed about leaving wet footprints inside Jeong Jin Wu's apartment. Whose fault was it for instilling fear and anxiety in a little child's heart and thwarting the hope of a young flower before it even had a chance to blossom? Just as people needed water to live, a child needed love from both his parents. But the parents who needed to nurture this child, how were they living their lives? Were they even aware that the love for a child came from the love between a mother and a father? And yet both of them would say that they loved the child and would be able to raise the child on their own.

Jeong Jin Wu and the schoolteacher approached a crossroads, one road leading to Seok Chun's factory and the other leading to their apartment complex. Jeong Jin Wu thanked the schoolteacher for helping him.

"Aren't you going to take these home?" the schoolteacher asked.

"Yes, but—"

"Then take the sand to your friend quickly. I will take these with me and leave them in front of your apartment door," said the schoolteacher politely. Then she made her way home with the bucket and shovel.

Jeong Jin Wu watched the schoolteacher walk in the other direction. He knew she was no ordinary schoolteacher but an extraordinary human being. She possessed the secret riches of humility, gentleness, and virtue that won the respect of her colleagues, students, community members, and husband. She was a pure, dignified, and honest woman who valued the worth of her students and the nobility of her occupation. She understood that sacrificing her life for the students of this generation was fulfilling not merely her duty as a schoolteacher but her destiny. Her love for the nation and her compassionate spirit for the people were admirable qualities that forced Jeong Jin Wu to reflect deeply upon himself and reassess his own state of mind. The schoolteacher was a beautiful woman, both inside and out. She wore the same old sweater from a couple of nights before, but today a soft aura of grace illuminated her entire being.

# 12

Jeong Jin Wu saw the factory on the horizon.

He desperately wanted to rest, but he knew that if he did, he would not get there before closing time. He picked up his pace. The backpack was weighing down his shoulders as heavily as ever. His wet pants and shoes were getting muddy from the dirt path.

Suddenly, a man called out, "Aren't you Judge Jeong Jin Wu?" Jeong Jin Wu recognized the thick voice.

He saw Chae Rim holding a suitcase. It was the man for whom he had been waiting, the man from whom he could gain more insight into the investigation on the fraudulent science fair. It was quite a coincidence to meet him on his way to see Seok Chun. Jeong Jin Wu lowered the backpack onto a patch of grass.

Chae Rim approached Jeong Jin Wu with a pompous air of confidence. Chae Rim sported a fashionable suit and a light gray necktie with colorful polka dots. It was fastened to his shirt by a clip so that even if he had to run, it would not move. Chae Rim looked suspiciously at Jeong Jin Wu's wet pants.

"Did you fall into the river?"

"Are you just now returning from your business trip?" Jeong Jin Wu responded with a question of his own.

Jeong Jin Wu's response was supposed to be a greeting, but he could not force himself to say it in a warmer tone. Furthermore, he did not want to explain why he had been in the river collecting sand. Animosity toward Chae Rim was brewing inside Jeong Jin Wu as he thought about the embezzlement scheme.

Avoiding the judge's penetrating glare, Chae Rim put his suitcase on the grass as well.

"I'm coming from the train station. Instead of going to my office, I decided to go home and rest. But I thought I should call the office to check for any messages, and my secretary said that you had stopped by to conduct an investigation and had asked for me. So then I went to your office, but your assistant said that you might be going to the factory. So that's why I'm here."

*As the old saying goes, a criminal always returns to the scene of the crime,* Jeong Jin Wu thought.

"Well, it's not *that* urgent. You could just come by whenever we call you," said Jeong Jin Wu, subtly cutting Chae Rim down to size.

But it did not affect Chae Rim, who coolly responded, "I don't feel comfortable pushing back unresolved issues. They should be dealt with right then and there."

"Is that right? Then let me get right to the point, Comrade Chairman. Did you tamper with the science fair evaluations?" Jeong Jin Wu said sternly.

"Ah, I see what this is about. No, I did not *tamper* with the evaluations, as you put it. The evaluations were handled by the judges at the fair. But I did process the paperwork for the cash prize and tax waiver, which have already been approved and signed by the board members. You must have seen those in my office."

"Let me rephrase my question. Do you value the inventions that were presented at the exhibition? And do you believe that they will enable progress in our society?"

"Progress in our society?" Chae Rim repeated. "Well, we're going to have to wait and see about that. But, overall, I do value the inventions. Yes, I do."

"Liar," Jeong Jin Wu scoffed.

"Excuse me?"

"You're a thief!"

"I would watch what you're saying, Comrade Judge," Chae Rim warned.

"Isn't it true that you took the cash prize and used it to purchase office furniture and build a new fence around your office building?"

Chae Rim averted his eyes from Jeong Jin Wu's face and replied, "We redistributed the funds."

Jeong Jin Wu was utterly confused.

"What do you mean by *we*? Who else was in on this?" asked Jeong Jin Wu, raising his voice.

"Let's just say that I had to pay *up* . . . uh . . . forget what I said . . . let's just say it was me. Anyway, Comrade Judge, what's the problem here?" said Chae Rim in a tone that indicated a desire to terminate this conversation.

*Pay up* . . . thought Jeong Jin Wu. He realized that Chae Rim was involved in a conspiracy worse than he had imagined. He was so enraged that he could not breathe properly. He nearly lost his senses and wanted to yell at Chae Rim.

"Comrade Chairman, as you know, the government distributed the exact amount for each of the inventions and the inventors. However, you decided to control those funds on your own. You pocketed the cash prize that was meant for the inventors and instead handed out vases and plaques. Please explain to me why you did that."

Chae Rim, evasive and shifty-eyed, hurriedly searched his pockets for his pack of cigarettes. For some unknown reason, as soon as he found it, he put it back. Chae Rim cleared his throat and regained his composure.

"There are two reasons. First, a portion of the cash prize was an allocation for us to refurbish our office and put up a metal fence around our building. However, we may have overdone it by using more than originally allocated. Second, instead of awarding our inventors with just a cash prize, we commended their work with a vase and a plaque. We did this to encourage our inventors to work harder. If they produce better machines, then we will give them more next year. Moreover, I realized that this year's inventors did not care about a cash prize. These were the kind of loyal people who care only for the progress of our society. I figured there's no need to give out cash prizes to these kinds of noble-minded inventors. Comrade Judge, that's the reason we used the funds to do some work on our office building. I did not put a dime in my pocket."

Chae Rim was so amazed and satisfied with his own logic and reasoning that he pulled out his cigarettes and smoked one slowly.

Furious and extremely irritated, Judge Jeong Jin Wu fired another charge.

"You cunningly sabotaged the noble minds of the inventors."

"What are you talking about, Comrade Judge?"

"You've not only sabotaged them, but you've insulted them and trampled all over them," added Judge Jeong Jin Wu, piercing Chae Rim with his acerbic words.

"Comrade Chairman, do you know what Comrade Lee Seok Chun went through in order to produce his machine? Do you have any idea what kind of days he has had to endure for the past five years? Have you seen the hundreds of blueprints that he went through to build that machine? Did you know that he basically slept at the factory and paid for every experimental failure out of his own pocket? He could not bring home a decent salary because of all this, but he persisted and finally succeeded. Did you know that?"

Jeong Jin Wu did not skip a beat.

"The country desires precisely this kind of loyal worker and considers his efforts to be valuable. And that is why the country holds these kinds of exhibitions to honor these types of workers, and that is why the country rewards them with cash prizes. The country tries to support the technicians and experts with the prizes so that they can enjoy an abundant life. However, you, Comrade Chairman, took the cash prize and refurbished your office with an expensive desk, luxurious sofa, and comfortable chair—the kind of furniture that you can't buy from just anywhere. How is that different from putting the cash prize directly into your pocket?"

Chae Rim appeared uncomfortable and loosened his tie.

"You, Comrade Chairman, stole from the people, who have spilled blood and sweat for their work. You have abused your authority. You have insulted the energy and talents of the people who participated in the exhibition, and you have hindered the Party's demands to improve technology and the country's economic advancement! You have committed a crime, comrade. And I will do everything in my power to prosecute you!"

"Um . . . Com- . . . Comrade Judge. Wait a minute, now. The other offices are furnished with the same kind of furniture." Chae Rim's face turned red.

"No more excuses! Criminals like you need to receive a harsh sentence. Our penal law clearly states that anyone who intentionally violates the socialist principle of equal distribution and infringes upon the people's efforts, creation, and inventions will be duly imprisoned. The penal law applies to everything you did."

"How . . . how does it apply to me?" Chae Rim's bright red face had turned a ghostly white.

"I'm actually taking your case lightly. Lee Seok Chun's marital problems are, of course, his own. However, you are also responsible for insulting him by not awarding him a cash prize at the exhibition, thus mocking his years of suffering over his invention. You fanned the flames of his marital discord by convincing Chae Sun

Hee to think of her husband as a lowlife. You will also duly receive punishment for interfering with another family's life."

Chae Rim drew an awkward smile as he stuttered, "Comrade Judge, I . . . I just came back from my business trip. I . . . I don't know what's going on."

"What is there not to know here? Sun Hee is your second cousin, and so is Seok Chun. Why would you sabotage family? You were also once a technician. And now you are a man of executive power. You should have helped him. If you knew that he was struggling with the engineering aspect of his machine, then you should have called some professional engineers to help him or encouraged him to enroll at the Engineering College. Isn't it your duty as a chairman to increase the expertise level of the workers rather than to increase profit?

"Comrade Judge, allow me to think about this for a few days, and then I will come see you at your office," replied Chae Rim, wiping the beads of perspiration off his forehead.

"Fine. You do that."

Jeong Jin Wu picked up his backpack and headed toward the factory. He no longer wanted to converse with the repulsive man. It was obvious to Jeong Jin Wu that Chae Rim had manipulated the science fair and profited from the scheme, a hypocritical gesture from someone who claimed to appreciate the toil and effort of this generation's inventors. When he cornered Chae Rim and did not allow him to slip away, Jeong Jin Wu felt the sublimity of justice reign over humanity. His heavy backpack felt light, and he walked with a spring in his step.

Meanwhile, Chae Rim picked up his luggage and trudged in the opposite direction with his shoulders slumped.

Clouds of greasy smoke billowed from the casting area as molten metal was poured into the molding container. The metal did not solidify in the molding container and remained golden. Bits of molten metal had splashed onto the walls, leaving a burned scent. The fan from the air ventilation system was spinning, but Jeong Jin Wu still felt the heat of the molten metal and smelled the stale air.

Jeong Jin Wu lowered his backpack, disappointed and unnerved. He feared he had come too late. The factory was lifeless. He did not see nor hear anyone working. The empty molten metal basin held to the ceiling by long steel beams was inactive, and moldings were scattered across the floor of the casting area. In the corner, there was an untouched pile of scrap moldings. The factory was empty; the machines were soulless.

Jeong Jin Wu searched the factory for workers on the night shift or workers about to start the night shift, but none was to be found. He went to the lathe sector, then to Seok Chun's station and tool cabinet, and then to the factory recreation center. He felt more and more helpless as he roamed the seemingly abandoned factory. His backpack felt heavier and heavier with each step. Just then, he heard movement in the back part of the factory. He made his way there and found Seok Chun sitting in front of the furnace, chipping away at a brick. Seok Chun rested his chin on his hands, deep in thought. A long ladle, a pair of tongs, and a scraper-like tool used to remove metal bits were scattered on the floor next to Seok Chun.

Then Seok Chun got up without realizing that Jeong Jin Wu was standing there. He opened the furnace and shoveled some fuel inside. Afterward, he sat back down on the stack of bricks. The golden blaze of the fire from the furnace was reflected on Seok Chun's pitiable face and disheveled hair. His entire body was covered in ash and soot.

Jeong Jin Wu was relieved to find Seok Chun after restlessly searching the factory.

"Comrade Seok Chun, why are you sitting here alone?" asked Jeong Jin Wu warmly.

When Seok Chun saw Jeong Jin Wu, he stood up immediately. He tried to come up with some excuse. "The night shift workers will arrive soon. I volunteered to watch over the molten metal by managing the furnace heat." But this was an obvious lie.

There were dark circles, traces of his exhaustion, around Seok Chun's eyes.

"Does a lathe worker know anything about working the furnace?"

"I've been working on the casting for a while now, so—"

"So you've learned the ropes. Were you successful in making the remote control?"

"It's such a sensitive piece that if it bubbles or if there's a rupture, then you have to just throw it away. The sand I'm using is also pretty old, so it causes additional problems."

"Speaking of which, I brought some sand. Would you care to have a look?"

"You did? From where?"

"If it's of any use, I'll tell you."

Jeong Jin Wu lowered his backpack. His shoulders and lower back ached intolerably, but he did his best not to reveal his pain. He did not want Seok Chun to be concerned. Seok Chun quickly unzipped the backpack and picked up a handful of sand. He spread the soft white sand on his hand and brought it in front of the furnace for a better look. Then he turned around and looked at Jeong Jin Wu's wet and muddied pants and shoes.

"So, will it be useful?" Jeong Jin Wu asked, unable to contain his curiosity.

Seok Chun was careful not to spill any of the sand on the floor. He put the handful of sand back inside the bag and stood up. Tears welled in his eyes.

"Comrade Judge, the sand is really good. Did you get this from the river?"

"You guessed correctly. I got it from under a large boulder below the small footbridge."

"It's really deep there and really cold," muttered Seok Chun, trying to hold back his tears.

"Nonsense. It was actually quite refreshing. Never mind that. So, then, you're telling me that it's useful?"

"It looks better than the one they haul by train from the other factory. I will go with the other workers to the river and dig up some more."

"Great! Then my efforts were not in vain," Jeong Jin Wu exclaimed.

Jeong Jin Wu had hesitated to bring the sand to Seok Chun at first, but now he felt relieved and lighter on his feet. From his backpack, he pulled out a pack of cigarettes and a match. He had wanted to smoke a cigarette ever since he had gotten out of the river, but the cigarette and match were soaked.

Seok Chun quickly offered one of his cigarettes. Then he grabbed a long wooden stick and got a flame from the furnace.

"You're quite talented," said Jeong Jin Wu, complimenting Seok Chun as he brought his cigarette close to the flame. "Why don't you smoke one, too?"

Seok Chun smiled glumly and returned to the furnace.

The two sat for some time without saying anything, and it seemed as if only the furnace listened to their deep thoughts. The radiance from the blaze reflected on the faces of the two men.

Seok Chun carefully broke the awkward silence.

"Comrade Judge, I don't know what to say. You've been so helpful and . . ."

"No need to say more. I know how you feel."

Jeong Jin Wu picked up a steel ladle and twirled it around. "But I do want to know if you've been thinking about what I said in my office the other day."

When Seok Chun did not answer, Jeong Jin Wu said, "Something still seems to be bothering you."

Seok Chun remained silent.

"Before you think about divorcing your wife, you have to consider what she wants from you. Don't be so antagonistic. It's time for you to think objectively about how she feels about you. I was deeply moved by your tireless efforts on the lathe without coveting awards or recognition. However, you cannot apply the same kind of fervor you have for your work to your family. A family may be small, but it's connected to one's world. You cannot think that yesterday's feelings for your wife will remain the same today. You need to constantly renew those emotions, your vows, and continue to paint your ideal family—*those* make up your world. But what are you doing in this respect? You have not changed with the times. You love Sun Hee the press worker and not the renowned mezzo-soprano of the performing arts company. She has progressed and become a new person. Times have changed, and so must you. Our entire society is actively progressing toward becoming intellectualized in scientific technology and the arts. But you, comrade, have fallen behind the times. Your so-called love for your wife is outdated. You're trying to measure your wife's love for you with a yardstick used in the old days, tallying all the good and bad things she has done for you. And then you try to work on your invention with all this baggage. How well do you think you will be able to perform your duties at the factory? If you had listened to your wife and gone to the Engineering College, then you would be a technician by now and would not have wasted all those years trying to figure out the complex engineering components of your invention."

Seok Chun took off his worn-out hat and started fidgeting with it. Jeong Jin Wu continued.

"Since you couldn't properly assess the changing times and only looked disdainfully at your wife with your nearsighted views, you criticized her for being vain. You think she's been acting superior to you for recommending technical college. Comrade Sun Hee's concern for you derived from your aimless life and technical stagnation. Can you really blame her after all? I believe that her demands are aligned with the demands of society, which is to raise the consciousness of the people in our country. She understood that the family is a unit of society, and that is why your self-improvement is absolutely required. You really have to correct your erroneous and ultra-conservative thoughts."

The hat in Seok Chun's large hands became like a small lump of cloth.

"Comrade Seok Chun, then, do you feel superior to Sun Hee? Yes, you do. It emerges from your narrow-minded pride. You act like you're the only one working loyally for the factory and for society, and, in doing so, you've trampled all over her dignity. You have to acknowledge that your wife's voice moves the hearts of the people. Your wife is our society's cultural representative, an artist."

Seok Chun rested his chin on his fist like Rodin's *The Thinker*, immersed in deep thought.

Jeong Jin Wu took the hat from Seok Chun's hand and dusted off the ashes. He returned the hat to its original form and put it on Seok Chun's head.

"Comrade Seok Chun, you've been criticizing Sun Hee. But for so many years, she's been by your side, suffering with you, feeling your pain when your invention goes awry. She believed that you would progress the same way she has progressed. That is why she was frustrated with you. As a man responsible for the stability of his family, if your wife says things like that, can't you just accept it? She wants to be proud of her husband because she truly loves you."

Seok Chun was at a loss for words.

"I am advising you, not as a judge, but as your elderly friend. Starting today, try to think progressively like the youths of this generation and create your own path. Don't be like an old factory worker set in his ways. Get your act together like an intelligent expert technician. Start by taking care of your appearance. Go to the Engineering College. On Sundays, take your son to the theater and watch your wife's performances. You've been wrong to think that these things are pretentious. I know you can do it, and I look forward to that day."

Seok Chun covered his face with his dirty hands as if he had been hit. He bit his thick lips to hold back his frustration. He didn't like what the judge was saying because he didn't feel he was at fault. The judge's words were too much for him to bear; they pained him greatly, and his bitterness toward his wife resurfaced.

Judge Jeong Jin Wu knew that Seok Chun's antagonistic feelings toward Sun Hee would not last much longer. This was because he knew that Seok Chun was honest, strong-willed, and a true man of character. Without these admirable qualities, he would not have been able to carry out his duties at the factory during this period of marital strife; he would not have been able to do the simplest and most ordinary task.

"Ah, Judge Jeong Jin Wu. You're back," interrupted the old equipment manager.

Jeong Jin Wu and Seok Chun stood up to greet the elderly man.

"Here, take this," said the equipment manager, handing Seok Chun a pot. "The old man said that you would be here."

Seok Chun's face turned red with embarrassment as he received the pot. The soup in the pot gave off a deliciously rich aroma. Seok Chun spoke as if he were sorry about something. He bit his lip and mumbled his words.

"Sir, starting from today, I will go home on time."

The old equipment manager looked at Judge Jeong Jin Wu in shock. Then the two smiled at each other.

"Oh, I see." The equipment manager nodded, and then added, "I need a cigarette."

Seok Chun humbly offered the old equipment manager a cigarette.

Jeong Jin Wu put the wooden stick into the furnace, just as Seok Chun had done before. But when he pulled it out, the tip was burned even without a flame.

The old equipment manager laughed and told Jeong Jin Wu the technique, "Comrade Judge, you have to put it in and pull it out in a flash."

Jeong Jin Wu did as he was told. The tip of the wooden stick lit up like a matchstick.

# 13

After a couple of days, Sun Hee came by the court. Judge Song noticed that she was lingering in front of Jeong Jin Wu's office, hesitating to knock, so he opened the door for her.

Jeong Jin Wu set aside the legal documents he was perusing.

Sun Hee paused uncertainly at the threshold. Jeong Jin Wu warmly invited her in. She had her hands in front of her as if they were powerless, and her body curled in on itself as if she was cold. She quietly pulled up a chair and sat before Jeong Jin Wu.

Jeong Jin Wu pulled out the file that had "Divorce File of Chae Sun Hee" written across the top and waited for her to speak. From the expression on her face, he did not think she was going to talk about her husband's backwardness and refusal to change along with society. However, Jeong Jin Wu felt uneasy about the hopelessness and defeat he saw in Sun Hee's face. Her eyes revealed her brokenness and many sleepless nights, very much as on the day she first entered his office.

Jeong Jin Wu regretted not calling Sun Hee into his office yesterday after his visit with Seok Chun the day before. He thought she would come to him with the cheerful news that the divorce was off, everything was back to normal, and things were fine. He was wrong.

There was no doubt that her colleagues and her husband had caused her much pain all these years. It was evident that she had many things on her mind, many complicated issues as convoluted and complex as a spiderweb with which she had been struggling, causing her to become emaciated and pallid. Jeong Jin Wu looked at Sun Hee with sympathy and tried to guess her thoughts.

Sun Hee regained her composure and spoke respectfully. "Comrade Judge, I am really grateful that you are spending your time and energy trying to keep my family united. But I still can't live with my husband. It's my fault. That's why, after the divorce—"

Jeong Jin Wu lowered his eyes to the documents and said, "Comrade Sun Hee, it doesn't seem that you've learned anything from your deputy director."

"I acknowledge my faults at my company. But that's an entirely different matter from my problems with my husband."

Tears stifled Sun Hee's voice.

"Is Seok Chun behaving the way he used to again?" Jeong Jin Wu asked.

"What's the point of his changing now? A leopard can't change his spots. I'm tired of living like this."

The tears that had welled up in her eyes streamed down her cheeks.

Jeong Jin Wu closed her divorce file and stood up. He began to pace back and forth in the office.

He stopped next to Sun Hee and said in a low, reproachful voice, "Your family discord will not be resolved with a divorce. I'm telling you this honestly. If you proceed with the divorce case, all you'll do is lose money from paying the legal fees. There is not enough evidence for a divorce, you see."

"Comrade Judge, why can't you help me?" asked Sun Hee, choking up with frustration.

"Please, calm down, Comrade Sun Hee. While I was objectively investigating your family problems, I realized that you have the ability to lead your family toward harmony. However, somewhere along the line, you lost faith in yourself. Your fanciful idealistic ideas about your husband and family life are lingering somewhere, but you were unable to anchor those thoughts to reality."

Sun Hee lowered her eyes.

"You cannot place those kinds of unrealistic expectations on your husband. Such fantasies create deep ethical problems in a family, wouldn't you agree? Even though Seok Chun is behind the times and tactless in expressing his love for you, he is still your husband and the father of your child. That is why you cannot disregard the time when you guys first expressed your innocent love for each other. You have to consider that moment to be precious and build from there, renewing your love for each other and for your son. However, you, Comrade Sun Hee, keep looking down on your husband. You have left him standing by the riverbank in your home village."

Tears rolled down Sun Hee's face.

Jeong Jin Wu stood next to his desk. Even though he saw that the poor woman was heartbroken, he proceeded in the name of justice.

"Comrade Sun Hee, you learned the trade of operating the lathe from your husband. The other workers recognized your singing talents and adored you. With the blessing of the grease-stained workers, you two got married and even found a nice place to live. The sincere emotions in your singing derived from your days working the lathe. Then, the factory recommended that you become a professional singer. But now, you have forgotten your roots. You have forgotten the very people who first loved you and supported you. Thereafter, you began to isolate yourself from the other singers at your company.

Sun Hee dabbed the corners of her eyes with her trembling hands.

"I hate to say this, but you've been looking down on your husband, to the extent that you've become arrogant and pompous. You must realize this. If you quit your singing career, then what's left for you? You have abandoned the one person in society who's closest to you—your husband. So what if he goes to the Engineering College and becomes a technical expert? So what if he one day becomes a foreman at a factory? Will it bring harmony to your family? Will it bring *rhythm* back to your family? Character does not derive from social position, occupation, or physical appearance. He who diligently carries out the Party's directives is the true bearer of noble consciousness and character. Look in the mirror. You say that you are an artist. But you know very well that you don't automatically become an elegant, sophisticated person just because you are a singer. In order for you to move the audience with the ideological lyrics of your music, you have to make the music yours. If you reprioritize and live the correct lifestyle, and if you have an affectionate relationship with your husband, then your goals will become a beautiful reality and your family will live in harmony."

Sun Hee could neither muster the courage nor find the words to counter the judge's logic.

Jeong Jin Wu sat down and pushed aside Sun Hee's divorce file as if to dismiss it. He did not think it was necessary to pursue the case when it was clear to him that she was shedding tears of self-reproach.

Sun Hee stopped crying, but she did not lift her head. She pulled an elegant silk handkerchief from her purse and dabbed the tears from her eyes. She took a deep breath and let out a sigh of despair. She pushed back her chair and stood up. With her eyes still lowered, she turned to leave the office.

"You're leaving without saying good-bye?" Jeong Jin Wu asked softly.

It was not a question that indicated her lack of etiquette but a question that anticipated Sun Hee's new beginning—bidding farewell to the past and welcoming a new day.

Sun Hee hesitated momentarily and then realized that she had broken the code of etiquette. She bowed to Jeong Jin Wu. Her eyes were swollen from crying, and her face was pale.

"Comrade Sun Hee, what are you going to do this Sunday?"

"I'll probably do whatever I feel like doing that day. Actually, I'll be leaving for Seong Gan District tomorrow for our tour."

Jeong Jin Wu was overjoyed because the deputy director had done as he had been told.

"When will you return?"

"Friday will be our final performance there, so I guess on Saturday. Why do you ask?" asked Sun Hee.

"I'm asking because this Sunday is May 10," said Jeong Jin Wu as he looked at the calendar. "Isn't that your tenth wedding anniversary?"

Sun Hee was shocked. She had her hand on the doorknob, but now she lost the strength to so much as grasp it. A shadow of remorse covered her pale face. She tried to avoid making eye contact with Jeong Jin Wu by focusing on one corner of the room. Tears began to fill her eyes again.

"That day . . . those kinds of days are only meant for normal families," Sun Hee replied.

"Would it be okay for me to stop by your house on that day?"

"Please, who can stop you, Comrade Judge?"

"No, I'm not going to your house as a judge, but as a friend. It'll also be fun to see my friend Ho Nam." Jeong Jin Wu laughed.

Jeong Jin Wu could not transfer his joviality to Sun Hee, who met his amicable gesture with seeming indifference.

He went over to Sun Hee and opened the door for her.

"Then have a great time on your trip. I wish you the best," said Jeong Jin Wu, trying to be encouraging.

Sun Hee left without saying a word. The clicking of her high heels faded down the corridor. Then there was silence.

Jeong Jin Wu's entire body was on the verge of collapsing. His throat was parched. Layers of fatigue and worry weighed his body down. He drank a cup of water and then sank deep into his sofa. As he closed his eyes, he thought about how Seok Chun's family life contrasted with his own marriage. He had harbored various resentments whenever his wife traveled for her research, leaving him with the housework. He had expressed disappointment and indignation before showing patience and affection.

Jeong Jin Wu missed his wife.

Since the cold weather had lifted and the warmth of spring had come, his wife could also be on her way back home.

The mountainous roads in that area were dangerously steep and windy. There was only one bus a day that came from that direction.

*If she missed the bus, then she would have had to hitch a ride on a truck. She's probably sitting in the back of a bumping truck with a towel around her head, thinking about something. What was she thinking about?*

She had never once expressed her difficulties in doing her research to her husband but instead kept them to herself. The tall peaks, the bright blue sky, the magnificent evergreens, and the dark river flowing below the steep mountains made for a picturesque view on first sight. But since Eun Ok traveled this road often, they no longer had the power to refresh her. That was why she would close her eyes and doze to allow time to pass. However, the bumpy roads would prevent her from truly resting.

*What was she thinking now?* Jeong Jin Wu thought.

Before she got married, when she had traveled the mountain road, she probably had great expectations. But then disappointment followed her failed experiments, and her complaining husband added to her distress.

Jeong Jin Wu recalled the last time he had greeted Eun Ok when she returned from her field research. He had been stern and cold, like an executive administrator. He had said things he should not have said to her. It was because he had been utterly fed up with what he considered her hopeless research. But even then, Eun Ok just smiled and caught up on the housework. How could he complain about such a saintly person?

The phone rang.

Jeong Jin Wu picked up the receiver. It was Chae Rim. He sounded like he wanted to pacify the judge.

"Comrade Judge, will you be in your office for a bit?"

"I will. In fact, I've been meaning to give you a call. Come by my office now," said Jeong Jin Wu in an authoritative tone.

"I'll be there. Comrade Judge, I haven't been able to sleep for the past couple of nights. I'm really sorry, and the more I think about my wrongdoing, the more I can't sleep."

Jeong Jin Wu wanted to discipline him right then and there, but he held his tongue. Chae Rim had hindered the country's technological advancement and trampled on the inventors' sincere efforts. Did he think that a few sleepless nights would be enough to absolve him of his crime and guilt?

"Comrade Judge, I am truly sorry before the law and I regret my misdeeds. This morning, I returned all the furniture that I had bought with the money meant for the cash prize. And then I decided that our administrative building does not need a metal fence and that a brick wall would do."

"Comrade Chairman, are you trying to exonerate yourself with a single phone call?"

"No, not at all," Chae Rim responded quickly. "I will be there soon."

Judge Jeong Jin Wu hung up the phone and pursued another line of thought. He needed to punish Chae Rim harshly for his illegal conduct. He had no choice but to consider Chae Rim's misdeeds a crime. He had sabotaged the inventors for profit and was apathetic about the country's technological advancement. He still was not completely truthful and remained a hypocrite, but he sounded as though he was prepared to rectify his mistakes. This was his first count of misconduct, and coming to the court-house to confess his crime would be an amazing sight in itself if he carried it out. Jeong Jin Wu considered lessening the sentence if Chae Rim came to the courthouse to confess. Chae Rim would have to award the cash prize to the inventors after all, and then it would be up to the court to decide whether he would be pun-ished for violating the moral codes and principles of his admin-istrative work.

# FAMILY

# 14

It was late in the evening when Jeong Jin Wu finished talking with Chae Rim. Jeong Jin Wu drilled the law into Chae Rim for several hours, revealing to him how seriously the nation disapproved of his embezzlement.

Chae Rim sat still like frost-covered grass when he realized that he would be severely punished and have to answer to Party leaders. He sighed with regret. He dared not contest the judge's criticisms; there was nothing for him to contest. He was fortunate not to be in prison for his crime.

Jeong Jin Wu led Chae Rim to the door.

Chae Rim held the doorknob and glanced at the judge with forlorn eyes. But it was not a look that expected Jeong Jin Wu to lessen his punishment.

"Comrade Judge," Chae Rim spoke, "I have a question. Are you going to tell Sun Hee about this issue?"

"Sun Hee and Seok Chun are trying to work things out for themselves. Go to their place and apologize to them."

Chae Rim slouched his broad shoulders and left the courthouse.

Jeong Jin Wu watched Chae Rim walk toward the small park in front of the courthouse. He fixed his gaze on the trees, where

Chae Rim had disappeared into the wooded park, with a feeling of unsettled dissatisfaction. Jeong Jin Wu was making Chae Rim pay the price for his crime, but he still did not feel at ease. He recalled the first time Chae Rim had stepped inside his office, exuding an aura of imperious pride and unassailable power. *How do people become like that?* thought Jeong Jin Wu. There were still too many people like Chae Rim who did not respect the country's efforts to advance technologically and improve the economy, who instead flaunted their authority as they sat on the throne of bureaucratic power. Jeong Jin Wu wondered if those selfish individuals with no conscience realized that their salaries and the benefits they received from being in those positions came from society's hardworking technicians and researchers.

Jeong Jin Wu headed home after another difficult day at the courthouse. Neon signs began to light up the city as the crimson sun retired behind the hills. A gentle wind blew through the trees, rustling the budding leaves and giving off the fresh scent of spring. Lights appeared in apartment windows one by one, creating a mosaic of changing patterns. Cars, buses, and trucks brightened the evening streets with dazzling headlights. Jeong Jin Wu's indignation toward Chae Rim began to subside as he found solace in the animated nightscape.

People on the pedestrian path were going about their business, some walking with the swiftest of paces while others strolled without the least concern in their lives. Some raced urgently to their destinations, while others sauntered, at liberty to observe and admire the wonders of spring. Some passed shops and restaurants without interest, while others stopped to peer into the windows. Some fixed their eyes on the ground, while others surveyed the town. On this brisk evening, on these cheerful streets, people seemed to be content with their lives.

"Hello."

Jeong Jin Wu turned around when he heard a familiar voice.

It was the coal miner, the husband of the schoolteacher, who lived on the second floor of his apartment building. This man had two loves in his life: his wife and liquor. He had on a tattered brown suit and held a black lunch box under his arm. His hat came down to his eyebrows. His broad shoulders, thick neck, and the wrinkles around his eyes and mouth were a testament to his years of hard work, and yet his eyes still beamed like a young worker's. It was clear that the coal miner was tired from a long day's work. His clothes showed that he had been inside a deep cavity in the earth.

Jeong Jin Wu asked, "Are you just now coming back from work?"

"Yep. Another day's work finished," replied the coal miner proudly. "I worked the crane today."

The coal miner paused and looked at Jeong Jin Wu. Then he continued, "By the way, Comrade Judge, something seems to be bothering you."

Jeong Jin Wu smiled wryly at the miner's keen observation.

"It must be another divorce case," the coal miner conjectured.

"You've guessed correctly."

"Your job must be difficult with these cases lingering in your head even after you get off work," said the coal miner. Then he asked the judge, "Is your wife still away doing research?"

Jeong Jin Wu smiled and nodded his head. What began as housework for him to do became fodder for gossip throughout the apartment complex, and now it had become a conventional part of greeting him. The coal miner's question was mixed with sympathy and understanding, which made Jeong Jin Wu feel grateful rather than spiteful. His wife's research at Yeonsudeok was important not only for producing vegetables but for inventing a new type of hybrid, which made her work all the more important. Other people seemed to have realized this, but Jeong Jin Wu had forgotten about Eun Ok's significant contribution to agriculture.

"Comrade Judge, would you care for a drink?"

Jeong Jin Wu raised his head to discover that they were standing in front of a pub with green neon lights flashing "Fine Liquor." He saw a few customers through the window with their elbows on the table, hands clasped, and heads hung low.

The coal miner said, "Just one pint."

"Let's go home," Jeong Jin Wu responded.

"Why? There's no one at your place anyway, and you seem to be lonely. Let's just have one pitcher."

Even before Jeong Jin Wu could make up an excuse, one pint of beer had already increased to one pitcher.

Jeong Jin Wu dragged the coal miner away from the pub. "Aren't you concerned about your wife? She waits for you every night in front of the building. She already worries enough about her students. You don't have to add to her problems."

The coal miner guffawed and headed toward the pub. But then he smacked his lips at the thought of his wife and turned around. He pulled out a cigarette and tried to justify himself.

"Comrade Judge, as you can see, I'm quite healthy. But my wife thinks I'm sick and nags me about my drinking."

"That's because your wife loves you."

"It gets pretty tiresome, if you ask me. I tried to put my foot down as a man, but it was no use. Her nagging continued, and now it's to a point where I can't handle it anymore. These days, I just keep my mouth shut. It's better this way. You see, rain comes and goes, and the clouds eventually roll away."

"So, you're still drinking."

"Comrade Judge, a wife is different from the law. She is far more generous and forgiving. When I promise her that I will quit today and then drink again, she just shakes her head and lets it go. That's how we live."

"I always thought that the two of you were happily married."

"Of course we are," responded the coal miner enthusiastically.

Jeong Jin Wu said gently, "If your wife has to worry about your drinking, how will she be able to focus on her teaching?"

The coal miner averted his eyes from Jeong Jin Wu.

"On the outside, it may seem like your wife is fine, but can you imagine how much she has cried over you? Think about when you first met her, and the times the two of you spent together in the first couple years of your marriage. I'm sure you didn't drink as much then."

The coal miner dug his hands deep into his pockets as he continued walking. He had a pensive demeanor. He felt that a fellow male comrade was betraying him. He then turned to the judge and shouted, "Drinking is not my life! I can quit! What's so hard about that?"

The coal miner strode away quickly.

Jeong Jin Wu grinned. He was impressed with the coal miner's curt but honest reaction. He was relieved to know that the coal miner had not wasted his life on liquor.

"You don't have to get upset about it," said Jeong Jin Wu. "Wait for me!"

Jeong Jin Wu caught up to the coal miner.

The coal miner lowered his distraught eyes and stared at the ground. The lunch box at his side was on the verge of falling. Jeong Jin Wu helped the coal miner with his lunch box and regretted admonishing someone who was joyfully on his way home from a hard day's work.

Jeong Jin Wu spoke to assuage the coal miner's feelings. "I seem to have interfered in your marriage. I can't seem to take off my legal hat. I've hurt many friends this way. Please forgive me."

The coal miner raised his head and looked deeply into Jeong Jin Wu's eyes. The coal miner's virtuous eyes were a telling sign that he was not a simplistic man who cared only about working and drinking. His eyes projected a light of determination that had

lain dormant for all these years, a promising sign of no longer suc-
cumbing to the yoke of alcoholism.

"Comrade Judge, I blame myself," mumbled the coal miner in
a subdued tone. "I respect you more than any of my drinking bud-
dies. Actually, I used to think that your wife kept you on a tight
leash and forced you to do all the housework while she was away
doing research. I thought doing research was easy, so I asked
myself, 'Why can't she do both, research and household chores?'"

Jeong Jin Wu nodded as he, too, had those thoughts about
Eun Ok.

"This is coming from me who hasn't done anything productive
with my education. I've wasted my life by drinking and taking my
wife for granted. In the corner of our closet, there is a dusty trunk
full of my old research notes."

The coal miner continued speaking in a melancholy tone.

"For the longest time, my wife wiped the dust off that trunk
every day. I guess she was expecting me to do something with it.
Whew! That was a long time ago. And now, there's no way for me
to retrieve those bygone days."

Jeong Jin Wu responded, "Isn't there a saying 'Start over with
a clean slate'? Don't be so down on yourself. It seems you've realized how precious time is. If you start now, you can still be productive. You have a strong-willed teacher as your wife who is more
than willing to assist you."

The two walked in silence. They made a right turn at the fork
in the road and walked toward their apartment complex.

From the front gate of the apartment building, a woman in an
old sweater walked out to meet them. It was the coal miner's wife.
The schoolteacher greeted the men warmly, but the coal miner
kept his eyes on the ground. He was in a pensive mood, regret-
ting his unproductive past. He then lifted his head and looked at
his wife in shame for his irresponsible habit of drinking but also
with a sense of determination to greet the new day ahead of him.

The schoolteacher bowed to Jeong Jin Wu and then walked slowly beside her husband into their apartment.

Jeong Jin Wu did not want to interfere with the couple, so he walked past them and went up to his apartment. He trudged slowly up the stairs, reluctant to enter his empty apartment. When he got to the third floor, he was overcome with loneliness. He knew he had to tend the vegetables in the greenhouse and prepare his own dinner. These responsibilities took time away from analyzing legal documents and thinking about other cases.

Nevertheless, Jeong Jin Wu decided to let go of every last complaint about his wife.

*So what if I have to sleep less to finish the housework and work on my cases? Can't I help Eun Ok, who's probably walking the steep paths of Yeonsudeok? I must not become like those who forget the noble purpose of life promised during the wedding ceremony. I did not marry for my own complacency or pleasure.*

Jeong Jin Wu fondly remembered that day, that beautiful day, the day of his wedding, the snow-covered day in March twenty years ago.

# 15

Jeong Jin Wu searched his pockets for his keys, but then he heard footsteps inside the house. The door was flung open. Eun Ok stood in the doorway, wiping her hands on her apron, pleased to see her husband and yet apologetic at the same time. With a rueful smile, she greeted him, wordless but filled with gratitude.

Eun Ok had lost weight conducting research in the mountains. She had more wrinkles on her face, and her cheeks were chapped from the cold wind. It appeared she had rushed to complete some of the household chores as soon as she had returned home. Perhaps it was because she felt sorry for leaving so urgently ten days ago, but it was hard to tell.

Jeong Jin Wu was pleased to see Eun Ok's unpretentious attitude. He had always loved how Eun Ok never complained about the monotony of their married life, never acted entitled but instead always presented herself as a simple-hearted, gentle woman. He had always loved her for these qualities, but, for some reason, tonight they felt new to him.

Jeong Jin Wu found traces of fatigue on Eun Ok's face.

"You must have had a hard time up there." He tried to speak tenderly, but it sounded curt and with no affection at all.

"Forget about me. I see that you didn't take a lunch to work this morning," said Eun Ok worriedly, noticing that Jeong Jin Wu was not carrying his briefcase or his lunchbox.

"I woke up late this morning, so I couldn't prepare lunch. I ate at the cafeteria instead."

"What about breakfast?"

"I had some leftovers from last night."

Eun Ok felt sorry about not preparing his breakfast and lunch. She put his shoes away.

"Something smells great!" Jeong Jin Wu exclaimed as he handed his coat to Eun Ok.

The aroma of stir-fried vegetables filled the apartment, which made Jeong Jin Wu feel welcomed. He felt his weariness from spending endless hours at his office and living the life of a widower for the past ten days dissipate. How wonderful it was to reexperience the days when his wife used to stay home! The early days of their marriage flashed through his mind. He remembered how his heart had raced throughout the day of their wedding and on their first night together, and, like an ocean that never sleeps, he had lain awake filled with inexplicable happiness. However, tonight was incomparable, tonight Jeong Jin Wu was overwhelmed with feelings of joy, encouragement, and tranquility.

Eun Ok went to and fro in the kitchen and prepared the dinner table. Her rough hands were sunburned and calloused like men's hands, unlike on the night of their wedding, when he had held Eun Ok's small, soft hands and gazed at her beautiful wedding dress. Her hair, once voluminous, black, and silky, was now dry and lackluster, thinning, with bristly strands of silver around her ears.

"I'm not sure how the vegetables are doing in the greenhouse," Jeong Jin Wu said worriedly.

"You did a really great job. You even recorded their growth."

Eun Ok spoke as if Jeong Jin Wu was not her husband but her assistant.

"Was it cold in Yeonsudeok?" Jeong Jin Wu asked, changing the subject.

"It snowed. The wind blew hard, but although the fields froze at night, they slowly defrosted by the afternoon. It was unusual weather for this time of year."

"Didn't the vegetables freeze?"

"No, they all grew well. This year's cabbage grew especially well."

Eun Ok described the vegetables as though they were her children. Whenever she talked about her vegetables, her eyes and smile were like those of a mother gazing at her infant. Jeong Jin Wu looked at her expression as she described the vegetables and thought back to how she used to hold their son in her arms, breast-feed him, and comb his hair back with her fingers. The way Eun Ok expressed her maternal love for their son then was no different from the way she was talking about her vegetables now. This moved his heart.

Jeong Jin Wu rubbed his hands excitedly and said, "This year, I have a feeling that the cabbages will be large and tasty. The ducks will stay away from the radishes. And since you sowed the tomato and cucumber seeds early, they will be able to grow with little problem. I hope none of the flowers have fallen off the vines."

Jeong Jin Wu tried to encourage Eun Ok's research. He wanted to say something optimistic and hopeful, something that would move her. However, this was the only way that he was able to express himself.

Eun Ok lowered the empty tray in her hands and gazed at her husband. As she smiled, wrinkles formed around her eyes and mouth. The cabbages, the radishes eaten by ducks, the early sowing of tomato and cucumber seeds, the inland weather, strong winds, seedlings, plant growth and development—these were all complex problems that derived from the ecological conditions of the plants' natural habitat. But Jeong Jin Wu naively desired only the best results for Eun Ok.

Eun Ok felt her husband's steadfast love for her. Although Jeong Jin Wu's promise to support Eun Ok's research was the covenant on which their marriage was founded, Eun Ok felt grateful for his unchanging attitude and the work he put into maintaining their family's harmony. Eun Ok looked back on the countless nights of doing research away from home. She knew that Jeong Jin Wu resented her each time she left. But on her return, she would notice that he had become an even more affectionate family man. This revitalized her fatigued spirit. Despite the hardships on the road and at Yeonsudeok for the past ten days, her weariness dissipated like a passing fog.

Eun Ok said, "Your soup's going to get cold. Please eat."

"You, too, dear," said Jeong Jin Wu as he sat down. "What a feast! There are so many side dishes. Seasoned greens and vegetables. When did you have time to pick these?"

"The villagers at Yeonsudeok gave them to me. They packed them in bundles and loaded them on the truck."

Jeong Jin Wu acted surprised.

They had had this conversation right around this time last year, the year before that, and the year before that. Every year, the villagers handpicked various greens, bundled them, and loaded them on the truck for Eun Ok. Both of them took a moment to thank the villagers and then proceeded to eat their dinner.

The rays of the sun spread their arms one last time before sinking into the horizon.

A breeze brushed across the newly budding trees lined up along the street, forcing the young branches to tap on the windows of the apartments as though they wanted permission to enter. The wind had traveled a great distance, rushing down from China's tall mountains, through the valleys, and across the vast plains. Yet, the wind did not appear to be tired after its long journey. As the evening grew darker, the brisk wind roamed the lonely city in search of a place to rest. However, there was no home for it to enter. The wind envied the lovely flowers resting in their pots in the warm apartments. It pushed the tree branches to tap incessantly on the windows, seeking attention.

From whence, from whom, for what reason was the wind running, like a fugitive, like someone who has abandoned his family? Who will ever know its point of departure, who will ever know its lonesome fate? It wanders the earth aimlessly, seeking refuge among the trees in the depths of a forest or by a river in an open meadow. It dashes by without looking back, or it lurks around a single spot. At times, it affectionately embraces life, sharing warmth and love with everything near and far. At other times, it bellows with rage and devours everything in sight with a destructive force that makes the earth shudder. It gets soaked in the cold rain and freezes in the icy blizzard. It moans in agony and howls into the lonely night. But then, on a quiet day, it wakes from the warmth of the sun and embarks on its journey yet again, looking forward to the promise of a new day, a new adventure. This is why it can never find a mate and, therefore, lives a most miserable life.

The night grew darker.

Eun Ok had finished washing the dishes and doing the laundry. After tending each vegetable in the greenhouse, she realized how late in the evening it had become.

Even at this hour, Jeong Jin Wu was sitting at his desk with his head buried in books and documents. He consulted the legal texts before raising his pen. After thinking deeply, he began to write.

Eun Ok approached her husband quietly. Jeong Jin Wu put his pen down and began to massage his temples. Eun Ok placed her hands on his shoulders.

Jeong Jin Wu held his wife's rugged hands and pulled her next to him.

Eun Ok placed her hands on his cheeks and gazed at her fatigued, hardworking husband.

"Are you writing an essay?" she asked softly.

"It's something like that. I'm trying to submit this article to the *Journal of Legal Theory*, but something's not right."

Eun Ok's countenance changed from admiration to concern. Jeong Jin Wu noticed this change and smiled brightly.

She picked up Jeong Jin Wu's article from the desk. More than the content of the article itself, Eun Ok noticed her husband's tireless research in every word and every sentence and on every page.

"Will you read it over for me?" asked Jeong Jin Wu, half-jokingly.

Eun Ok read through the text with admiration. She read the entire article carefully and then put it down.

"I see that you're going to use those as well," said Eun Ok, referring to the other legal documents fanned out on Jeong Jin Wu's desk.

"I'm not sure yet . . ." Jeong Jin Wu trailed off. But it was certain that he had much to do.

Eun Ok opened the desk drawer and took out two tickets to the Bongjeol Movie Theater. She smiled with her lips pursed and looked at her husband. Her eyes were those of a young girl—bright and lustrous.

Eun Ok spoke excitedly, "Take Sunday off. We'll go on a boat ride at the amusement park and then a stroll around the park and the river. In the evening, we can catch this film."

"You think we're still in our twenties to go out on a date like this?" Jeong Jin Wu laughed wholeheartedly. "Have you forgotten that we're in our fifties?"

"What does age have to do with it? We're still young at heart."

"You're right. We're still young, passionate, and full of life." Jeong Jin Wu gazed at Eun Ok tenderly. "Thank you very much. However, Sunday is not a good time."

"Why not?"

"I have to stop by a house in the Gang An District."

"Is it another divorce case?"

Jeong Jin Wu nodded silently.

Eun Ok did not say anything. She sighed and brushed her disheveled hair behind her ear. She never interfered with his work and never asked about other families' marital problems. Eun Ok couldn't handle the very idea of divorce. She knew the sleepless nights and torment he had to endure trying to resolve the agony of marital problems. She realized that she would not be able to help by sympathizing or analyzing the matter with him. She did not want to burden him with more problems, so she did not ask any more questions about it.

Divorce.

The very word cast a dark shadow across her face and changed the atmosphere in the room.

The two sat quietly.

The weekend date that Eun Ok had planned, a rare occurrence for the couple, was postponed. The two sat pensively, worrying over this divorce case as if the divorcing spouses were their closest friends.

Outside the window, the wind shook the branches frantically and bellowed mournfully.

Jeong Jin Wu returned his attention to his article and spoke softly to Eun Ok, "You must be tired from your long journey. Get some rest."

When there was no reply, Jeong Jin Wu raised his head. "Do you have something to say to me?"

"It must be hard for you to stay home by yourself, right?" asked Eun Ok cautiously.

"What, are you thinking of divorcing me?" Jeong Jin Wu chuckled. Eun Ok did not.

"Don't you worry about me," Jeong Jin Wu reassured Eun Ok. "Now, get some rest."

But Eun Ok could not retire to her room just yet. "You prepare your own breakfast, lunch, and dinner . . . you take care of the vegetables in the greenhouse . . . you write your article . . . It must be very hard for you."

Jeong Jin Wu knew how Eun Ok expected him to respond. He put down his pen and rested his elbows on his desk.

"It seems as though you've read my mind," said Jeong Jin Wu.

Eun Ok lowered her eyes.

Jeong Jin Wu caressed Eun Ok's coarse hands. He spoke frankly, "It is difficult at times . . . and I get angry and frustrated . . . but it's been a rewarding life. This is beyond the expectations of our wedding night. I'm very pleased with how our lives are in unison every step of the way. To think of someone frail like you in that harsh terrain . . . It brings me happiness to see you on that path of pursuing knowledge, persevering through the intolerably cold weather."

Jeong Jin Wu took a moment before he proceeded, "To be honest with you, a few days ago, I was not too happy. In fact, I was extremely upset. In the early days of our married life, I was more than willing to support your research, but after many years, I felt like I was forced to support you because that is what a husband is supposed to do. I began to envy other families whose wives stayed at home. I wanted that, too, a simple, ordinary, happy family."

Eun Ok began to caress her husband's hands, a gesture of regret and apology.

When Jeong Jin Wu saw Eun Ok's misty eyes, he said, "Why are you crying when I'm trying to compliment you? You're the one who must be more tired than me. You must be very tired. Look at your hands. I told you to wear gloves. You may not be able to wear gloves when you plant each seed, but after that, please wear them."

"Yes, I will."

Eun Ok wiped the tears with her finger.

Jeong Jin Wu continued. "Don't be discouraged. Look how much your research has advanced since you've started. The radishes and cabbages have to be considered a success. Now you have a better idea of what to do with the cucumbers and squash. Yes, indeed. Do you think the villagers at Yeonsudeok will be able to enjoy the cabbages and radishes by next year?"

"Yes, I think they will." Eun Ok nodded and smiled.

"When were you planning to leave for Yeonsudeok again?"

"If it's all right with you, I was thinking of leaving on Monday."

"Monday? Ah, that is why you arranged our date on Sunday." Jeong Jin Wu nodded as though he had solved a mystery case. Then he sighed. "It's fine. Go on Monday. And next time, you don't have to leave notes. I already know what to do. I'm your best research assistant." Jeong Jin Wu chuckled again.

From outside the window, the wind noticed Jeong Jin Wu and Eun Ok enjoying each other's company by the single lamp on the desk and respectfully left them in peace.

# 16

After Sun Hee prepared dinner for Ho Nam, she collapsed on her bed. As the hours passed, she grew more overwhelmed by mixed feelings of shame, bitterness, regret, and desperation. The intensity of her mental pain left her empty and dejected, as if she had been banished to a deserted place. It seemed dark everywhere, and the only flame of life left seemed to be fading away. The flame flickered whenever the wind blew, and then it went out. The dying wick also soon vanished into obscurity.

Suddenly, Sun Hee opened her eyes, terrified. The room was tranquil, and Ho Nam was still awake, sitting on the floor by the desk making a pair of glasses out of wire. Sun Hee cuddled Ho Nam in her arms and tried to assuage his loneliness.

"Won't you go to sleep now?" whispered Sun Hee.

"After I finish making this."

"Come, let's get ready for bed."

"No, I'm going to wait until Dad comes home."

Sun Hee did not oppose her son's desires. She sighed and closed her eyes. All of a sudden, a memory of the judge's acute eyes and his words, as sharp as surgical tools, flashed before her. The judge's keen assessment of her was like a mirror that reflected her innermost thoughts, like an X-ray that had peered into her soul. She realized that there was no use hiding her flaws from the judge, and there was certainly no use in crying in front of him.

*Why did I really become a singer? How have I truly treated Seok Chun all these years?*

When Ho Nam finished making his glasses, he put them on and sat next to Sun Hee.

"Mom, look at my glasses."

"They're really nice."

"Is Dad coming home tonight?"

"Well, I'm not sure. If he's busy at the factory, then he may not."

In the past, Sun Hee would bark at Ho Nam whenever he asked about his father. But tonight, she replied in a gentler tone, which gave him the courage to ask, "Mom, did you prepare Dad's dinner?"

"Uh huh."

"You see, you think he's coming home, too."

Sun Hee embraced her son, and he remained in his mother's arms. Sun Hee caressed his shoulders and back. She realized that she would not be able to detach her son from his father, that his burning love would never be extinguished. The more Sun Hee mocked Seok Chun, the more Ho Nam distanced himself from his mother. But the more Sun Hee commended Seok Chun, the more Ho Nam was willing to accept his mother's love. Ho Nam's genuine loyalty to his father stung Sun Hee's heart. The loneliness and sadness that had overwhelmed Sun Hee disappeared, and instead a warm feeling lightened her heart.

The night was growing deeper, and the wind blew harder. Suddenly, the dog barked gleefully. From the front yard came the sound of familiar footsteps approaching the house.

"It's Dad!" shouted Ho Nam as he jumped out of bed. He flung open the door.

Seok Chun reacted to the swinging door and said excitedly, "Hey, you better be careful. You might hit me in the face."

Seok Chun picked up Ho Nam and carried him into the house. The cold air from outside and the stench of grease from his clothes entered the room.

Seok Chun's voice and the factory stench, both of which had sickened Sun Hee for the past few years, filled the room. She felt that a change of heart was not possible and that their lives would continue as they had been. Then, all of a sudden, her anger flared within her. Sun Hee kept her head down and went into the kitchen. As she was preparing dinner for Seok Chun, she heard an affectionate conversation between father and son. This added to her anger. Regardless of how she felt, father and son continued their jovial conversation.

"What's that kid's name? Se Pil? So, what's he doing to you?" asked Seok Chun.

"Whenever I come out of the school, he hides behind a wall to scare me. If I don't share my lunch with him, he hits me."

"Didn't he finish kindergarten? How could a kid like that be so mean to you? I better go say something to him. But then again, if he asks you for some lunch, give him some. You have to know how to share."

"I always give him some. He's greedy."

Sun Hee entered the room carrying the round dinner table.

Seok Chun said quietly, "There are a lot of side dishes tonight." But he did not look up at his wife.

Sun Hee thought that her husband was just trying to be friendly without any sincerity in his words, and that he was acting like there never had been marital problems between them. Everything he said sounded awkward and contrived, which annoyed her greatly. She preferred that he be his usual self—cold, obstinate, and rough around the edges.

There were a lot more vegetable side dishes than on other nights. The next-door neighbor had given Sun Hee some vegetables, and the neighborhood leader had bought some from the marketplace for the family as well. It appeared as if Sun Hee had prepared a hearty dinner as a sign of reconciliation, even though this was not the case. She did not want to give Seok Chun the wrong impression. She wondered why she had not felt like this when she was preparing dinner earlier. She could not understand why her feelings for him were vacillating.

Seok Chun pushed a backpack in Sun Hee's direction. "Can you wash this for me? It's Comrade Judge's. I have to give it back to him."

He glanced quickly at Sun Hee from the corner of his eye and continued. "He brought this backpack full of sand from the river. He wanted me to use it for my molding. The water must've been cold. His clothes were wet, and his pants were muddy. His face had turned blue from the cold water."

Sun Hee felt her hair stand on end, as she immediately recalled the day when she was washing her clothes by the river and saw the judge shoveling sand. She thought that he was going to use the sand to fix something in his apartment. Sun Hee recalled snickering at him for his absurd behavior.

"So, were you able to use the sand he brought you?" asked Sun Hee in a low voice.

"I couldn't. You can't use that kind of sand for molding. I didn't have the heart to tell him. Instead, I used the sand that our purchasing manager had ordered from the Eastern Sea."

Seok Chun sighed at the thought of having to tell Jeong Jin Wu the truth one day. How would the judge take it? He had gone to the trouble of digging up the sand, which was useless. Nonetheless, Seok Chun understood that the sand represented Jeong Jin Wu's attempt to unify his family. This alone made Seok Chun grateful to the judge.

*     *     *

It was Sunday.

Sun Hee and her troupe had finished their tour in Seong Gan District and were on their way home. They had planned to leave on Saturday, but the locals had insisted that they stay for one more night.

The train sped along the tracks.

Sun Hee sat by the window with her elbow on the armrest and her chin resting on her hand. The half-opened window let in the fragrance of the countryside—the fresh scent of the soil and the melting snow. The air that blew in would normally have bothered her, but today, it did not seem to affect her. It also did not seem that she was going to strike up a conversation with anyone on the train. She sat motionless, like a statue staring blankly at the passing mountains, valleys, and fields. The lush, warm, natural scenery appeared cold and bitter to her. The brisk breeze made her hair fly uncontrollably. It seemed to be the only part of Sun Hee that was alive.

"You're thinking about it again, aren't you?" asked Eun Mi, who was sitting across from Sun Hee. Just like a few days ago when they had argued at the theater, Eun Mi broke the silence by speaking first. Eun Mi examined Sun Hee, who was wallowing in her own sorrow.

Sun Hee envied Eun Mi's virtuous, gentle heart. Misery, worries, or agony seemed to melt away, and only new buds seemed to blossom from Eun Mi. Sun Hee turned her head away from her friend and sank back into her anguish, dismissing whatever Eun Mi had to say.

All of a sudden, Sun Hee missed Ho Nam. She wondered if, in these past few days, he had eaten properly, or had gone to school on time, or if Se Pil, the kid who lived behind them, had hit Ho Nam again. As Sun Hee was thinking about her son, she also thought about Seok Chun. As if they were two leaves on a branch, there was no way for her think about her son without thinking about her husband. Yet she did not yearn for or miss him. She did acknowledge the fact that he must have had a difficult time trying to take care of Ho Nam by himself for the past few days. She wondered how his multispindle machine was coming along. That man, who could not stay away from his work for more than a second, must have had a stressful time juggling Ho Nam's meal preparation and drawing up his blueprints. She also could not overlook the difficulty that he must have faced these past years in having to deal with a woman like herself. The night before she went on her tour, Seok Chun held Ho Nam in his arms as though there were no problems between them, and that had made her feel at ease. She regretted thinking him foolish for trying to lighten the gloomy atmosphere in the house, though it turned out awkwardly at times. Ho Nam had sulked the entire evening until his father came home. After Seok Chun had eaten his dinner, he and Ho Nam went into the master bedroom and made various things out of wire. Later, Ho Nam slept in Seok Chun's arms.

Sun Hee desperately wanted to see her son. However, longing faded into grief because she knew that Ho Nam would not be able to come out to the train station to greet her. Ho Nam had never once come to greet Sun Hee at the station when she returned from a tour. Since Seok Chun never came, there was no way for Ho Nam to come.

Sun Hee asked quietly, "Eun Mi, I was pretty bad, wasn't I?"

"We've been on this train for an hour, and these are your first words?" said Eun Mi jokingly. She then turned serious. "Yes, you looked really depressed. You weren't moved by the songs at all, and you looked like your mind was elsewhere." Then Eun Mi tried to be encouraging. "But still, you sounded good. The audience requested several encores."

Sun Hee turned her face toward the window again. She recalled the locals who gave the singers boxes of tomatoes on the day they were leaving, and the factory workers who showered her with applause and flowers. She recalled the joyful faces of the workers and their generous hospitality that overflowed like a mountain spring.

"Hey, Sun Hee. Get your things together. We're almost at the station," said Eun Mi.

As soon as the train came out of the tunnel, it began to slow down with the abrupt sounds of gears changing and the screech of the wheels grinding against the tracks. The singers, actors, and other passengers got up from their seats, laughing and chattering while reaching for their luggage.

Sun Hee remained seated and closed her eyes. She waited for the others to get off the train first and meet with their waiting family members. Sun Hee would get off the train when they had all left the platform. She would then head home by herself. She knew that no one would come to greet her at the station, so she would hide her melancholy and pain from her comrades by remaining in the car until everyone had left. And now, that moment of insurmountable pain was approaching as the train pulled into the station.

The people waiting on the platform took a step back when the train came to a halt. The other comrades and Eun Mi moved down the aisles and got off the train, immediately greeting and being greeted by their loved ones. Some frantically looked for family members, standing on tiptoe and bobbing their heads for a better opportunity to identify their loved ones in the crowd. And some shouted names with the hope of an answer, even the faintest one. The many hands waving in the air made it impossible to distinguish to whom each was directed.

*How affectionate and harmonious does a family have to be to receive that kind of welcome?* thought Sun Hee.

"Ma'am, wake up, please. This is the final stop," said the conductor, passing along the aisle.

Sun Hee looked out the window. All the people bustling around on the platform made it through the turnstile in an instant. Sun Hee sighed, brushed her hair with her hands, and reluctantly grabbed her luggage. She was the last one on the train. She exited onto the platform and was greeted by loneliness. It no longer terrified her as it used to because she had grown accustomed to its spectral presence. It was the only faithful adversary that had never failed to greet her at the station in all these years. The station was completely desolate, and so was Sun Hee.

Sun Hee composed herself and had headed out of the station when she noticed two men and a child standing by the turnstile.

She felt a rush of electricity running through her limbs, momentarily paralyzing her. Without a doubt, the two men were the judge and her husband, and the child was unquestionably Ho Nam.

"Mom!"

In the midst of her dejection, Sun Hee heard the distinct and familiar voice of her son. Ho Nam ran toward Sun Hee at full speed, like a rolling ball.

"Ho Nam!"

Sun Hee dropped her luggage and ran toward her son. Ho Nam launched himself at his mother, making Sun Hee nearly fall backward. She held her son tightly while still standing, but then she crouched down to hug him, securing him deep in her warm embrace.

Ho Nam whispered to Sun Hee, "Mom, that man came to our house. We told him that you weren't home. And then he told us to go to the train station."

Sun Hee was at a loss for words.

"You know what?" Ho Nam continued. "Dad said he will go to night school."

"Really?"

Sun Hee, overwhelmed by mixed emotions, choked up with tears, unable to speak any further. She held Ho Nam's small hand and slowly stood up. The mist in her eyes obscured her vision; she could not make out the judge and her husband.

Jeong Jin Wu stayed back, and Seok Chun walked up to Sun Hee. Without saying a word, he helped Sun Hee with her luggage.

It had been a while since the two had looked at each other. One appeared detached, and the other doleful. Their eyes reflected resentment and understanding, forgiveness and hope as they looked deeply at each other and felt the other's pain.

Ho Nam stood between them and held each parent's hand like a child desperate for his parents' love. He missed holding both their hands.

Jeong Jin Wu looked warmly at the family as they approached him.

Sun Hee kept wiping away her tears.

Jeong Jin Wu greeted her with "How was your trip?"

Sun Hee lowered her eyes. She felt the utmost respect and gratitude for the elderly representative of the law. She appeared enraptured at the thought of starting a new life.

They walked out of the station and onto the square.

Judge Jeong Jin Wu held Ho Nam's hand and asked, "Would you like to come to my house?"

"Really?"

"Of course."

"Did your mom come home, too?"

"Of course," Jeong Jin Wu replied, chuckling. "In fact, she's waiting for you."

"Then, let's go!" shouted Ho Nam.

Sun Hee gave Ho Nam a sign of disapproval. Ho Nam hid behind Jeong Jin Wu's legs.

Jeong Jin Wu laughed and said to the couple, "Comrade Seok Chun, Comrade Sun Hee, you two go home. I'll go for a walk with Ho Nam. I will bring him back around dinner time."

Jeong Jin Wu wanted to give the couple as much privacy as possible. Seok Chun and Sun Hee must have so much to talk about on their tenth wedding anniversary—falling in love, the early days of their marriage . . . memories, life lessons, hope . . .

Jeong Jin Wu took Ho Nam's hand and walked down the path toward a small park.

All the apartment buildings along the street had their windows open to welcome the sunlight and fresh air.

The sun was warm in May, and the leaves on the trees gave off the fresh fragrance of spring. The trees along the street waved their branches in the light breeze and provided shade on the path. Another small path led to a park surrounded by tall pine trees and flowers that blossomed late into the spring season.

They stopped at a newly painted blue bench.

"Do you want to rest a bit?" asked Jeong Jin Wu.

"Uh huh."

Jeong Jin Wu helped Ho Nam up onto the bench. They both took a deep breath of the sweet scent of flowers, grass, and pine.

Between some trees and a grassy path, a newlywed couple was walking with an entourage escorting them. They took a picture amid the beautiful scenery with the apartment buildings in the background.

The newlyweds walked toward Jeong Jin Wu and Ho Nam. The groom's face was as bright as the flower on his lapel. The bride had a corsage pinned to her dress and a crown made of roses. She lifted her long dress so that she wouldn't trip over it as she walked. Each time she took a step, the tips of her shoes poked out. The bride and groom stood affectionately next to each other. The bride then rested her head on the groom's shoulder.

The photographer knelt and focused his lens.

Ho Nam seemed entertained by the sight. He stood up from the bench and said, "Isn't that nice?"

"Uh huh."

Jeong Jin Wu was immersed in such deep thoughts that he answered without knowing what had been asked.

The photograph of the young couple captured life's most beautiful artwork, the union and excitement of a new family on this joyous day. For older couples who had endured marriage through the seasons, the wedding ceremony was a fond memory, but for young couples, it was their reality. For the next generation, it would become tradition, society's gift. The course of human history may seem uneventful, but the joy of one's wedding day never grows old. This was the everlasting tradition of humanity that no one or nothing could destroy.

"Hey, mister."

Ho Nam looked serious and continued, "It would be nice for mom and dad to have a wedding."

Jeong Jin Wu thought Ho Nam would be disappointed if he told the child that his parents had already had their wedding ceremony, like this young couple, long before he had been born. He tried to change the subject.

"Would you like to have some crackers and delicious food?"

"No."

"Then, what?"

"If there is a wedding, then mom and dad will be better."

Jeong Jin Wu's eyes began to sting with tears.

*You're right, child. If your parents had another wedding, then they would be more affectionate with each other, and you would be able to rest secure in their love and be the happy child that you deserve to be. However, what can I say? The wedding that you're looking at with envious eyes happens only once. One day you will understand the meaning of marriage.*

Jeong Jin Wu looked at Ho Nam and tried to temper the child's hopes. *Don't worry, child. Your parents will remarry. They may not have a wedding ceremony again, but they will renew their wedding vows. It will be a spiritual wedding.*

People began to fill the park to enjoy the mild Sunday afternoon.

There are people who dream of building a family, and there are people who already live in one. There is no one without a family. A family is where the love of humanity dwells, and it is a beautiful world where hope flourishes.

# AFTERWORD

Paek Nam-nyong's *Friend* is one of the few North Korean novels that has reached an international audience. First published in Pyongyang in 1988, the novel was picked up by the South Korean press Sallimteo in 1992, and the French publisher Actes Sud produced a translation by Patrick Maurus in 2011. One reason for this interest is surely the subject matter. In a review in *Le Monde*, Philippe Pons writes, "[*Friend*] is revealing of a literary approach that began in the 1980s, aimed at getting rid of 'socialist realism' and 'revolutionary romanticism'—idealizing the heroic struggle and sacrifice—to deal with the lives of ordinary people." Almost all the North Korean writing we have access to in English translation is by dissidents or defectors. *Friend* is unique in the Anglophone publishing landscape in that it is a state-sanctioned novel, written in Korea for North Koreans, by an author in good standing with the regime.

But *Friend* is not only of interest for what it can tell an Anglophone reader about North Korea. It is a novel constructed on powerful dialogues, internal monologues, and strong personalities. Paek's Judge Jeong Jin Wu is concerned with the strength of the North Korean state, but he is equally concerned with universally thorny questions, such as how to balance work and family life and how to allow adults, especially women, the self-determination offered by divorce without causing the affected children undue suffering. Household chores and the social expectation that women will shoulder them even as they pursue careers outside the home are a recurring theme. And as the work's title hints, *Friend* also explores the possibilities and limits of a helping hand, whether in the form of official government intervention or social or familial well-wishers, when an individual is struggling or a marriage is on the rocks. That Paek's vivid psychological portraits also give readers a glance into a famously closed society is an unintended bonus.

## History and Style of North Korean Fiction

*Friend*, of course, did not appear in a vacuum. As a rule, literary works in North Korea show the process of individuals acquiring "correct" political consciousness. Literature translates Party directives into entertaining narratives and models how one should adapt to new sociopolitical situations. The Party, Writers' Union, and literary critics prescribe guidelines and ensure that artists adhere to them in both the form and the content of their work. Writers like Paek are able to operate within this framework of prescriptions and produce literature that fulfills the Party's directives while challenging the reader.

Historically, the Party has seen literature as a significant part of national campaigns to materialize Party directives. The Cheollima campaign, for example, in the late 1950s and throughout the 1960s focused on the collective effort of the people to reconstruct the country in the aftermath of the Korean War. A typical book from this period has an optimistic plotline, as the utopian socialist state was projected to be within reach. No problem was too big and no task was too tiresome for the gung-ho heroes and heroines whose nearly supernatural power and devotion to the nation were intended to increase morale among readers. This is the type of literature, with its glorification of work and workers, that will come to mind for many readers when they think of Socialist Realist or even Communist literature more broadly.

Narratives that praise Kim Il Sung became standard in North Korean literature only after the Fifteenth Plenary Meeting of the Fourth Central Party Committee in 1967. Until then, most works of fiction did not depict Kim Il Sung or even mention him. By this point, Kim Il Sung's supporters had decisively suppressed all other factions within the Party. The 1967 meeting codified the cult of personality that had grown up around Kim as well as officially adopted Kim's Juche, or Self-Reliance, ideology. Kim's words and image became commonplace in art and indeed in all public discourse, and writing the phrase "According to the Great Leader Kim Il Sung," thanking Kim Il Sung, expressing a desire to please him, or using numerous fawning monikers to describe his being became the normative writing practice in North Korea after 1967.

The 1970s was a period of heightened literary production, and to this day it remains the decade that saw the largest number of new works published in North Korean history. Two major national campaigns, the Three Revolutions Movement and the Speed Campaign, called on the people to reeducate themselves with the correct ideology, technology, and culture, along with increasing production at a rapid pace. During this period, writers scribbled madly to meet deadlines and fulfill quotas. At the same time, amateurs were encouraged to write in order to display the level of ideological education among the populace. This overproduction of literary works did not impress North Korean literary critics, who criticized the resulting narratives as trite and repetitive with flat characters. It was in this literary climate that Paek Nam-nyong made his debut.

## Life and Literary Career of Paek Nam-nyong

*Friend* is one of the novels I analyze in my book *Rewriting Revolution: Women, Sexuality, and Memory in North Korean Fiction*, and through the auspices of an independent organization in the United States, I was fortunate enough to be able to travel to North Korea in 2015 to interview Paek. I had sent more than fifty questions for our meeting before my arrival in Pyongyang. I met Paek in the lobby of my hotel, the Haebangsan. We were taken to a conference room where we could discuss my questions and converse about other matters pertaining to his life as a writer. We were scheduled to meet for a day but ended up spending three days together. Most of what follows is drawn from my conversations with him, particularly regarding his personal life. One of North Korea's most successful writers, Paek was humble, generous, and kind. I purposely refrained from asking sensitive political questions.

Most of Paek's works reflect his tragic upbringing and difficult journey to becoming one of North Korea's most celebrated novelists. Born on October 19, 1949, in Hamheung City in South Hamgyeong Province, Paek had not yet turned one year old when his father was killed in an American bombardment during the Korean War. Like most survivors of the war, Paek, his two older sisters, and his single mother lived in poverty. When Paek was eleven, his mother died of a terminal disease, leaving Paek to be raised by his older sisters. As soon as he graduated from high school, he entered the steel industry, learning to turn the lathe and work other heavy machinery. Although Paek claims that he had found his life's worth at the steel factory, his true passion was reading literature and writing short stories in his free time. These early stories were about his workplace and fellow workers.

After publishing his first short story, "High-Quality Coal" (*Goyeoltan*) in a magazine, Paek decided to major in literature at Kim Il Sung University. He passed the entrance exam and was accepted in 1971. However, instead of moving down to Pyongyang, Paek continued to work at his factory in Hamheung to support himself and took long-distance learning courses. Every spring and fall, he would spend two months in Pyongyang attending classes on campus. During the rest of the year, he would work and study before going down to Pyongyang again. Paek graduated with a bachelor's degree in Korean literature in 1976 and joined the Jagang Province Writers' Union near his hometown.

While he was content with his job at the factory, he followed the Party's Three Revolutions campaign, which called on the people to study political ideology, acquire the latest technical skills, and raise their cultural consciousness through literature, cinema, songs, theater, and collective activities. Paek chose a career in writing to educate his readers on the importance of self-cultivation, which entails lifelong learning, serving the country and the people, abiding by Party doctrine, and participating in collective community initiatives.

After working at the Jagang Province Writers' Union for many years, Paek received an invitation to join the Writers' Union in Pyongyang. Paek, his wife, and three children moved to the capital city and adjusted to their new living conditions. However, tragedy revisited Paek when his wife died of brain disease, leaving him to raise his three children on his own.

Paek was later promoted to the April 15 Literary Production Unit, an elite group whose primary task is to write historical novels based on the lives and accomplishments of Kim Il Sung and Kim Jong Il. These books are then published in a series titled Immortal History and Immortal Leadership. The April 15 Literary Production Unit was conceived by Kim Jong Il during the mid-1960s and was tasked with producing the first novel in the series by 1972, in honor of Kim Il Sung's sixtieth birthday. That novel is *The Year 1932*, and it recounts the formation of Kim Il Sung's anti-Japanese guerrilla army, which had been instrumental in fortifying Kim's political position during the colonial period. Thereafter, the writers of the April 15 Literary Production Unit produced numerous novels for the series, which continues to be published to this day. Paek's contributions to the series are in the Immortal Leadership track and include *A Thousand Miles to the East Sea (Donghae cheonni)*, *Prelude to Spring (Bomui seogok)*, and *Inheritors (Gyeseungja)*.

It is important to understand the difference between the practice of giving leaders cameos in a novel and the work of the April 15 Literary Production Unit. The unit is tasked with the specific duty of delineating the historical accomplishments of the leaders. According to Paek, each writer in this group chooses a specific moment in the given leader's life, researches the relevant revolutionary exploits, and creates a realistic narrative that dramatizes the events.

In his literary work outside the series, Paek demonstrates how people deal with the most mundane (but ever-so-difficult) situations. "Servicemen" (*Bongmujadeul*, 1979), "Workplace" (*Ilteo*, 1979), and "Young Party Secretary" (*Jeolmeun dangbiseo*, 1983) place the protagonists at the heart of workplace conflicts, in which they must deal with coworkers who prioritize certain self-interest groups over the welfare of the collective. Both *After 60 Years (60 nyeon hu*, 1982) and "Life" (*Saengmyeong*, 1985) reveal political corruption among colleagues and their self-aggrandizing ambitions to succeed in life at the expense of others. The heroes in these stories do not transform society into a socialist paradise. Instead, Paek identifies these problems in his society and creates characters who struggle but eventually choose the righteous path without necessarily imposing the Party's directives as the only panacea. There are didactic, propagandistic elements, as there are in *Friend*, but Paek's first concern in the majority of his work is individual ethical responsibility, a topic applicable to members of any society, culture, or nationality.

## On Writing *Friend*

The premise of *Friend* is based on observations Paek made of divorcing couples while he was working at the Jagang Province Writers' Union. His office was located on the top floor of a three-story building. The first floor was the municipal court, which handled civil cases, where couples would line up to file for divorce. He observed these divorcing couples for more than a year and regularly attended the court hearings. He befriended the presiding judge (the basis for the protagonist in *Friend*) and gathered detailed information about past cases. He took note of the judicial procedures and the legal language. He also witnessed the pain of divorce and the toll it took on the children, if there were any involved. Through his inadvertent field research, Paek had found the material for his novel. He decided to write *Friend* in a way that would reach deeper into the emotional and psychological world of his characters than any of his other stories.

*Friend* is set during the Hidden Hero campaign of the 1980s, which sought to recognize the extraordinary achievements of otherwise ordinary citizens, and elements of this campaign can be found in the novel. It is also influenced by Three Revolutions campaign mentioned earlier. Protagonist Judge Jeong Jin Wu admonishes the other characters for not abiding by the Party's directives of self-improvement through education. Manual labor was no longer seen as the pinnacle of achievement in North Korean fiction. By the 1980s, many stories portrayed characters with higher education and technical skills. The trend in fiction of this period was to delineate a new class of intellectual heroes who improved social conditions with their brainpower rather than their brute strength. Seok Chun is a lathe operator who refuses to pursue the education that could raise him to a managerial or executive position at his factory. Paek does not denigrate Seok Chun's achievements, but he does question whether the younger man could offer society more than the use of his hands. Judge Jeong Jin Wu rebukes Seok Chun's averse attitude toward change, which is a common literary and rhetorical style in North Korean literature, and encourages him to enroll in the Engineering College. Although Judge Jeong Jin Wu works to inspire the characters to change so that they can help develop a stronger nation, the conclusion of the narrative is more ambiguous than the prescribed formula used in many North Korean works of fiction. For Paek, even proper political indoctrinations cannot make individuals change overnight. Ultimately, Paek designs his narrative around individuals who navigate their agency through the thicket of political expectations and discover meaning in themselves, family, and the community.

In this sense, *Friend* is Paek's finest work, an achievement that has made him a renowned novelist in North Korea. The motif of the story is the catastrophic consequences of divorce that derive from individuals placing their self-centered choices above family unity in importance. Paek abides by the Party's ideology on family as a small unit that ought to preserve the moral fabric of society, but he also asserts that remaining happily married is a completely different story. No political ideology can force individuals to love and live happily ever after. He acknowledges that marriage is hard work and that maintaining the harmony of a family requires self-sacrifice. And through secondary plotlines, Paek is able to complicate even this assertion. Far from being a tidy morality play, *Friend* portrays a messy world of human emotions and relationships that is at once entirely alien and eerily familiar.

WEATHERHEAD BOOKS ON ASIA

WEATHERHEAD EAST ASIAN INSTITUTE,
COLUMBIA UNIVERSITY

LITERATURE

DAVID DER-WEI WANG, EDITOR

Ye Zhaoyan, *Nanjing 1937: A Love Story*, translated by Michael
Berry (2003)

Oda Makoto, *The Breaking Jewel*, translated by Donald Keene (2003)

Han Shaogong, *A Dictionary of Maqiao*, translated by Julia Lovell
(2003)

Takahashi Takako, *Lonely Woman*, translated by Maryellen Toman
Mori (2004)

Chen Ran, *A Private Life*, translated by John Howard-Gibbon
(2004)

Eileen Chang, *Written on Water*, translated by Andrew F. Jones
(2004)

*Writing Women in Modern China: The Revolutionary Years, 1936–1976*,
edited by Amy D. Dooling (2005)

Han Bangqing, *The Sing-song Girls of Shanghai*, first translated by
Eileen Chang, revised and edited by Eva Hung (2005)

*Loud Sparrows: Contemporary Chinese Short-Shorts*, translated and
edited by Aili Mu, Julie Chiu, and Howard Goldblatt (2006)

Hiratsuka Raichō, *In the Beginning, Woman Was the Sun*, translated
by Teruko Craig (2006)

Zhu Wen, *I Love Dollars and Other Stories of China*, translated by
Julia Lovell (2007)

Kim Sowŏl, *Azaleas: A Book of Poems*, translated by David McCann
(2007)

Wang Anyi, *The Song of Everlasting Sorrow: A Novel of Shanghai*,
translated by Michael Berry with Susan Chan Egan (2008)

Ch'oe Yun, *There a Petal Silently Falls: Three Stories by Ch'oe Yun*,
translated by Bruce and Ju-Chan Fulton (2008)

Inoue Yasushi, *The Blue Wolf: A Novel of the Life of Chinggis Khan*, translated by Joshua A. Fogel (2009)

Anonymous, *Courtesans and Opium: Romantic Illusions of the Fool of Yangzhou*, translated by Patrick Hanan (2009)

Cao Naiqian, *There's Nothing I Can Do When I Think of You Late at Night*, translated by John Balcom (2009)

Park Wan-suh, *Who Ate Up All the Shinga? An Autobiographical Novel*, translated by Yu Young-nan and Stephen J. Epstein (2009)

Yi T'aejun, *Eastern Sentiments*, translated by Janet Poole (2009)

Hwang Sunwŏn, *Lost Souls: Stories*, translated by Bruce and Ju-Chan Fulton (2009)

Kim Sŏk-pŏm, *The Curious Tale of Mandogi's Ghost*, translated by Cindi Textor (2010)

*The Columbia Anthology of Modern Chinese Drama*, edited by Xiaomei Chen (2011)

Qian Zhongshu, *Humans, Beasts, and Ghosts: Stories and Essays*, edited by Christopher G. Rea, translated by Dennis T. Hu, Nathan K. Mao, Yiran Mao, Christopher G. Rea, and Philip F. Williams (2011)

Dung Kai-cheung, *Atlas: The Archaeology of an Imaginary City*, translated by Dung Kai-cheung, Anders Hansson, and Bonnie S. McDougall (2012)

O Chŏnghŭi, *River of Fire and Other Stories*, translated by Bruce and Ju-Chan Fulton (2012)

Endō Shūsaku, *Kiku's Prayer: A Novel*, translated by Van Gessel (2013)

Li Rui, *Trees without Wind: A Novel*, translated by John Balcom (2013)

Abe Kōbō, *The Frontier Within: Essays by Abe Kōbō*, edited, translated, and with an introduction by Richard F. Calichman (2013)

Zhu Wen, *The Matchmaker, the Apprentice, and the Football Fan: More Stories of China*, translated by Julia Lovell (2013)

*The Columbia Anthology of Modern Chinese Drama*, abridged edition, edited by Xiaomei Chen (2013)

Natsume Sōseki, *Light and Dark*, translated by John Nathan (2013)

Seirai Yūichi, *Ground Zero, Nagasaki: Stories*, translated by Paul Warham (2015)

Hideo Furukawa, *Horses, Horses, in the End the Light Remains Pure: A Tale That Begins with Fukushima*, translated by Doug Slaymaker with Akiko Takenaka (2016)

Abe Kōbō, *Beasts Head for Home: A Novel*, translated by Richard F. Calichman (2017)

Yi Mun-yol, *Meeting with My Brother: A Novella*, translated by Heinz Insu Fenkl with Yoosup Chang (2017)

Ch'ae Manshik, *Sunset: A Ch'ae Manshik Reader*, edited and translated by Bruce and Ju-Chan Fulton (2017)

Tanizaki Jun'ichiro, *In Black and White: A Novel*, translated by Phyllis I. Lyons (2018)

Yi T'aejun, *Dust and Other Stories*, translated by Janet Poole (2018)

Tsering Döndrup, *The Handsome Monk and Other Stories*, translated by Christopher Peacock (2019)

Kimura Yūsuke, *"Sacred Cesium Ground" and "Isa's Deluge": Two Novellas of Japan's 3/11 Disaster*, translated by Doug Slaymaker (2019)

Wang Anyi, *Fu Ping: A Novel*, translated by Howard Goldblatt (2019)

## HISTORY, SOCIETY, AND CULTURE

### CAROL GLUCK, EDITOR

Takeuchi Yoshimi, *What Is Modernity? Writings of Takeuchi Yoshimi*, edited and translated, with an introduction, by Richard F. Calichman (2005)

*Contemporary Japanese Thought*, edited and translated by Richard F. Calichman (2005)

*Overcoming Modernity*, edited and translated by Richard F. Calichman (2008)

Natsume Sōseki, *Theory of Literature and Other Critical Writings*, edited and translated by Michael Bourdaghs, Atsuko Ueda, and Joseph A. Murphy (2009)

Kojin Karatani, *History and Repetition*, edited by Seiji M. Lippit (2012)

*The Birth of Chinese Feminism: Essential Texts in Transnational Theory*, edited by Lydia H. Liu, Rebecca E. Karl, and Dorothy Ko (2013)

Yoshiaki Yoshimi, *Grassroots Fascism: The War Experience of the Japanese People*, translated by Ethan Mark (2015)

Paek 1639813
2020